CASE OF THE
CURVED STAIRCASE

A MACARONI ON WHEELS MYSTERY

BOOK 2

S.K. Derban

COPYRIGHT NOTICE

Library Cataloging Data

Names: Derban, S.K. (S.K. Derban)

Case of the Curved Staircase: A Macaroni on Wheels Mystery, Book 2 / S.K. Derban

302 p. 23cm × 15cm (9in × 6 in.)

ISBN-13: 978-1-963188-09-7 (paperback) | 978-1-963188-11-0 (trade paperback) | 978-1-963188-10-3 (e-book)

Key Words: cozy culinary mysteries; cozy mysteries with cats; cozy mysteries with recipies; beach cozy mysteries; Italian cozy mysteries; female sleuths; femal detectives

Library of Congress Control Number: 2025913757 Fiction

DEDICATION

My heart flows with love and affection for Milagros,
my very special auntie...

This book is also dedicated to Sylvia, Monica, and Stefanie,
her beautiful daughters, and to the extended family who
continue to bring smiles all around...

Scott, Barry, Ken, Alyssa, Sierra, Michael, Alex, Nathan,
Sabrina, Zach, and Emmett.

I am blessed by the love and ongoing support from this
extraordinary family.

ACKNOWLEDGEMENTS

Thank you to Jesus, the Author of Salvation – El-Shaddai.

How do I find the time to write? All because of my wonderful, Godly husband who takes amazing care of me. Thank you, Mario!

How do I have the energy to write? All because of my fantastic family and friends. What a comfort to know you are always by my side.

God has blessed me with the very best in the publishing industry:

Adam Ramirez, your artistic talent amazes me! Thank you for the Macaroni on Wheels noodle. The logo you designed is perfect!

Leslie L. McKee, you continue to make the editing process fun! Thank you for taking such great care of my manuscripts.

Jessica Sisneros, you are an angel on earth! Thank you for your outstanding proofreading skills.

Mariah Sinclair, your talent for cover designs is truly amazing. I adore how you bring a seed of an idea to life!

Derinda Babcock, this is our fifth project together and you continue to astonish me. Your interior design skills are the best in the business. Working with you is a blessing! Thank you for always being available to me.

Slim Man, your music satisfies the soul like a glass of fine Italian red wine. Add one of your amazing meals and there's no better evening. Thank you for sharing your fabulous Pesto Recipe with all of us.

Grazie Mille to all!

SPECIAL MESSAGE FOR THE READER FROM S.K. DERBAN

Thank you for selecting this second book in the *Macaroni on Wheels Mystery* series.

Spoiler Alert Number One!

If you have not read *Case of the Bayfront Murder*, I would highly recommend you reading it first. Although the *Macaroni on Wheels Mystery* series have separate stories, there is a romantic suspense subplot throughout all three books. The suspense is resolved in *Case of the Paella Party*. And yes, it is romantic!

Spoiler Alert Number Two!

If you plan on reading my stand-alone novel, *Uneven Exchange*, please do so before you read *Macaroni on Wheels, Case of the Curved Staircase*. Numerous readers asked me to write a sequel to *Uneven Exchange* as there was some unfinished business. The questions are answered in *Case of the Curved Staircase*. I have a feeling you are going to smile! (And maybe shed a tear.)

Stay until the end!

Stay until the end! After the Epilogue of each Macaroni on Wheels Mystery novel, Terza Tiepolo shares a cooking tip straight from the Macaroni on Wheels kitchen. Enjoy!

TABLE OF CONTENTS

Copyright Notice ii

Dedication iii

Acknowledgements v

Special Message for the Reader vii

Introduction xi

Prologue 1

Chapter One: Plans Are Set 7

Chapter Two: Ruby Slippers 13

Chapter Three: It's Party Time 29

Chapter Four: Stairs Can Be Very Dangerous 45

Chapter Five: Talk of Murder 59

Chapter Six: Cameras, Cameras, and More Cameras . . . 67

Chapter Seven: Murder Board 81

Chapter Eight: Family Dinner 85

Chapter Nine: Medical Examiner and More 95

Chapter Ten: Avery Ellington – THE THIRD! 111

Chapter Eleven: Videos, Videos, and More Videos 117

Chapter Twelve: Lots of Lasagna 129

Chapter Thirteen: Conner to the Rescue 139

Chapter Fourteen: Catering Comes First 147

Chapter Fifteen: A Couple of Spies 157

Chapter Sixteen: Nico's Soft Side 171

Chapter Seventeen: Here Come the Kiddos 179

Chapter Eighteen: Uneven Exchange Returns 185

Chapter Nineteen: Mama Knows Best—Or Does She? . 199

Chapter Twenty: Confrontation 205

Chapter Twenty-One: Still Waiting. 217

Chapter Twenty-Two: Knight is Shining Armor 221

Chapter Twenty-Three: Alone at Last 235

Chapter Twenty-Four: Back to Work. 245

Chapter Twenty-Five: Special Memories 253

Chapter Twenty-Six: Date Night 257

Chapter Twenty-Seven: Wait on the Lord. 265

Epilogue: Case Closed. 267

Terza's Cooking Tips 277

Special Guest Recipe by Slim Man 279

About the Author. 283

Other Books by S.K. Derban 285

INTRODUCTION TO CASE OF THE CURVED STAIRCASE

Taken from the closing paragraphs of
Case of the Bayfront Murder
Little Italy, San Diego, California
The scene is set. After helping to solve the murder mystery, Terza and Moheenie review the list of suspects while erasing their murder board. When Moheenie leaves for the evening, Terza prepares to close up shop. The telephone rings...

"Macaroni on Wheels."

"Is this the catering company in Little Italy?"

"Yes, it is," Terza replied, instantly taking note of the man's British-sounding accent.

"Is it the one right next door to the Tiepolo Mercato?"

Terza chuckled. "Definitely yes, right next door. Who referred you? Was it Ezio or Benedette Tiepolo?"

"It was the butcher. I'm not sure of his name."

"That is Ezio Tiepolo, my father."

"Well, your father says you are the second-best chef in San Diego."

Terza's laughter continued. "Did he say that my mother is the first best?"

"As a matter of fact, he did. My name is Joshua Kamoze. I'm calling to see if you would consider catering a birthday party for my wife. Her name is Sloan."

"Of course," Terza said. "Birthday parties are my favorite. I will first need to check my calendar. When are you planning to have the party?"

"On the thirtieth of October, the day before Halloween," Joshua told her.

While Terza clicked on her calendar she asked, "Are you planning a Halloween theme?"

Joshua laughed. "Oh no! I'm planning just the opposite. Sloan complains that every year her birthday coincides with Halloween. This year I wanted to surprise her with a normal birthday."

"Good to know it is a surprise." Terza's calendar filled the computer screen. Using her mouse, she advanced the months to October. "You are in luck. I am booked for the thirty-first, but open on the thirtieth. How many people are you expecting?"

"Around forty. Is that too many?"

"No, forty is perfect. Will the party be at your home or another location?"

"At our home. It shouldn't be too far from you. We live in one of the historic homes close to Presidio Park."

"Oh, I love those houses. Is it a one, or two-story?"

"Two."

"Then, I bet you have a gorgeous staircase," Terza commented.

"Yes, we do. Sloan's favorite part of Christmas is decorating the wooden railing with garland."

"It sounds beautiful. Okay, I have you down for October thirtieth. I just need your contact information to get started. Then, I can send you menus and all the information you will need to plan the perfect party."

"That sounds great. I am glad I met your father, Terza."

After ending her conversation with Joshua, Terza telephoned her father.

"Tiepolo Mercato."

"Hi, Papa. I called to thank you for the referral. The man's name is Joshua Kamoze, although I forgot to ask him when you met."

"Hum," her father mumbled while obviously thinking. "Does he have a British accent?"

"Yes, yes he does. Well, it sounds British, but I caught the sound of another place."

"Jamaica!" Ezio announced with great enthusiasm. "He is a nice man."

"How do you know he is from Jamaica?"

"Because we had an enjoyable talk while I was making his sandwich. I think he walked over during his lunch break. If I remember correctly, he was at a business meeting downtown."

"Papa, you are a very special man. I adore how kind you are to absolutely everyone!"

"We're all God's children. Right?"

"You are correct." Terza paused a beat. "Guess what? He lives in one of the historic houses by Presidio Park."

"Your mother would love that," Ezio said. "Maybe he lives in one of the homes on the tour your mother took."

"He might. I cannot wait to see the staircase. They always look so beautiful decorated for Christmas with garland. Mr. Kamoze said that decorating the staircase is his wife's favorite part."

"I can imagine. It must be a grand staircase," Ezio said. "You know the ones that curve from the second floor down to the first."

CASE OF THE CURVED STAIRCASE

Autumn. The city lights reflected as ribbons of red, yellow, and white upon the water of San Diego Bay. Terza stood with her nose inches away from the expansive office building windows and looked down at the shimmering lights.

Moheenie remained more than a foot away from the thick glass. "How can you dare stand so close? Yikes! It's scary being twenty-four floors high."

Terza turned to face her best friend. "Don't be afraid, Mo." She extended her hand. "Come closer, and I promise not to let you go. You have to see how the city lights are reflecting off of the water. They're breathtaking."

Moheenie ignored Terza's hand and stepped farther back. "Yes, it is beautiful, and I can see the lights perfectly from right here."

Terza returned to her position in front of the window and tapped. "Do you really think you are going to fall through this thick plate of glass?" She glanced over her shoulder.

Moheenie kept her distance and shook her head. "Well, not really, but why take the chance?" She looked around the room as more of the book club members arrived. "It's almost seven. Let's take our seats."

Terza laced an arm around Moheenie's small waist. "Yes, let's get comfy."

They walked toward the same two swivel chairs they occupied at every meeting. Terza settled onto the luxurious leather. "Isn't it odd that we all sit in the same seats each and every month?"

Moheenie rotated her chair toward Terza. "Good question. I wonder what would happen if we missed a meeting."

"I bet our places would remain empty." Terza's forearms pressed against the armrests. "We are certainly creatures of habit, aren't we?"

"We are indeed."

Terza's gaze returned to admire the view provided by the floor-to-ceiling windows.

"There you go again, lost in thought," Moheenie said. "You are envisioning the autumn season, aren't you?"

Terza's head jerked sideways. "How did you know?"

Moheenie laughed. "Because I know you, Tee! There is something about this building that causes you to reflect upon every season of the year."

Terza nodded. "You're right. I think it is because we are high above it all. You know how much I adore San Diego. When I look out, I think about the time of year and the fun we always have being outdoors."

"The ocean water is still warm," Moheenie offered.

"And the tourists are few and far between," Terza added with a sly grin. "Although I don't think we should blame them for all of our traffic woes. The students are the biggest culprits."

"Whether it's the tourists or students, at least we can finally drive to the beach in less than an hour!"

"Exactly." Terza watched Barnaby walk into the board room. In his typical, formal British style, Barnaby Paddington came dressed in gray wool slacks, a crisp white shirt, and perfectly knotted bowtie. She appreciated the specks of color in his selection of tie this evening and admired his matching suspenders.

"Good evening, ladies and gents," Barnaby began.

"Quit smiling," Moheenie whispered.

"I can't help it. I get a kick out of his British accent. Plus, look, he is even wearing suspenders."

Moheenie followed Terza's gaze. "He looks so cute, and kind of like a professor."

Barnaby studied the room before continuing. "Welcome to the October meeting of our San Diego Murder Mystery Book Club." He motioned to his left. "As always, there is coffee, tea, soft drinks, and water on the credenza. Our gathering is informal so please feel free to pop up and partake of refreshments whenever you desire." Barnaby acknowledged Terza with a nod and placed a palm over his heart. "Once again our resident chef, Miss Terza Tiepolo, has brought us a lovely assortment of Italian cookies." He rubbed his stomach and chuckled. "I know from experience that they are quite delicious. Thank you very much, Terza. I'm positive it is a great deal of work. Please do not feel obligated to bake for us every month."

Terza pushed her palm through the air. "It is no trouble at all. Baking is just a small way of thanking you for allowing us to invade your law firm."

Barnaby adjusted his bowtie. "Now that is *my* pleasure. This stuffy corporate law firm needs a bit of excitement."

"Speaking of excitement," Ramsey chimed in from the far end of the board room table. He ran his fingers through both sides of his thick auburn hair. "Terza, please don't tell me you won again!"

Terza turned her head from one side to the other. "No, I didn't. I thought that you won!" She watched Ramsey's focus turn to Barnaby and then followed his lead.

"Let me see." Barnaby grinned and rubbed his chin.

Ramsey laughed. "I can tell you're stalling!"

Barnaby focused on Terza. "You were two wins up on

Ramsey in July, and then he won in August. That gave you a lead of just one. Case won in September, and now we have another new winner for October."

The room instantly became *pin-drop* quiet. "Congratulations to"—Barnaby stretched out his pause— "Moheenie Brickman!"

"Congratulations!" Terza reached out a hand to Moheenie. "Why didn't you tell me?"

"I was too excited." Moheenie squeezed Terza's palm. "I just couldn't believe it, and I wanted to hear from Barnaby first."

"Wonderful job," Barnaby told her. "You are now tied with Case. Hopefully you two will continue to give Terza and Ramsey some much needed competition."

"Congratulations, Moheenie!" Case called out.

"Yes, congratulations," Ramsey echoed.

A chorus of congratulatory comments sounded from around the conference room table.

Moheenie's gaze circled the room, thanking them all.

Barnaby centered his attention to the group. "Let us begin. I do not believe we have any new members this evening. Therefore, we may forgo the introductions. Now as you all know, you must name the murderer and then also explain exactly how you knew who committed the murder. Approximately one half of you did name the correct person, but this time only Moheenie accurately explained how she knew who did it." Barnaby turned his focus back toward Moheenie. "You now have the honor of telling our club members who committed the murder and how she carried it out."

Moheenie stood to address her fellow book club members. When she finished, Moheenie received a round of applause. Once again Barnaby took the floor.

"Thank you, Moheenie. Fortunately, we still have more than twenty mysteries to solve in our delightful whodunnit book. Now let us begin the discussion on our current murder mystery novel. Since we just started this new book, I am hoping all of you have completed reading through chapter seven. May I please see a show of hands?"

Everyone raised a hand.

Barnaby smiled. "Excellent. Has anyone read more than seven chapters?" He looked around the table to a motion of turning heads. A lively discussion then followed for just over an hour while the members speculated on solving the current crime. As the time neared 8:30 p.m. Barnaby circulated a five-page handout to each member.

"Five pages?" Ramsey asked, sounding surprised.

Terza laughed. "Game on, Ramsey. The longer the pages, the harder the mystery."

"Not necessarily," Barnaby countered.

"Have you already read it?" Moheenie asked him.

"No, in fact I have not. As all of you, I was a bit surprised by the length. Our previous murder mysteries have been on three pages." Barnaby made eye contact with several of the members. "You know your challenge. Do your best to solve the murder, and then explain exactly how you solved it. As always, my email address is located on the first page. Remember, you must email me your complete answer within three weeks in order to participate. That would be prior to the fifth of November." Barnaby adjusted his horn-rimmed eyeglasses. "Is there any other business to discuss?"

Terza raised her hand. "Shall we talk about our November and December schedules?"

Barnaby nodded. "Yes, that is a great idea. Our next get-together on the sixteenth of November will be a combined November and December meeting. Since many of us are extra busy from Thanksgiving until the end of the year, there will be no book club meeting in December. We will resume in January."

"Do we have a date for January?" Case looked at his phone. "I have my calendar pulled up."

"Not as yet," Barnaby answered. "I will distribute the annual schedule for next year at our meeting in November. Does that sound like a plan?" After a combination of thank you, yes, and nods, Barnaby continued, "Right-oh, then. Let us call it an evening. Thank you for coming, and drive safely."

Terza stood and pushed in her chair. "Thank you, Barnaby. We'll see you next month."

"See you next month," Moheenie added. "Thanks, Barnaby!"

"You both are most welcome. Goodbye, ladies."

Terza and Moheenie entered the elevator on the firm's twenty-fourth floor and rode it to the parking garage. As they walked toward Terza's Fiat she lightly tapped Moheenie's shoulder. "Great job, Mo! That was one of our hardest mysteries. How did you know who did it?"

Moheenie looked toward the garage ceiling. "I'm not sure." When she turned her focus to Terza, Moheenie's dark eyes sprang alive. "Maybe it had something to do with Doctor McCool's murder. My mystery-solving skills must be on overdrive."

Terza nodded. "Yes, they must be." She flipped through the pages of the latest handout and then arched her brows. "This looks like fun."

"Are you going to begin tonight?"

"Of course I am. Are you?"

Moheenie chuckled. "Yes, especially now that I have tasted victory."

CHAPTER ONE

PLANS ARE SET

LITTLE ITALY, SAN DIEGO, CALIFORNIA

Wednesday

After another end to a busy day of catering, Terza stood in the office of her Macaroni on Wheels catering company, or *MOW* as they commonly called it, and stared out the window. She blindly watched the sidewalk activity as both tourists and locals made their way along the main street. She blinked several times to clear her mind. Today was eventful, but not too difficult, as *MOW* catered another downtown baby shower. Her jumbled thoughts centered on the two big weekend events, beginning with Joshua's surprise birthday party for his wife Sloan on Friday and the pizza party on Halloween night.

From previous experience Terza knew she should mentally isolate each event. The surprise party came first, so that is where she set her focus. *I need to call Joshua.* Still looking outside Terza noticed several couples obviously going to dinner, while others were out walking their dogs. Thinking it was time for her own dinner, Terza sat behind her office desk to make her final catering call for the evening. She dialed Joshua Kamoze's telephone number.

"Hello, Terza. How are you this evening?"

"I'm fine, thank you, Joshua. How are you?"

"Excellent, thank you."

"Are you able to speak freely right now, or is Sloan within earshot?"

"It's safe to talk. I'm still at the office. Sloan has no idea what we're planning."

Terza checked the clock on her office wall. "It's after six. Are you working late?"

Joshua guffawed softly. "I wish. Typically Sloan and I roll in together around seven. It makes for very long days."

"What do you have for dinner?"

Joshua sighed. "Not much, I'm afraid. That is one thing Sloan and I are determined to change. We need to think ahead and plan out our meals. We even talked about taking cooking lessons."

Terza chuckled. "Funny you should say that. Setting up a cooking school has been in the back of my mind."

"Sign us up! Sloan and I will be your first students."

"You are very kind, but it is just a seed of a thought right now. When and if it sprouts, I will let you know." She used her computer mouse to click on her calendar. "I called to coordinate our meeting for tomorrow morning."

"Coordinate away."

Terza smiled as Joshua sounded even more British than usual. "Okay, are you absolutely positive Sloan will be gone when Moheenie and I arrive?"

"Yes, I am absolutely positive," he echoed her question. "A few of Sloan's coworkers are coming to the surprise party. They have been extremely helpful and have assured me Sloan has a busy day tomorrow. She will be leaving the house by eight and will not be home until after six."

"Is there a chance she could return home during lunch?"

"No, not at all. Her friends are taking Sloan out for a birthday lunch since she's off work Friday."

"That is perfect, Joshua. I do have a number of other questions, but they can hold until we see you tomorrow." Terza checked her notes on the computer tablet resting on the desk.

"The only other question for this evening is about the menu. Do you have any last-minute changes?"

"No, I think everything sounds perfect just the way we planned."

Terza smiled with relief. She always asked about menu changes before a catering event but also held her breath hoping none would come. "I believe that is it for now. Moheenie and I will see you tomorrow morning at nine. Are you taking the entire day off?"

"Yes, I am taking both Thursday and Friday off. Of course Sloan will have no idea as she always calls my mobile instead of the office."

"Perfect. Thank you, Joshua. Have a great evening."

"You, too. I'll see you in the morning."

Terza disconnected her call and returned her attention to the party menu. She inhaled deeply knowing how much was involved and then dialed her sister Angeline.

"Hi, Tee. What's up?"

"Hey, Ange. You are still helping me on Friday, right?"

"Of course I am. I wouldn't back out at this late notice."

"You're a lifesaver. Thank you."

"Why do you sound so stressed, Terza?"

"It's not stress." Terza's neck stiffened. "I'm just a tad bit concerned. There are so many things to plan."

"Would you like me to bring Mom? I know she'd be happy to help."

"I don't know." Terza hesitated. "Mom would be a huge help, but—"

Angeline chuckled. "But she would try and take over?"

"Exactly."

"Well since you have me for one night only, I will allow you to be the boss. Let me know if you change your mind about Mom."

"Thanks, big sis."

"You're welcome, little sis. Now, am I still meeting you at the Kamoze's house?"

"Yes. Are you able to make it by five?"

"Five is just fine. I decided to only work half a day on Friday. It will be nice getting off at noon. Do you need me any earlier?"

"No, Angeline, but thank you anyway. The setup is no problem. We just need extra hands come party time. Please remember to park down the street. Joshua doesn't want any cars near the house."

"I will. What about the other guests? If I remember correctly that area doesn't have a lot of street parking."

"You're right, it doesn't, but Joshua certainly knows how to host a party. Since he often uses a car service when traveling for work, he decided to hire the same company for the entire evening. I believe he booked seven cars to chauffeur the guests to and from the party."

"I love it! What a great idea. As your attorney I'm also happy none of the guests will be driving."

"Amen to that, especially since we are providing the wine. Joshua is taking care of the balance of the bar, but I do get concerned whenever *MOW* is the provider of alcohol."

"You can never be too careful," Angeline cautioned. "Call if you need me before Friday. Love you!"

"Love you more!"

"Ciao, ciao, Tee."

"Ciao, ciao."

Terza's shoulders relaxed after speaking with her older sister. She also realized that the empty feeling in her stomach was due to hunger, but she lacked the desire to cook or sit in a restaurant. Thinking about her options, Terza rested her palms on the arms of her desk chair and tilted back. *What do I feel like eating?* With her mind finally made up Terza pressed the number for Buon Appetito, one of her favorite restaurants in Little Italy. This particular one specialized in an amazing mushroom and asparagus risotto baked in a nest of parmesan cheese.

After three rings Terza heard the familiar, *"Buona sera."*

"Buona sera, Sophie. It's Terza."

"Terza, how lovely to hear your voice."

"Thank you. I was wondering if the restaurant is extra busy."

"We are never too busy to make Risotto Alla Piemontese for our favorite customer. Would you like to place an order?"

"You are too kind, and you know me very well. Yes, please, I would love an order to go. I am closing up shop as we speak, so I can be there in about fifteen minutes."

"Fifteen minutes is perfect. Would you like me to pour you a glass of wine?"

"Hum," Terza murmured. "Thank you very much for the offer. It sounds tempting, but not tonight. I am in the mood to just hang out at home."

"I get it," Sophie told her. "I will see you soon. Ciao."

"Ciao, ciao."

Now with the thought of the scrumptious risotto on her mind, Terza checked to make certain her stove was turned off. She then finished wiping down the counters, closed the blinds, and turned off the lights. "Ten minutes down and five to go." Terza exited her front office door, turned the lock, and headed out.

She attempted to walk briskly to Buon Appetito but found herself having to dart around the slow-moving dinner crowd. Instead of being frustrating, their leisurely pace made her smile. It pleased Terza when others also appreciated her favorite town. Oftentimes she would stroll along the main street in Little Italy and take specific note of all the community offered. The former four-block fishing village had transformed into a vibrant destination for residents and tourists to enjoy. The city planners were careful to provide parks along with the housing, and many different types of restaurants lined the boulevard. Some were upscale dining, and yet others were one window, to-go-only pizza stops. Her family's Tiepolo Mercato even provided the groceries for dining at home.

Inside Buon Appetito, Terza accepted the white paper bag with enthusiasm and hurried the few blocks home. When she opened the door of her fourth-floor condominium Terza was surprised to see her cat waiting out in the open.

"Well hello, Olive!"

Olive purred loudly.

"To what do I owe this pleasure?" Terza walked to the kitchen and placed her dinner on the counter. "You rarely show your beauty until you know the coast is clear."

Olive's purring intensified when Terza walked toward the pantry cabinet.

"Are you hungry, my precious little lady?" Terza opened the door and selected a can of Olive's favorite wet food. She lowered the salmon selection to the counter, crouching down to rub Olive's back. Terza placed her palm on Olive's head and slowly moved her hand toward Olive's tail. She smiled as Olive seemed to be mesmerized by her touch. Terza then stood to pop the top of Olive's dinner. "Would you like some salmon?"

Olive lifted a paw as if offering to help. Loud, persistent meowing replaced Olive's purring after Terza lowered the dish. Moments later all turned quiet.

Terza then transferred her own dinner to a ceramic plate. With the steaming risotto piled high, she slid onto a counter stool and inhaled the enticing aroma. Her fork captured the perfect bite of rice, asparagus, and mushrooms. Terza allowed the mixture to momentarily rest on her tongue before chewing. When her attempt to cut a section of the toasted parmesan nest failed, Terza used her fingers to pull off a piece. She dropped the melted cheese into her mouth and moaned. *This has to be the best risotto on the planet.*

CHAPTER TWO

RUBY SLIPPERS

Thursday

At the home of Joshua Kamoze, Terza rang the doorbell and waited with Moheenie on the front step. Moments later Joshua opened the door.

"Hello, Terza." Joshua beamed. He was casually dressed in khaki shorts and a white linen shirt with rolled-up sleeves. Terza appreciated how the bright white accented Joshua's dark skin tone. "Please, please, come in." He then extended his hand to Moheenie. "You must be the fabulous Moheenie I've heard about. It is nice to meet you. I am Joshua Kamoze, and please just call me Joshua."

Moheenie intercepted his outstretched palm. "It is nice to meet you, too, Joshua." She looked sideways at Terza and then laughed. "I'm fabulous?"

"Of course you are!" As they stepped through the doorway, Terza surveyed the beautifully decorated living room, thinking that it looked like a designer showcase home. The attention to detail was amazing. Terza first noticed the tan paint with several scarlet red accent walls. The chenille print sofa and coordinating side chairs housed more throw pillows than Terza could count, with each outlined by red and gold loop fringe. "Your home is absolutely gorgeous."

"Thank you, but I must give Sloan all the credit. She has great taste. As you can tell she adores the British West Indies design."

Moheenie looked toward the ceiling. "Wow! Check out the amazing fan."

Terza followed Moheenie's gaze to a large spiral of bamboo-style blades. "Now this fan definitely has an island feel. I love the way it turns like a barrel. What is the material?"

Joshua shook his head. "I'm not certain. The fan blades look like wood, but I think they may be pressed bamboo. Sloan knows how much I like fans and surprised me when I returned home from a business trip. It was already spiralling beautifully when I arrived."

Terza returned her focus to Joshua. "It looks fantastic—a definite statement piece."

"I agree." Moheenie blew out a breath of air. "Are you certain that Sloan will not mind having a party in this perfect home?"

Joshua laughed. "I'm positive. We entertain all the time. What good is a house if it is not a home?"

"Great point." Terza gestured with her hand. "Lead the way. We are now on to the most important room."

"I am guessing you are referring to the kitchen?" Joshua asked.

"Always," Moheenie answered.

As the trio made their way through the dining area, Terza and Moheenie continued to admire the decor. When they entered the kitchen, Terza stopped. "Wait a minute." Both hands shot to her hips. "I thought you don't cook very much?"

"We don't." Joshua's dark eyes narrowed. "Why do you ask?"

Terza spread her arms wide. "Because of this catering-company-sized kitchen. It is astonishing!"

Joshua shrugged. "What can I say?"

Moheenie chuckled. "With a kitchen like this I think you need cooking lessons."

"We already discussed it," Terza added. "Who knows? Maybe Joshua and Sloan will be our first students."

"I'm hoping." Joshua lifted his crossed fingers. "When Sloan and I decided to remodel we just wanted to get it right. Even though neither of us are big in the kitchen, we have dreams of one day knowing our way around."

"You did a fantastic job." Terza placed her computer tablet on the generous-sized granite counter. "We have a lot to go over, so we better get started." She swiped the screen and then opened the *Sloan Surprise Party* window. "Let's begin by reviewing the menu."

Joshua leaned against the counter. "I'm all ears."

Terza inhaled while reading from her screen. "I know you wanted plenty of appetizers first."

Joshua nodded.

"As discussed, we plan on serving Crispy Polenta Bites, which are basically fried polenta rounds topped with marinara sauce and shaved parmesan cheese."

"They sound delicious," Joshua commented.

"Trust me," Moheenie said. "They are!"

Terza looked up and smiled before continuing. "Our next appetizer is melon wrapped with prosciutto. On this appetizer I toss the cantaloupe slices with a balsamic vinegar dressing. It really adds to the flavor."

Joshua chuckled. "Let me guess. I bet your prosciutto comes from the Tiepolo Mercato?"

"Of course." Terza grinned. "We serve nothing but the best."

Moheenie pinned her eyes on Joshua. "Wait until you hear about the Brussels sprouts. They are my favorite."

"I adore Brussels sprouts."

"Then hopefully our third appetizer will also be a favorite of yours as well, Joshua," Terza said. "The Brussels sprouts are tossed with honey, olive oil, and fresh herbs. I then build a skewer of sprouts alternating with pancetta. Together they are baked until crisp."

Joshua rubbed his flat stomach. "Yum! Those sound delicious. Now I can't wait to hear the last two."

Terza checked her notes. "Roasted mushrooms with walnuts is the fourth appetizer. I wanted to have at least two vegetable dishes."

Joshua nodded. "Good idea."

"The last appetizer is for the bread lovers," Terza announced.

Moheenie and Joshua simultaneously raised their hands.

"It is fried fennel bread made with pizza dough." Terza looked to Joshua. "What do you think?"

"I think we are going to be too full for dinner, but that's a good thing. I am hoping our guests feel pampered. Where are you going to place the appetizer platters?"

"We were planning on passing them while walking throughout the different rooms," Moheenie explained. "It's fun for the guests to mingle and let us come to them."

Joshua placed a palm over his heart. "I like that idea."

Terza smiled. "I'm glad. We also need to decide on the dinner service. If my notes are correct you do *not* want us to set up tables?"

"That's right. I hope our guests will feel free to sit anywhere." He motioned toward the rear of his home. "Our back patio has heaters and is quite comfortable. A minimum of twelve guests can enjoy their meals on the two large tables." Joshua looked toward the dining table. "That table can easily sit ten guests, and another five can get comfy here at the bar. The rest of our guests can sit throughout our home."

"Aren't you concerned about guests eating on your beautiful furniture?" Moheenie asked.

"Not in the least. According to Sloan we have slipcovers, although I'm not certain I know what that means."

Moheenie and Terza exchanged a smile. "We do," Moheenie said. "Slipcovers are a great way to go."

"And they can be washed." Terza walked over to the long dining room wall with a huge glass window facing the street. "What do you think if we set up the pasta station beneath this window?"

Joshua joined her side. "Sounds good to me. Do you have enough room?"

Terza measured with outstretched arms. "I think it will work perfectly. There will be plenty of space between our worktable and the dining table." She stepped closer to the living room. "If we set up right here, there should be no problem at all."

"I can always move the dining table more toward the kitchen," Joshua offered.

"Thank you, but I don't think it will be necessary." She remained by the window. "In this area we plan to set up the pasta station. As you requested, we will have two selections of fresh pasta. Moheenie will be serving capellini with garlic, tomatoes, and basil, and I will be preparing spaghetti with shrimp and lemon."

"I'm hungry already!" Joshua looked toward Moheenie. "Is it hard to make the pasta dishes fresh for each guest?"

"Not now, but at first I was petrified! Terza has taught me so much."

"Where did you learn to cook, Terza?"

"First from my mom, of course, and then I went to culinary school."

Joshua clapped his hands together. "The food sounds incredible. Between the appetizers and the pasta stations our guests are going to be full."

Terza held up her hand. "Wait, you forgot about the gnocchi."

Joshua placed a hand to his head. "That's right. Where will that be?"

"Over there in the kitchen. My sister Angeline will be in the kitchen serving the gnocchi. It will be Cacio E Pepe style, which is basically cheese, pepper, and butter." Terza snapped her fingers. "Oh, and Angeline will also be serving the garlic bread."

Joshua touched his forehead. "That's right. I forgot about the garlic bread. Do you think I ordered too much food?"

"We can always skip the garlic bread," Terza suggested.

"I don't know." Joshua sighed. "Moheenie, what do you think?"

Moheenie lifted her arms in surrender. "Please don't ask me. When it comes to garlic bread I can never get enough!"

"I agree." He smiled at Terza. "The garlic bread stays."

"Okay, but remember we also have dessert."

"Didn't we decide on just gelato?"

"Yes, we have an assortment of three flavors, but I thought you also ordered a birthday cake."

Joshua rolled his dark eyes. "I did! Oh well," he said with finality in his voice. "Let's keep the menu as it is."

"Where should we set up the bar?" Terza looked around the room.

"The outside patio will be perfect. Would you like to see it?"

"Yes, please." Terza looked to Moheenie. "Why don't you go with Joshua, and I will be right there."

"Let's go through the living room. The glass sliders in the family room open the full width of the wall."

Moheenie followed Joshua as Terza typed a few last-minute notes into her computer tablet. She glanced up at the sound of the side kitchen door opening. "Hello," Terza greeted a female who she guessed to be in her late twenties. She was fair skinned and wore navy blue yoga pants and a baggy pink T-shirt. Her red hair was pulled back into a ponytail with several loose tendrils falling across her face. Terza watched her brush wet strands of hair away from her bright green eyes.

"You must be the caterer. Joshua said you were coming over. I'm his little sister, Ruby."

"It is nice to meet you, Ruby." Terza stepped closer and offered her hand. "Yes, I'm Terza, owner of Macaroni on Wheels catering."

Ruby ignored Terza's outstretched palm, opened the refrigerator door, and withdrew a bottle of water. "Oh." She stared blindly ahead while sipping from the plastic bottle.

Feeling uncomfortable, Terza returned to her computer tablet and turned off the screen. "Joshua and Moheenie are waiting for me on the patio. I'll be right back."

"I know what you're thinking," Ruby announced with zero emotion.

"Excuse me?"

"Joshua has dark skin and mine is light. How can we possibly be siblings?"

Terza shook her head. "That never even entered my mind."

"It is not polite to lie," Ruby said with a matter-of-fact tone. It seemed like Ruby was simply making a statement.

Uncertain how to respond, Terza decided to just ignore Ruby's comment.

"I was adopted." Ruby's eyes finally met Terza's. "When I was two, our mother and father adopted me. Joshua was only ten."

"Where did you live?"

"We lived in Charlotte, North Carolina. Our father is a banker."

"That's wonderful, Ruby." Terza was pleased to have what seemed to be a normal conversation.

"We moved to Los Angeles right before I started high school. Daddy got a job transfer."

"Is that where Joshua went to college?"

"Yes, he went to U.C.L.A." Ruby's blank stare resumed.

"Shall we join Joshua on the patio?" Terza suggested.

When Ruby failed to comment, Terza turned to lead the way. Without looking back, she hoped Ruby would follow.

Joshua's face lit up when Terza stepped outside. Looking behind her he said, "Ruby Slippers, how was your run?"

"It was nice." Ruby moved to him, leaning her head onto Joshua's chest.

"I see you met Terza, and this is Moheenie."

Ruby instantly stood erectly and extended her hand toward Moheenie. "Hi, Moheenie, it is so nice to meet you. I'm Ruby."

Terza could not believe the transformation in Ruby.

"My silly brother calls me Ruby Slippers. It's kind of our thing."

"I get it." Moheenie chuckled. "Since my maiden name was Lakalaka, my husband often calls me Lakalaka instead of Moheenie or Mo."

"Lakalaka. I like it!"

Joshua spread his arms widely. "Tell me, Terza, what do you think of our patio?"

She surveyed the outside patio and guessed the covered area to be at least twenty by thirty feet. It featured an outdoor built-in barbecue with a refrigerator and a large stainless-steel sink. "This is amazing." Terza looked toward the now opened wall. "I love how your family room just flows into this outdoor space."

"Look at these curtains." Moheenie stood holding onto the white sailcloth fabric. "Doesn't it feel like we are at an exclusive resort?"

Terza nodded. "It sure does."

"Originally Sloan and I added the curtains just to capture an overall look," Joshua said. "But I was surprised how often we use them. Sometimes we close one side if the sun is coming in too strong, and they even provide protection from the wind."

Moheenie released the fabric and angled her head toward Joshua. "Would you prefer us to set up the pasta station out here?"

Joshua rubbed his chin. "That's a thought." He looked to Terza. "What do you think?"

"It is such an inviting space, but I always prefer to separate the food from the bar area. Guests tend to congregate in those two sections. The party will spread throughout your entire home if you divide them."

Joshua nodded enthusiastically. "That is exactly what I wanted."

Terza smiled. "I'm glad." She walked over to the free-standing bar, made of bamboo with a high-glass resin top, which was located next to the built-in barbecue. "Ranger is going to love working here," she told Moheenie.

"Ranger is my husband," Moheenie explained to Ruby and Joshua. "His primary job is a San Diego Lifeguard, but he tends bar for us whenever he's available."

"Ranger is the best bartender ever!" Terza added.

Moheenie joined Terza at the bamboo bar. "I believe you have a friend bringing the beer. Did you also want Ranger to serve it?"

"Yes, if he doesn't mind. My friend Brady owns a brewery in the North Park area. He will probably bring ten times more than necessary." Joshua laughed. "But Brady will also want to enjoy the party. Please ask Ranger not to be offended when Brady gets overly excited."

Moheenie smiled. "Ranger is an easy-going guy. I'm sure he won't mind."

"When I last spoke with Brady, he said he was bringing numerous coolers filled with beer and ice. He also has made a list of the beer selection to have at the bar. But I know Brady. If someone asks Ranger a question about the selection of beers, Brady will jump in and explain way more than the person will ever want to know."

Terza smiled. "Brewing beer is an art. Brady is probably very proud of his accomplishments."

Joshua tented his fingers. "That he is."

"I think Brady and Ranger are going to get along great," Moheenie added. "Just watch, by the end of the evening they will be standing side by side bartending together."

"Mo, I think we should set up two water dispensers there"—Terza pointed to the barbecue counter—"and two in the kitchen."

"I stocked up on small water bottles and also tons of soda," Joshua said.

"That's great." Terza tucked a loose strand of hair behind her ear. "Ranger will keep a row of chilled water bottles on the bar, and then out here we will have two glass dispensers. One will be filled with ice water, rosemary, and cucumbers, and the other with lemons and limes. We always like guests to stay hydrated, and flavored waters are very appealing. Moheenie and I find that people will often choose a glass of water instead of soda or alcohol."

"I'm not surprised. Sloan and I could not get enough of the water at our last hotel."

"I think we are all set out here." Terza stepped away from the bar. "Shall we return to the kitchen? I have a few final questions."

Joshua extended an arm. "Follow me."

"I'll be right in," Moheenie called. "I want to double check a couple of things for Ranger."

"I'll stay with Moheenie," Ruby told her brother. "You know, just in case she has any questions."

"Thanks, Ruby Slippers." Joshua patted Ruby's shoulder. "You're the best!"

Back in the kitchen Terza touched her computer tablet to revive the screen and then swiped to retrieve her notes. She read a few lines before shifting her gaze to Joshua. "Are you still handling the decorations?"

"Yes." He angled his head. "Well, not me personally, but Sloan's friends. I'm kind of afraid to ask what they have planned."

"Ha!" Terza grinned. "Is this a big birthday?"

"Yes. Sloan is turning thirty. I just hope they don't go overboard with comical reminders."

"I'm sure her friends will know exactly what she likes." Terza glimpsed at her screen. "One of her friends is also bringing the cake, correct?"

Joshua nodded. "That would be Carnegie. She owns a bakery in the North County."

"I can't wait to meet her. Perhaps I will be able to send business her way." Terza read from the screen, and then turned her computer tablet off. "Would you still like us to serve coffee?"

"Most definitely, as I am a full-fledged coffee addict."

"Then you are going to appreciate Ranger's talents. He makes a mean cappuccino."

"Excellent." Joshua turned his attention to Ruby when she joined them in the kitchen.

Terza captured a flash of distress on Moheenie's face as she lingered behind Ruby. "I think we are all set. The two of us will be back tomorrow by three, and then Ranger will arrive no later than four. My sister, Angeline will be here by five."

Joshua slid an arm around Ruby's waist. "It sounds like you have everything planned perfectly. Please just remember to park out of sight from the house."

"No problem," Terza said. "After we unload, I will move the van several blocks away."

"Sometimes I park near the Palm Tree Inn," Ruby told them. "There is always plenty of parking along the street."

"Isn't that too far?" Joshua asked.

Ruby shook her head. "Not really, Joshua. It's barely three blocks."

"Well, hopefully you won't have to move your catering van that far, but if so, I can always follow you down the hill."

"Thanks. I'm sure we will find a suitable spot. I also reminded Ranger and Angeline to park away from the house."

"Thank you, Terza, and thank you, Moheenie. I think Sloan is going to be very happy."

"She is going to love her surprise," Ruby added.

"It is our pleasure." Terza and Moheenie moved toward the front door.

"Thanks again," Moheenie added. "We will see you tomorrow."

"Goodbye," Joshua said.

"Bye!" Ruby waved.

Terza and Moheenie walked toward Terza's red Fiat. After getting in, they looked at each other. It was obvious that each had something important to say.

"You first, Mo. I caught a look when you followed Ruby into the kitchen."

"That Ruby Slippers has a slipper missing. She is one psycho chick!"

"I was going to say the same thing. But she was crazy with me, not you. I couldn't believe how sweet she was when Joshua introduced you."

"Ha!" Moheenie's eyes ballooned. "That was only when her brother was around. She came completely unglued the moment you two left for the kitchen."

"What did she say?" Terza could see a lot happening behind Moheenie's dark eyes.

"She first asked, no wait, practically *accused* me of having a relationship with her brother."

"She accused you? That's crazy, Mo!"

"Well, almost. Ruby Slippers asked me how long I have known her brother. Of course, I told her we just met today."

"Didn't she believe you?"

"No! She told me to tell the truth and not to worry because she would keep it a secret from Sloan." Moheenie took a loud breath. "I insisted that I was telling the truth, then asked her not to call me a liar."

Terza's mouth shot open. "You said that?"

Moheenie shrugged. "'Please don't call me a liar' is exactly how I worded it."

"Good for you, Mo! I agree, she has more than one screw loose."

"Tell me, what did she say to you, Tee?"

Terza angled her head. "Come to think of it she basically accused me of lying, too. When Ruby—"

Moheenie laughed. "You mean Ruby Slippers."

"You're right. When Ruby Slippers first came into the kitchen she had this crazy stare. I wondered what was going on in her mind."

"She was probably looking for a butcher knife." Moheenie paused. "No wait! Forget I said that. Psycho chick is already crazy enough without me making up stories."

"It's forgotten. But listen to this." Terza grimaced. "After Ruby Slippers stares me down, she then informs me she knows what I am thinking!"

"Good grief!" Moheenie pressed her temples. "Now she's psychic? I guess psycho and psychic do go together. What did she say you were thinking?"

"That I didn't understand how she and Joshua could possibly be siblings. Ruby Slippers pointed out that his skin is dark, and her skin is light."

"So?"

"Exactly, Mo. It never crossed my mind."

Moheenie lowered her hands. "Did you tell her that?"

Terza nodded. "Of course I did, and in turn, Ruby Slippers told me it is not polite to lie."

"At least we're in good company!" Moheenie laughed. "She thinks we're both liars."

"You are right about that." Terza looked ahead, lost in thought, before shifting her focus back to Moheenie. "You know, Ruby Slippers must be insecure about her adoption. Joshua was ten when his parents adopted her."

"How old was she?"

"She was just a baby. Ruby Slippers told me they lived in Charlotte, North Carolina before moving to Los Angeles. Their father was in banking."

"Did he get a job transfer?"

"Yes. They moved just before Ruby Slippers started high school. Joshua attended U.C.L.A."

Moheenie rubbed her chin. "I wonder what brought them to San Diego?"

Terza rotated her head. "She didn't say. Plus I don't know if Ruby Slippers lives here in San Diego, too."

"You can always ask her."

"Ha!" Terza started the engine. "Buckle up. I'll leave that one up to you."

Moheenie fastened her seatbelt. "No thanks!"

The two friends laughed and talked on the return trip to Macaroni on Wheels but kicked it back into work mode when they reached the office. "We sure have a lot to do." Terza unlocked the door. "What time is it?"

Moheenie checked her phone. "I can't believe it is just after eleven. Doesn't it seem later?"

"Yes, much later." Terza dropped her bag onto the kitchen counter. "Shall we tackle a few things before lunch?"

"I'm game." Moheenie reached for their aprons, tossing one to Terza. "Let's power through for an hour or so then take a quick break."

"Sounds like a plan. I would like to have everything prepared before we leave for the day."

Moheenie nodded. "I agree. Tomorrow morning should just be for any last-minute details."

Terza tapped her forehead. "You can read my mind." She finished wrapping her apron strings from back to front and tied a quick bow.

Moheenie examined their catering whiteboard. "What shall I start on first?"

Terza joined her by the board. "Let's begin at the end by making the gelato. We can work on it together."

Moheenie raised her eyebrows. "We do get to taste test, right?"

"Of course we do!" Terza moved to a row of cupboards and selected several large stainless-steel bowls. "After we finish the gelato would you like to start on the polenta bites? You can fry the rounds, then leave them on a rack to cool. The marinara is made and ready to go. We will put them together at the party."

"That sounds easy. Which appetizer are *you* going to tackle?"

"Probably the Brussels sprouts. Do you agree?"

"I do." Moheenie grinned. "Now let's get this party started."

"You stole my line!"

CHAPTER THREE

It's Party Time

Friday

When Terza steered her Macaroni on Wheels catering van onto the Kamoze's driveway, Joshua stood at the opened front door. Wearing blue denim shorts and a lime green T-shirt, he appeared to be directing foot traffic. Their friends were funneling through, already zealously preparing for the big day. Moheenie waved before Terza walked up to greet him.

"Good afternoon, Joshua. Would you like us to use the side kitchen door?"

"Good afternoon, Terza. Please use whichever door you would like. May I help you unload?"

"No, thank you. Moheenie and I have this down to a science."

He tilted his head and smiled. "I will agree on one term: you let me carry the heavy items."

"Agreed." Terza grinned. "Talk later." She returned to the van and helped Moheenie lower their rolling cart to the concrete driveway. One by one, they filled the chrome cart with plastic food bins.

"Shall we stop and take this first load?"

"Definitely, Mo. I think we may be getting top heavy."

Moheenie looked from side to side. "Which way shall we roll?"

"Let's use the kitchen door." Terza wrapped both hands around the chrome handle. "I'll push and you guide."

The cart rolled smoothly along the front driveway, but the sidewalk narrowed when they reached the corner of the house. Terza slowed her pace, allowing Moheenie to steer them on a direct path to the kitchen door. Moheenie knocked and then opened the door without waiting for a response. She guided the cart toward the middle of the kitchen while Terza pushed. They both stopped and scanned the cheerful decorations.

"Wow!" Moheenie lifted her arms. "Everything looks fantastic!"

"Why thank you!" A smiling female walked into the dining area. "We wanted to make it colorful. Sloan loves color." She continued to the kitchen and held out a hand to Moheenie. "Hello there. My name is Carnegie."

Moheenie accepted Carnegie's hand. "Hi, I'm Moheenie, or just Mo, whichever comes out first."

Terza extended her right palm. "Carnegie! You are the wonderful baker."

Carnegie embraced Terza's hand. "And you must be the wonderful caterer?"

"At your service." Terza smiled. "I'm Terza. It's very nice to meet you. I cannot wait to see the cake."

Carnegie pumped her eyebrows as if preparing to reveal a secret. Her blue eyes seemed to sparkle. She tiptoed to the refrigerator and withdrew a large pink cake box. After carefully lowering it to the kitchen counter, Carnegie slowly lifted the lid. Terza and Moheenie both peeked in and saw a cream-topped cake with raspberries and orange slices.

"It is gorgeous," Moheenie said.

"Yes, it is," Terza agreed. "What type of cake did you bake?"

Carnegie pushed a blonde tendril behind her ear. "The cake is one of Sloan's favorites. It's a ricotta cake, with blood orange, raspberry, and cranberry whipped cream."

Terza angled her head. "The ricotta must lead to an extremely moist cake."

Carnegie nodded. "It does. Have you ever baked with ricotta?"

"Yes, but not in a cake. I must give it a try." Terza tapped at her head. "Or, come to think of it, I will probably just call you." She leaned in for another look. "The birthday placard is perfect. How did you make it?"

"The placard is made with marzipan, and then of course the writing is chocolate."

"Happy birthday, Sloan," Moheenie read. "It looks nicer than writing directly on the cake."

"I think so, too." Carnegie smiled at her creation. "Typically I like the outside of my cakes to provide a hint as to what is inside. As you can see, with this cake I used the raspberries and blood oranges as the decoration."

"Is the gold edible?"

"Yes, most definitely." Carnegie glanced Terza's way. "Even the placard is edible."

"We better leave that one to Sloan!" Moheenie laughed. "Only the birthday girl should chew on her own name."

Carnegie giggled. "Good idea." She closed the pink box. "Would you like me to save each of you a piece of cake?"

"That is so sweet," Terza said. "I would love to taste your cake, but we don't want to take any away from the guests."

"Nonsense, there will be plenty. The cake serves forty, and from what I hear they are probably going to be too full for dessert."

"I'm never too full for cake." Moheenie rubbed her stomach.

Carnegie looked sideways at Moheenie. "You can't eat much. I wish I had your slender waist!"

"I think you look great." Terza reflected on Carnegie's vibrant blue eyes. *She looks happy.*

"You are too kind," Carnegie told Terza. "I hear you are a fantastic chef."

"Thank you. I hope you enjoy every last bite." Terza turned to Moheenie. "Are you ready for the final load?"

"Ready."

"Do you need any help, Terza?"

"No, but thank you, Carnegie."

"If you need me, I'll be out back. We have finished decorating inside the house and are now working on the patio."

"I'm glad you didn't decorate with black balloons and the number thirty all around," Moheenie commented.

Carnegie chuckled. "Have you met Sloan?"

Terza and Moheenie both turned their heads.

"She is such a sweetheart and doesn't look a day over twenty. Sloan wouldn't mind black balloons, but they just wouldn't fit her personality. I wanted the decor to be bright and festive."

Terza glanced up at the colorful *Happy Birthday* banner. "I think you hit the mark."

"Me, too," Moheenie agreed.

"Thank you, ladies. I'll see you in a bit."

Terza and Moheenie completed their final trip, then went to move the van out of the Kamoze's driveway. When they returned to the house, Moheenie resumed working in the kitchen while Terza carried a case of wine from the counter to the patio. Carnegie introduced her to three other friends before Terza excused herself to help Moheenie. She passed Ruby sitting on the bottom of the stairs.

"Hi, Ruby! It's nice to see you again," Terza lied convincingly.

"Hello, Terza. Have you seen my brother?"

"Yes, he is out back on the patio."

"Is he talking with all those other girls?"

What an odd question. "Joshua is with Sloan's friends, if that's what you mean. They're all preparing for the party. You should join them."

Ruby did not reply. Instead, she looked to the floor while knocking several times on the wooden stairstep.

Unsure of whether to remain or leave, Terza stood with her tennis shoes frozen in place. After several uncomfortable minutes Ruby finally spoke. "Stairs can be very dangerous."

Terza nodded slowly and struggled to think of a response. Before she could speak, Ruby jumped to her feet and bolted toward the back patio.

"Hi, Ruby," Terza heard Carnegie say. Seconds later Carnegie stood directly in front of Terza. "Are you alright?"

Terza blinked hard. "I uh," she stammered. "Yes, I'm fine."

"What did she say?" Carnegie asked, obviously referring to Ruby.

Terza knew she should remain professional and not gossip about her clients. "It's nothing."

Carnegie placed a hand tenderly on Terza's arm. "Honey, Sloan knows all about Ruby. It's okay, you can tell me."

Terza narrowed her eyes. "Does Joshua also know?"

"I don't think so. When it comes to his beloved Ruby Slippers, I think he purposely remains in the dark. Please don't let her bother you."

"It wasn't really anything specific, just weird. Ruby was sitting on the bottom stair. She knocked on the wood several times and told me that stairs can be dangerous. Then she jumped up and rushed outside without saying another word."

Carnegie sighed audibly. "Darn that girl. I don't know why she has to bring it up, especially on the day of Sloan's party."

"Bring what up?"

"Joshua's first wife, Yvette, died by accident," Carnegie spoke softly. "She fell down a flight of stairs and broke her neck."

Terza's hand shot to her mouth. "That's horrible! Poor Joshua, poor Ruby."

"You can feel for Joshua, but not Ruby. I mean, Yvette and Ruby were not close, but Joshua loved Yvette dearly. From what I understand, they knew each other in Jamaica."

"Ruby said they lived in North Carolina."

"Joshua's father was a banker in Jamaica. I believe they moved to the United States right before they adopted Ruby. I'm not sure though. They must have moved away from North Carolina because Sloan told me Joshua and Yvette lived in Los Angeles. That is where she died."

"You and Sloan sound very close." Terza interlocked her fingers.

Carnegie smiled warmly. "We are. When Sloan and Joshua fell in love, she was hesitant about marrying him. They talked a lot about Joshua's first wife, and Sloan shared a great deal with me. In the end she realized that Joshua truly loves her, and it is okay for him to have also loved Yvette."

Terza nodded at the sweet sentiment. "Thank you for helping me understand Ruby a little. I better go, though. Duty calls."

Carnegie followed as Terza made her way back to the kitchen. Moheenie had three of the four appetizers semi-prepared and positioned on sheet pans. "The prosciutto-wrapped melon is in the refrigerator."

Carnegie walked over to peek at each pan. "These appetizers look amazing. I still can't figure out how you two stay so slim."

Moheenie shrugged. "No idea."

"I think it's because we are constantly grazing," Terza suggested. "Half the time we forget to eat a regular meal because we have been tasting food all day."

Moheenie nodded. "I think you're right, Tee."

"I cannot wait to taste these Brussels sprouts." Carnegie moved to the refrigerator and withdrew three plastic bottles of water. "I'm back to work. See you in a bit."

Terza waited until Carnegie was out of sight before whispering, "I just had another Ruby Slippers adventure."

"What happened?"

Terza turned her head from side to side. "I better wait to tell you. Who knows when she will sneak up?" Terza studied each of the appetizer pans. "Thank you, Mo. They look great. I'm going to set up our pasta stations."

"What should I do next?"

"Just continue to organize each course. You are such a pro now."

Moheenie grinned. "Thanks, Tee!"

For the two pasta stations, Terza set up rectangular tables and covered them with red-and-white checkered tablecloths. On each table Terza placed dual electric countertop burners. She carefully positioned the cords so they would not accidently pull them from the wall while working. Terza looked up. "Mo, I gave each of us a large burner for the water and a small burner for mixing the pasta. What do you think?"

"That's perfect. Thank you."

"Remember to keep the water at a constant boil. Since you are using capellini, each serving will cook in less than three minutes. Are you comfortable with the progression?"

Moheenie walked closer to her pasta station. "Let's see, I first coat my hot pan with olive oil and then add the tomatoes." She looked to Terza who smiled and nodded. "Then I drop the pasta into the boiling salted water while the tomatoes are cooking down. When the pasta is ready, I add the garlic first, then the pasta, and toss them both with the tomatoes. Right before serving I add the basil."

"You've got it. Just remember to add a touch of pasta water if you feel it's needed."

Moheenie inspected the table contents. "Do we have ladles?"

Terza pulled them from a crate. "One each."

"Perfect." Moheenie tented her long, shapely fingers. "And do we have enough food for both stations?"

"We are prepared for thirty servings from each, for a total of sixty. Since we only have forty guests, I'm sure we'll be fine.

Besides, not every guest is going to have a pasta selection. Some may just enjoy the gnocchi.”

“I think we’re going to have a lot of food left over.”

“Yes, but fortunately, it won’t go to waste. We’ll leave any leftover gnocchi for Joshua and Sloan to enjoy another time. Your tomatoes and my shrimp will be perfect for tomorrow’s pizza night.”

Moheenie shot Terza a smile. “Plus, they are already prepared and ready to go.”

“My thoughts exactly.” Terza nodded.

Joshua returned to the dining area with Ruby close behind. “Wow, you ladies are fast workers.”

Terza chuckled. “Practice.”

“Joshua, I just love your accent,” Moheenie told him.

Terza looked to Ruby in time to see her eyes roll and her face scowl.

“Thank you, Moheenie. It comes from a combination of my mother and father. She is French, and he is British. They both attended the same college in England.”

“Did you ever live in England?”

“No, Terza, my parents had already moved to Jamaica before I was born. My father was hired as the president of a London-based bank located on the island.”

“What a great gig!” Moheenie said.

“I know.” Joshua nodded. “Typically banking does not come to mind when one thinks of Jamaica. But it was a fun place to grow up, and I had some wonderful school chums. The combination of French, British, and Jamaican resulted in this crazy accent of mine.”

“How did you feel about moving to North Carolina?” Terza asked.

“We were ready.” Joshua slowly rocked his head. “Jamaica is amazing, but there is something to be said for city life. Believe it or not, I actually got tired of wearing shorts and flip-flops every single day.”

Moheenie chuckled. "You mean as you are right now?"

Joshua joined her laughter. He looked down at his outfit. "Don't worry. I will be changed by party time." Joshua cupped his arm around Ruby and drew her close. "Ruby Slippers is the best part about moving to Charlotte."

Terza watched Ruby gaze adoringly at her brother. "You then moved to Los Angeles, right, Ruby?"

"Yes. Our parents still live there now, and I live in Long Beach."

"Will they also be joining us for the party?"

Joshua turned his head. "No, Moheenie, unfortunately they were not able to make it. But we will be spending time with them during Christmas." He walked closer to Terza's pasta station and waved the scent toward his nostrils. "This already smells amazing. What is that incredible aroma?"

"Most likely you are smelling the fresh garlic marinade we used for the shrimp, but I also am getting a whiff of the basil. Moheenie will be serving capellini with garlic, tomatoes, and fresh basil. At this station, I will be preparing spaghetti with shrimp and lemon."

"Please remind me to taste absolutely everything."

Terza smiled. "I'll try."

"You too, Moheenie," Joshua instructed playfully, much to Ruby's obvious disdain. He then took Ruby's hand. "Shall we finish up outside and then get ready?"

Ruby's former frown turned into a bright smile as she stared at Joshua. After the duo disappeared, Terza and Moheenie spoke volumes to each other with just one glance. When Moheenie's phone chimed her eyes moved to the screen.

"It's Ranger. He wants to know what we are wearing tonight."

"Dressy. Tell him to come as he is. His clothes are ironed and waiting here in the closet."

"That's right." Moheenie typed her response. She immediately started laughing. "Ranger says that he's naked. Do you still want him to come as is?"

"I don't believe it. Tell him to send a photo." Terza thought for a brief moment and then shouted, "Wait!"

Moheenie stopped typing.

"Don't you dare tell him to send a photo! I know Ranger, and I'm guessing he just might!"

Moheenie grinned. "Don't worry. I know him, too, and I wasn't about to request a photo. I was just reminding him about the time. He has fifteen minutes to get his rear here."

Ranger arrived in twenty minutes and worked quickly to set up the bar and coffee station. Brady appeared shortly thereafter, and the two acted like old friends. Terza's sister, Angeline, arrived less than thirty minutes later. By quarter past five, the Macaroni on Wheels foursome excused themselves and headed for the prearranged guest bedroom. Angeline, Terza, and Moheenie changed into their dress uniforms while Ranger used the adjoining bathroom.

"These are nice skirts," Angeline commented with a sly smile. "I need a new black skirt for work."

Terza joined Angeline at the full-length mirror. "Would you like the white shirt, as well?"

Angeline inspected her outfit. "No, I think the skirt will be perfect. Some black tights, a pair of new black boots, and a caramel-colored sweater." She captured Moheenie's face in the reflection. "What do you think, Mo? Wouldn't that make a great outfit?"

Moheenie nodded aggressively. "Yes, it would. I really like brown and black together."

"You are as bad as Mom." Terza hugged her sister. "Do you know what happened the last time she helped us with a catering event?"

Angeline faked a confused expression.

"Oh come on. I bet you already know."

Angeline's smile grew.

"You do know!" Terza accused, pointing her finger toward Angeline's reflection. "Mom *took* one of my skirts."

"I think you actually *gave* it to her."

"You're right." Terza lowered her hand. "I did give it to her. Now I suppose you would like me to give you one, too?"

"It would look nice with my new boots."

"What new boots?"

Angeline laughed. "The ones I'm going to buy when you give me this skirt!"

Terza folded her arms, turning to directly face Angeline. "You know I will have to replace my stock of uniforms."

Angeline nodded.

"Would this be considered payment for your services tonight?"

Angeline continued to nod.

"Okay then. You can have the skirt."

Angeline stepped back, closer to Moheenie. She offered her a high five. "You are way too easy, Tee. You know I work for free."

"I know you do, Ange. I just admire your persuasion skills."

"No wonder you make a good attorney," Moheenie added.

"Why thank you, Mo. I will always be happy to represent you."

Ranger knocked on the bathroom door. "Is it safe to come out?"

"It's safe!" Moheenie called.

He opened the door. "How do I look?"

"Like the best bartender ever," Terza told him.

"I like your hair, honey." Moheenie brushed her hand along the top of his shaved crew cut. "I see you used gel."

"Nothing but the best for my favorite bosses."

"You look great. I really like those black pants."

"Stop it, Angeline," Terza warned playfully. "I don't have any in your size!"

Surprised is an understatement on how Sloan acted when she walked through her front door. Shock, disbelief, and amazement more accurately described her feelings. For a fleeting moment, Terza wondered if she should search the house for smelling salts.

Wearing an ear-to-ear grin, Joshua rarely left Sloan's side as he sampled each and every appetizer. Terza's heart warmed when she saw him offer Sloan the first bite before taking one himself. She also observed Ruby slide farther and farther away from the merriment. At one point when Sloan was stolen by her friends, Joshua took a plate of gnocchi and joined Ruby on the sofa. It took some coaxing, but Joshua finally got Ruby to smile.

Moheenie was right about Ranger and Brady getting along. From the very beginning, the two men stood side by side and bartended together for the entire party. Brady promised to teach Ranger how to brew beer, and Ranger promised to show Brady his favorite, and very secret, surfing spot.

When the party goers moved from dinner to dessert, Terza thanked her sister and gave her the rest of the night off. But instead of leaving, Angeline hung out at the bar for at least an hour. Terza wondered if she would be seeing even more of Brady than his time with Ranger. Angeline seemed quite infatuated with the beer connoisseur.

As the festivities simmered to a close, Sloan walked into the kitchen with both hands circling a coffee mug. Her eyes met Moheenie's. "Your husband makes the best latte."

Moheenie grinned. "He does, doesn't he? I was just thinking about placing an order."

"Would you like me to bring you a cup?"

"No, Sloan, but thank you. You're the birthday girl. It is our job to serve you, not the other way around."

While Terza listened to Sloan and Moheenie, she found herself drawn to Sloan's softness. Carnegie was correct in her statement that Sloan did not look a day over twenty. Sloan's deep brown skin tone seemed free of facial lines. Even the skin around her dark eyes was smooth and free from laugh lines, and her bright smile appeared radiant. The soothing quality of Sloan's voice made Terza yearn to listen and hear more.

"You both have done so much already." Sloan smiled. "The party was absolutely perfect. Thank you very, very much."

"It was our pleasure." Terza adjusted her ponytail. "You have such fun friends."

Sloan nodded. "I do. I am very blessed." She angled her head. "You have great hair, by the way. I wish I could wear mine long like yours."

"Thank you, but this wild mess?"

Sloan chuckled. "Why do you think I cut my hair so short?"

"You have a wild mess, too?"

Sloan nodded. "More like a wild fro!" She laughed from her gut.

"Your haircut is amazing," Terza told Sloan. "Every time I watch one of the entertainment shows, I practically drool over how cool some of the actresses wear their hair. You even have it shaved on the side."

Sloan rubbed her fingers over the light stubble. "I took a photograph to my stylist. It was one of the celebrities, but I am not sure which one right now. There are some interesting cuts."

Carnegie joined Sloan at the kitchen counter. "Happy birthday, Sloanie baloney!"

Sloan giggled. "I'm surprised you didn't write *Sloanie baloney* on my cake."

"I thought about it." Carnegie winked at Terza.

"I'm sure you did."

"Would you like another piece?"

Sloan touched her stomach. "Carnegie, it was amazing, but I'm officially stuffed."

Carnegie looked to Moheenie and Terza. "Ladies? How would you like another piece of cake?"

Terza and Moheenie shook their heads in unison. "No, thank you," Terza said. "I'm full, too, but it was one of the best cakes I have ever tasted."

"It was delicious," Moheenie agreed. "Thank you very much, Carnegie."

"You're both welcome." Carnegie hugged Sloan. "Well, birthday girl, it's time to call it a night. I was the first guest here, and now I'm the last."

Sloan slid off the counter stool. "I'll walk you out."

"Good night, Terza. Goodnight, Mo. It was nice meeting you both."

"Good night, Carnegie," Moheenie called out.

Terza waved. "Ciao, ciao."

Several minutes later Sloan returned to the kitchen. "You should call it a night, too. You must be very tired."

"We're almost finished. We just need to load the van," Terza explained.

"You probably parked down the street?" Sloan guessed.

"We did, but don't worry. It won't take us long."

Sloan held up a palm. "No, no, please don't misunderstand me. I'm concerned about you two, not me. I really wish you would leave the rest until the morning."

Terza looked to Moheenie. "We could leave the espresso machine. That way we won't have to wait for it to cool down."

"Are you sure you don't mind?" Moheenie asked Sloan.

"I don't mind at all, and it would make me feel better just knowing you can go home a bit earlier."

"Okay then. Mo, do you want to let Ranger know? Perhaps he can get the van for us." She looked directly at Sloan. "Thank you very much. I will come over in the morning. Would you like to text me when you get up?"

"What time were you thinking?" Sloan asked.

"Not before nine."

"Then just come on by. Ruby would like to get on the road by seven, and Joshua has a meeting at eight-thirty. We will definitely be up early."

"Would you like me to call you before I leave my condo?"

"No, not at all, Terza. Please feel free to stop by. I will be home all morning."

Terza smiled. "Sounds like a plan."

Half an hour later, Terza, Moheenie, and Ranger had said their goodbyes and were standing beside the Macaroni on Wheels van. Ranger opened the driver's side door for Terza before walking Moheenie to the passenger's side. "I'll see you lovely ladies back at *MOW*." He kissed his wife before closing her door.

"See you there." Terza buckled her seatbelt. "It was a great party. Thanks for your help."

"Of course. A good time was had by all."

"Aloha, honey."

"Right back at you, Lakalaka."

During the short return drive to Macaroni on Wheels, Terza told Moheenie about her second run-in with Ruby.

"She just knocked on the stairs?"

"Yes, and it was so weird, Mo. Ruby Slippers sat on the bottom stair and knocked on the wood."

"How many times?"

Terza thought back. "I don't know, maybe seven or eight."

"All without saying anything?" Moheenie pressed.

Terza nodded. "She stared straight ahead and knocked. She then suddenly said, 'Stairs can be very dangerous,' jumped to her feet, and left."

"That girl is creepy!"

"I agree. Good thing she is going to be gone by the time I pick up the espresso machine."

"Are you sure you don't need any help?"

"I'm positive, but thank you. If you can, get to *MOW* by noon so we can prep for the pizza party."

"No problem. Noon is easy."

CHAPTER FOUR

Stairs Can Be Very Dangerous

Saturday

A noisy purring woke Terza from an unusual dream. She pressed her eyelids closed and strained to revisit the events. Instead of remembering, Terza felt Olive's paws as they kneaded the small of her back. "Let me sleep," she told Olive, while being pushed closer to the edge of her bed. But when Terza moved Olive followed, and the paws continued their soft punches. Terza reached behind and pulled Olive close. "What are you doing, sweet pea?"

Olive purred loudly.

"Now I will never remember my dream."

The purring intensified.

"Are you hungry?"

Olive jumped from the bed.

Knowing that Olive was headed straight for the kitchen, Terza rubbed at her eyes, stretched out her arms, and finally stepped onto her plush throw rug. Terza joined Olive in the kitchen and set out making breakfast for them both. While waiting, Olive used her paws to push her empty crystal bowl from side to side.

Terza laughed. "I'm working as fast as I can."

Olive's breakfast consisted of wet cat food, her favorite, and Terza opted for a banana, coffee, and a ginger scone.

Holding her coffee in one hand, she opened the door of her fourth-floor balcony and placed the glass mug on a small round patio table. Terza then retrieved her scone before settling onto one of the two patio chairs. After Olive finished her breakfast, she nudged up to Terza's leg and sat directly on top of her foot.

Terza finished her scone, refilled her coffee mug, then brought her Bible out to the balcony. She read several chapters before calling her mother.

"*Buon giorno*," Benedette answered.

"*Buon giorno*, Mom. What do you have planned for today?"

"I am helping your father with his costume. You know how he likes to dress up for the children."

"That's right. I forgot today is Halloween. What is Papa going to be this year?"

Benedette laughed. "Take a guess."

"Please do not tell me he's going as a butcher again!"

"No, he decided to get creative this year. Your father is dressing up like a cow!"

"A cow?" Terza shouted. "A butcher dressing up like a cow? There is *definitely* something wrong with that. Where did Papa get a cow costume?"

"At the thrift store! I still cannot believe it. Last week your father went to visit his friend at the bakery over by Old Town."

"Oh, I think I know the one. It's the Italian bakery, right?"

"Correct. The one next door to the thrift store. And when your father returned home, he had an enormous smile on his face."

"Papa doesn't like thrift stores," Terza announced.

"I know that, and you know that, but for some reason he walked inside. While looking around the store he caught sight of the now famous cow costume!" Benedette could not stop laughing.

"Who else knows about this crazy cow outfit?"

"Just your brother, Dom. He stopped by on his way home from work last night. Your father wanted to surprise everyone, but Damiano walked in while I was making some alterations."

"Darn, I missed it!" Terza slapped her thigh. "I would have loved to see Dom's face."

"It was priceless, that's for sure. But he's not telling the kiddos. Damiano wants them to be surprised when they come over to trick or treat this evening."

"Have you told Ange?" Terza asked.

"Not yet, but I will when she calls. I want to make sure she stops by the Mercato sometime today."

"I'm sure Ange will also stop by this evening to see Charley and Caleb in their costumes. Do you know what Rain has planned for them?"

"No idea," Benedette answered. "But she always comes up with something good. I am sorry you are going to miss all the fun."

"Me, too, but we have a busy day and night in front of us. Please, please take photos for me."

"I will. Are you planning on dressing up?"

Terza grunted. "There is no way, Mom. You know I really don't care for Halloween."

"You did when you were little."

"I probably just wanted extra candy."

"That's a thought."

"Please tell Papa I'll definitely stop by to see him later. You know, I'm surprised he found a costume so close to Halloween."

"I was very surprised when he brought it in the door," Benedette agreed. "I'm guessing it might have been made for a school play. It looks like someone designed the costume from scratch. Whoever did, was a great seamstress."

"I can't wait to see it. Have a wonderful day, Mom."

"You as well, my love."

"Ciao."

"Arrivederci."

Terza had just enough time to shower and change before leaving for the Kamoze's house. Dressed in well-worn, boyfriend jeans and a white T-shirt, Terza went in search of her leather flip-flops. "Olive, where are you?" she called. "I know, it's my fault," Terza spoke lovingly. "I should not have left them out." Terza bent down to look under the coffee table. There she found Olive, practically smiling, while sitting on top of Terza's new Hawaiian flip-flops.

Terza tilted her head. "I do not understand you, missy. You look comfy, but how can that be so?" Terza gently pushed Olive aside, and reached for both shoes. She held them eye level. "How can you possibly enjoy lounging on these?"

Olive meowed one time, as an obvious announcement of displeasure. She then crawled behind the sofa.

"Don't worry, I get it," Terza told Olive. "You're mad and you do not plan on saying goodbye." Terza chuckled. "Enjoy your day."

At 9:10 a.m., Terza drove her cabernet-colored Fiat out of the parking garage, and by 9:25 a.m. she pulled into the Kamoze's driveway. Terza stepped out and walked to the front door. She rang the bell, waited several moments, and rang the bell a second time. Terza then knocked loudly and pressed her ear against the wooden surface. Since no one answered, she half-expected to hear the sound of a loud vacuum, but the house was quiet.

Terza walked around to the kitchen door and knocked again. Finally, she tried the door and found it unlocked. Unsure whether to go inside, Terza opened it slightly and called out. "Sloan, are you home?"

No response.

"Sloan, it's Terza! I came to pick up the espresso machine."

No response.

Terza hesitated before stepping fully into the kitchen and tried to listen for the sounds of water running. *Perhaps Sloan is still in the shower.* She looked around the kitchen and dining room area. Everything appeared to be spotless, and yet there was a trace aroma of bacon. It was evident the family was up early, had breakfast, and washed the dishes.

Terza again called Sloan's name as she walked through the dining area toward the living room. She noticed fresh vacuum lines on the expansive floor rug. Terza also felt a presence and turned to her left. She instantly saw Sloan, flat on the floor at the bottom of the stairs.

"No," Terza moaned, rushing to Sloan's side. "No!" Terza screamed. At first, she panicked, not knowing what to do. Sloan could be alive and need help. Terza knelt, touched the side of Sloan's chambray shirt, and gently pushed her shoulder.

"Sloan, can you hear me?" Terza asked loudly. "Sloan!" Praying for positive results, Terza checked for a pulse by touching two fingers to Sloan's neck. Nothing.

"Dear God, no." Terza immediately began to sob. "This cannot be happening." Terza dropped to both knees next to Sloan's lifeless body and wept. She blinked hard, struggling to regain control. Finally, Terza stood and slid the phone from her pocket. She stared at the screen wondering who to call first. Terza scrolled through and stopped at the listing for Nicolas Garza. She depressed the call button.

"Terza," Nico said with genuine enthusiasm. "It is nice to hear from you. How are you doing?"

His reaction surprised her. She had not heard from him in over a month and suspected he was not interested. "Not very well." She sniffed. "She's dead, Nico. Sloan is dead."

"Did you call nine, one, one?"

"No, not yet."

"Terza, listen to me. I am not on duty right now. You must hang up immediately and call nine, one, one."

"Okay," Terza spoke absently.

"Terza," Nico said with authority. "Did you hear me?"

She continued to stare at Sloan's body.

"Terza!" he shouted.

Terza turned her head toward the window and looked outside. The sunlight seemed to help her focus. "Yes, yes," she said quickly. "I'll call them now."

Without saying goodbye, Terza ended her call and dialed 911. After providing the necessary information to the dispatch center, Terza went outside to wait in her car. She considered calling Moheenie and pondered who should call Joshua. Instead, she elected to do nothing but wait.

Screeching sirens alerted Terza, and the entire neighborhood, of the police's arrival. Two cars with flashing lights parked haphazardly in front of the Kamoze's home, followed by a fire engine. Terza stepped out of her vehicle and met the officers on the driveway.

"Did you make the call?" the first male officer asked.

"Yes." Terza slowly nodded.

"Is the victim inside?" the female partner looked toward the house.

"Yes, she is." Terza watched a second male officer walk along the driveway. "The kitchen door is open."

The female officer spoke up. "Thank you. Please remain here."

Terza first watched the two partners walk away, followed by three firefighters. She then saw another police officer approach. He extended a card. "My name is Officer Abraham Barbour," he spoke gently. "May I have your name please?"

She accepted his card. "My name is Terza. Terza Tiepolo."

"Thank you, Terza." He printed on a small pad and then showed Terza his paper. "Did I spell it correctly?"

Terza read his chicken scratch and nodded.

"And what is your address, Terza?"

Terza provided the officer with the address of her condominium, as well as her Macaroni on Wheels business. Per his request, she also recited her telephone numbers.

"So tell me, Terza, what were you doing here?"

Why does he keep emphasizing my name?

"Please explain your reason for being here, Terza," Barbour repeated.

Terza exhaled loudly. "We catered a birthday party for Sloan Kamoze last night. I came back this morning to retrieve my espresso machine."

"Was Sloan Kamoze expecting you?"

"Yes. I told her I would come by after nine this morning."

"At what time did you arrive?"

"It was closer to nine-thirty," Terza explained.

"Did you call first?" Barbour asked.

"No." Terza turned her head to look at him. "I asked Sloan if she would like me to, but she said to just come over."

"Is it typical for you to leave your catering supplies behind?"

Terza felt like she was being interrogated. "No, it is not typical. We usually clean up everything before we leave. Sloan seemed tired and kept insisting that we finish this morning. I agreed to leave the espresso machine because it takes a while to cool."

"I see." Barbour wrote more than she could have possibly said.

Terza grew agitated. "I feel like you're accusing me of something."

Barbour's hazel eyes drilled through her. "Do you have a reason to feel guilty?"

"Of course not," Terza snapped.

The questions and answers continued until the police duo emerged from the kitchen door. The female officer walked closer to Barbour, and the two then moved toward the rear of their vehicles. Terza could see them referring to Barbour's notes. Ten minutes later they returned to where Terza stood.

"Ms. Tiepolo, my name is Julia Cantore," the female officer finally introduced herself. Instead of a handshake, Cantore offered Terza a business card.

Terza accepted the card and read the officer's name. It did not match her overall appearance. The name of Julia Cantore sounded soft and feminine, while the officer looked harsh and austere. Cantore wore her auburn hair in a tight bun, and she had on little to no makeup. She was a medium height, large-boned woman who appeared to lift weights. Terza guessed her age to be somewhere in the late thirties.

"Please come inside with me." Cantore led the way.

Terza followed without speaking and then slowed when Cantore approached the corpse. The firefighters moved away, exiting through the same kitchen door.

"Is this exactly how you found Mrs. Kamoze?"

"Yes," Terza squeaked.

"Did you touch her?" Cantore asked.

"I checked for a pulse." Terza paused. "On her neck."

"Did you find one?"

Terza's mind raced. She thought, *of course not! Why do you think I called?* "No, I did not," she replied.

"What did you do next?" Cantore pressed.

Terza quickly considered whether or not to mention Nico. "I called Detective Garza," she finally responded.

"I see." Cantore's eyebrows shot upward. "Is there a reason you called Garza before the police?"

"He *is* the police," Terza said, rapidly growing frustrated.

"I mean, the actual police department," Cantore snarled. "You did use his private number, I assume?"

"Yes, I did. Nicolas Garza is a friend of mine. Is it a crime to have the private number of a friend?"

Cantore ignored Terza's question.

"Did you touch Mrs. Kamoze in any other location?"

"No."

"Did you touch anything in the house?"

"Not this morning, but we did cater her birthday party last night."

"Alright, let's go back outside."

When Terza turned to leave she noticed something amiss with the sofa pillows.

"What is it?" Cantore watched Terza.

"Do you see the vacuum marks on the area rug in front of the sofa?"

"Yes," Cantore's yes sounded more like *so what*.

"Everything in this living room is perfect." Terza turned in a circle to survey the room. "In fact, everything in this house looks perfect. Sloan must have gotten up early this morning and cleaned."

"Do you have a point?" Cantore asked.

Terza briefly considered holding on to her idea. Instead, she ignored the officer's sarcasm and continued. "Sloan Kamoze is an amazing decorator and an obvious perfectionist. Every little thing has its place. And yet,"—Terza gestured toward the sofa—"that throw pillow on the end is upside down."

Cantore moved closer to the area rug without stepping on the carpet. "There is no distinctive pattern. How can you tell it's upside down?"

"By the fringe. Do you see the minor difference in the fringe of the pillow to the left? The zipper causes the fringe to slightly separate."

"May-be," Cantore stretched out the two syllables.

"Look at the carpet as well." Terza pointed.

Cantore knelt.

"The pile has been disturbed, but only in a direct line to the pillow."

"I don't know." Cantore stood. "Wait here. I'll be right back."

A split second after Cantore walked away, Terza whipped out her mobile and took a three-hundred-and-sixty-degree video. She also snapped several photos of the area rug and pillow. By the time Cantore returned, Terza's phone was tucked inside her back denim pocket.

"What do you think of this?" Speaking to her partner, Cantore related Terza's previous comments.

"I say we take a few photos and then leave it up to the techs."

Cantore nodded. "Sounds good."

"What about her?" Her partner motioned toward Terza.

Terza groaned silently. *I can hear you. I'm standing right here!*

Cantore turned to face Terza. "You can take your coffee maker and head on out. We know where to find you."

"Thank you," Terza said politely. *It's an espresso machine, not a coffee maker.* Without voicing her thoughts, Terza lifted the espresso machine from the counter and walked toward the kitchen door. She paused at the sound of the two officers whispering.

"Shouldn't we take her to the station?" the male officer asked.

"She's a friend of Garza's," Cantore said.

"So?"

"I don't want him up my butt. She's easy enough to find."

Terza continued to her car, with thoughts of Sloan, Nico, and Joshua rolling through her mind. Suddenly she wanted to cry again. She reversed her car out of the driveway, trying to avoid all eye contact with the many neighbors. Terza needed to speak with Moheenie, but it had to be in person. Instead of returning home, Terza drove straight to Macaroni on Wheels.

She parked, brought the espresso machine through the back door, and rested it on the concrete counter. Terza inhaled deeply, held her breath, then exhaled loudly before dialing Moheenie's number.

"Hey, Tee."

"Hi, Mo."

"What's wrong?"

"Are you almost ready?" Terza asked.

"Almost. It's just about eleven. I was planning on leaving in about a half hour. Tell me what's wrong."

"It's Sloan. She's dead, Moheenie," Terza sobbed. "I found her dead."

"We'll be right there. Are you at *MOW*?"

"Yes."

"Get some water and sit down. Ranger and I are on the way."

Terza nodded into the phone as she ended their call.

Time suspended while Terza waited for her friends. When they walked through the rear door, she felt as if they had arrived within minutes. Moheenie rushed to Terza's side.

"Bring it in." Moheenie hugged Terza tightly. Ranger moved closer and wrapped his arms around both of them.

The trio stood together, breathing as one, until Ranger asked, "How are you doing?"

Terza sighed while pulling free. "I cannot believe it. Sloan is"—she paused—"*was*, so nice. How could this happen?"

"Was it an accident?" Ranger asked.

Terza slowly shook her head. "I don't know. I just don't know."

Moheenie reached for Terza's hand. "Tell us what you do know. Start at the beginning and tell us everything."

Terza relayed her visit, how she entered through the kitchen door when no one answered the front bell, and then how she found Sloan's body. She finished with the saga of Abraham Barbour, Julia Cantore, and the unnamed partner. Terza felt her face flush. "But now I'm starting to get mad."

"I don't understand."

"This cannot be an accident, Mo. You know and I know what is always said about a coincidence."

Moheenie nodded. "There is no such thing."

"Exactly." Terza squeezed her fists. "Joshua's first wife was found dead at the bottom of the stairs, and now Sloan, his second wife, was found dead at the bottom of the stairs. This is not a coincidence. This is murder."

"But Joshua loved Sloan," Moheenie countered.

"Wait just a minute." Ranger blocked the air with his opened palms. "Don't even *think* about getting involved. You two stay out of this. Way out!"

"Ranger," Terza spoke bluntly, "someone has to look out for Sloan, and those officers seemed to be clueless."

"Yes, someone does, but not the two of you. Is Garza on the case?"

"No." Terza's voice softened. "That's a whole other story."

"Well, I better come with you tonight," Ranger told them.

"Thank you, honey." Moheenie reached for Ranger's hand.

"That's not necessary. It's a make your own pizza party, and there are a lot of kiddos and parents to chaperone. I'd love to have you, but we don't need a bartender."

"I wouldn't go as a bartender," Ranger explained. "I can go with you for moral support."

"Aren't you bowling with Conner and Mando?" Terza asked. "Isn't it supposed to be blacklight bowling with florescent balls?"

Ranger nodded. "Yes, but I can cancel."

"Are you kidding? Conner would kill me!"

Moheenie cringed. "Terza! Don't say the K-word!"

"Sorry." Terza grimaced. "Ranger, you have to go. Conner would be very upset if I dragged you away. Besides, tonight will be one of the easiest events ever. We are in charge of the pizza, and the pizza alone. *MOW* has nothing to do with the beverages or desserts."

"You said it is a make your own party?" Ranger asked.

"Yes." Terza nodded. "It starts out that way but typically fizzles quickly. Each guest has the opportunity to roll out their own pizza dough and then add the toppings. The children like cheese, cheese, and more cheese. Soon, they all get bored and will most likely want to spend extra time trick or treating. Moheenie and I will take over the pizza preparation."

"Are you going in costume?" Ranger asked.

"Of course not." Terza shook her head. "Plus, why does it matter?"

Ranger shrugged. "It doesn't. I was just curious."

"Come on, Tee. Let's dress up," Moheenie pleaded, with a glint in her coal black eyes. "It will be fun. We need a laugh, especially now."

Terza's spirit lifted. "You just want to go as a hula dancer," she playfully accused.

Moheenie grinned. "So? You can go as a chef. Just wear your white jacket and the hat thingy. What's it called again?"

Terza smiled. "A toque blanche, but you can simply call it a chef's hat."

"Whatever it is called, will you wear it?"

"We'll see. Let's talk about it later, Mo." Terza looked at Ranger. "Thanks for coming to the rescue. I feel much better now."

"That's good. You know I'm always here if you need me."

"I know, Ranger. Thank you. You're a dear friend." Terza glanced at Moheenie. "Did you drive together?"

"Yes, but I can easily walk home," Ranger said. "It's less than two miles."

"Why don't you take your car, and I will drive Moheenie home after our party?"

"Okay, but let's talk about that." Ranger sounded protective as he looked at their whiteboard on the kitchen wall. "I see your pizza party starts at five. Where is it?"

"La Mesa," Terza answered. "It is about a twenty-minute drive."

"What time do you think it will be over?"

"We should be finished by nine. Moheenie and I will be home before ten."

Moheenie dropped Ranger's hand. "What's with the interrogation?"

"Quiet, Lakalaka." Ranger laughed. "I need to make certain my special ladies are safe."

"Seriously, Ranger, we'll be fine."

"Okay, Terza, but there are a lot of crazies out and about on Halloween. Promise me that you will both stay together when you unload, and then please make certain Moheenie is safely inside the lobby before you drive away."

"What about Terza?" Moheenie asked. "Don't you care that she is driving home by herself?"

"Of course I do, but she has a gated garage." Ranger directed his next statement to Terza. "Please look around when you drive through the gate. Make certain you're not followed."

Terza saluted. "Aye, aye, captain."

Ranger rolled his eyes. "Enough already. I'm out of here." He kissed Moheenie on the lips and then kissed Terza on the forehead. "Behave, you two."

"Always," Moheenie said. "Have fun!"

"Ciao, Ranger."

"Bye."

CHAPTER FIVE

Seconds after Ranger left, Terza lifted her phone from the concrete kitchen counter. She slid her fingers quickly across the screen and held it toward Moheenie. "Check this out."

Moheenie drew closer. "I think that's the Kamoze's sofa. So what exactly am I looking for?"

"Put your detective hat on and concentrate."

Moheenie accepted the phone and used her thumb and forefinger to zoom onto the image. She looked up at Terza. "The pillow on the right side is upside down."

"Exactly." Terza took her phone and swiped to the close-up photograph of the carpet. She returned it to Moheenie. "Now, talk to me about this area rug."

Moheenie scrutinized the photo. "The rug has fresh vacuum marks with the exception of one area." She lifted her eyes to Terza. "The rug has been disturbed right in front of the sofa where the upside-down pillow is located."

Terza nodded slowly.

Moheenie returned Terza's phone. "Did you show the officers?"

"Yes, but they didn't seem very interested."

"You should tell Nico," Moheenie suggested.

Terza sighed. "I'm not sure, Mo. I just don't know what to think."

"What to think about Sloan or about Nico?"

Terza reached for her apron. "About everything." She tied the red strings. Feeling in a fog, Terza went to the refrigerator and inventoried the pizza toppings. She then scrolled through her computer tablet and finally looked directly up at her best friend.

"Did you talk to him?" Moheenie asked, obviously referring to Nico.

Terza dropped her head. "What is wrong with me, Mo? How selfish can I be? I should be thinking about Sloan, and only Sloan, and yet I can't get Nico out of my head."

"You're human, Tee. You thought something might happen between you and Nico. Don't beat yourself up about it."

Terza reached for her butcher knife and began slicing the pepperoni.

"Shall I grate the cheese?"

"That would be perfect. Thank you." While Terza's sharp knife sliced through the round meat, she paused and drew a breath. "Why didn't it happen? When Nico went overboard with the champagne, the flowers, and the chocolates, I thought for certain we would go out again."

"You did go out once."

"Once and then nothing." Terza groaned. "Nico took me out for dinner, and I thought we had a great time. I felt positive he would call me for a second date, but Nico never did. That was over two months ago."

"Earlier you told Ranger that Garza was another story. What did you mean by that? Did you talk to Nico?"

"Yes." Terza stopped chopping. "Like an idiot I called him when I found Sloan."

"What happened?"

"Not what I expected." Terza bit her lower lip. "I guess I imagined him coming to my rescue, you know, rushing right over. Instead he asked me if I had called nine, one, one."

Moheenie drew in an audible breath. "Oh, that's cold!"

Terza clenched her jaw. "Tell me about it. There is only one thing that makes me feel a tiny bit better."

"What's that?"

"I think the officers were going to take me down to the station."

"Do you mean for questioning?" Moheenie's eyes grew wide.

"Yes, I believe so. I mean, they don't know me. Anyway, when Cantore's partner asked, she basically told him to let me be. She insinuated that I was a friend of Garza's."

"Now that's a good sign." Moheenie raised her dark eyebrows. "He must have called them, Tee."

Terza's shoulders relaxed. "That's what I'm thinking. So part of me is pleased that he at least intervened on my behalf, but then I am still so confused why Nico never called me after our date."

"I'm so sorry. I know you liked him."

"I thought I might." Terza resumed her chopping. "I just never got the chance."

"What about Conner? I know you feel an attraction for him."

"You're right. I do. Conner is very sweet and surfer-boy cute. For some unknown reason I don't think of him as marriage material."

"Conner would make a great husband." When Terza hesitated, Moheenie continued. "Don't say it. I know you have a thing for dark and handsome."

Terza finally chuckled. "Of course you're right, but if Nico is going to give me the cold shoulder, I just might give Conner a second look."

"That a girl!" Moheenie grated the cheese into a stainless-steel bowl. "And speaking of marriage material, aren't you two going to a wedding together next week?"

Terza nodded. "Yes, we are. It is an evening wedding this upcoming Saturday."

"Oh, I adore evening weddings. Are they getting married in a church?"

"The actual wedding ceremony will be held at the Catholic Cathedral just north of downtown, and the reception is at the Grand Hotel." Terza looked up from her food preparation. "It should be fun. Conner told me that we'll be taking limos from the wedding venue to the reception, and if the weather holds, the bride and groom will be traveling by horse and carriage."

Moheenie's palm covered her heart. "Oh, I love that idea! What are you wearing?"

"I still don't know." Terza groaned. "I have a tea-length silver dress, but I really wanted to buy something new."

Moheenie's eyes shot open. "Let's go shopping!"

"I'm too busy to shop."

"Then make the time. How about tomorrow afternoon?"

"We'll see." Terza moved from slicing the pepperoni to slicing ham for the Hawaiian-style pizzas, while Moheenie continued grating the mounds of cheese. Half an hour later the duo decided to take a break.

"Let's go and see my pop. Mom says he's dressed like a cow!"

"Like a cow?" Moheenie giggled. "There is something very wrong about a butcher dressing up like a cow!"

"That's what I said." Terza pulled Moheenie by the hand. "Come on. We need a good laugh."

The girls walked through the adjoining door between the Macaroni on Wheels kitchen and the Tiepolo Mercato. Instead of his predictable place behind the butcher's counter, Terza's father, Ezio, stood in the middle of the market talking to three young boys and two little girls. His costumed covered his entire body with an oval cut-out for his face and openings for his hands. Ezio's gestures were animated as he pretended to be grazing like a cow.

"Look at you, Papa!"

Ezio wore an ear-to-ear grin as he looked up from his routine. "Come, come, my little Gnocchi. Do you like my cow costume?"

Terza leaned on her back foot with arms folded across her chest. "That I do, but a cow? Really, Papa!"

Ezio placed his hands around his padded middle. "What's wrong with a cow?"

Moheenie started laughing. "There's nothing *wrong* with a cow, but there is something amiss when a butcher dresses up like a cow."

Looking confused, Ezio angled his head. "There is?"

Terza and Moheenie exchanged crazed looks and then turned back to Ezio. He withdrew candy from his costume and handed several pieces to each child before saying goodbye.

"You even have a pocket?" Terza followed her father toward the butcher case. He stepped behind the counter while Terza and Moheenie remained in front.

Ezio chuckled. "Your mother added one for me."

Moheenie's mouth shot open. "Ha! A cow costume with a pocket, no less!"

"Isn't it great?"

"It is," Moheenie told him.

"Excuse me, ladies. I have a customer."

"Nice seeing you, Papa."

"Did you read your Bible this morning?"

"I did."

"Did you call your mother?"

Terza grinned. "You know I did."

"Then you, my little Gnocchi, are my favorite daughter."

"Thanks, Papa."

Moheenie waved. "Bye, Mr. Tie."

Still smiling, they returned to the Macaroni on Wheels kitchen and stared at the catering whiteboard. With narrowed eyes, Terza looked sideways at Moheenie. "We still have our other whiteboard alongside of the refrigerator." She lowered her voice to a whisper. "What do you think?"

"Oh my gosh! Do you really think Sloan was murdered?"

Terza shrugged. "It's a definite possibility, but at this point we can't be sure."

"You could go see the Medical Examiner."

"I could, but Sloan's body might not even be there yet."

"Go on Monday," Moheenie suggested.

"Good call." Terza nodded. "I will check in with Doctor Radovan on Monday. If Sloan Kamoze was in fact murdered, then we will get out our murder board. If Joshua did this, we have to prove it. Maybe we can help solve the murder of his first wife, too."

"Do you really think it might be Joshua?" Moheenie grimaced. "I thought he loved his first wife. I also thought he loved Sloan. Plus, what about Ruby Slippers?"

"She was gone long before Sloan died."

Moheenie lowered her chin. "Are you sure?"

"I can only go by what Sloan told us last night. She was supposed to leave early in the morning."

"Was Ruby Slippers even around when Yvette died?"

"We don't know, but we need to find out." Terza touched a palm to her phone as it rested on the kitchen island. "Maybe I should call Joshua."

Moheenie's hand shot to her mouth. "Oh my! What would you say?"

"That I'm sorry, of course. Since I found Sloan's body, isn't it only natural for me to call?"

Moheenie hesitated. "I guess so." She tapped her fingers on the counter. "But what do you hope to gain?"

"I'm not sure. Maybe it would be helpful to judge his reaction."

"It might be."

Terza lifted her phone and pressed the contact number for

Joshua Kamoze. After several rings his voicemail answered. "Hi Joshua, it's Terza."

Moheenie's eyes bulged.

"I just wanted to say that I am so sorry about Sloan. I'm really sorry. Goodbye."

"Was that his voicemail?"

"Yes. I was caught off guard, Mo, and I didn't know what to say. Did it sound stupid?"

"No, you sounded just right."

Terza's phone chimed with an incoming text. She looked at the screen. "It's Joshua!"

"What does he want?"

Terza read the text:

Thanks for your call, Terza. I just cannot talk right now.

Moheenie moaned. "I still feel sorry for him."

"I do, too, but only if he didn't do it." Terza looked around the kitchen. "Okay, let's finish up, grab something to eat, and then load the van."

Moheenie grinned. "What about our costumes?"

Terza crossed her arms.

"Come on, Tee. It will be fun." Moheenie opened the pantry door and withdrew Terza's chef's coat. She then took the toque blanche down from the top shelf and handed both to Terza. "You look so cute in these."

"Why are you so set on dressing up?"

"It's either my hula skirt or our casual catering clothes." Using her palms, Moheenie pretended to be weighing each choice. She looked to the left and bounced her palm. "Khaki pants and *MOW* shirt." She motioned with her right palm. "Or hula skirt and cute Hawaiian halter top."

"Won't you get cold?"

"We are going to be standing in front of an oven all night. No, I won't get cold!"

"Okay, my Hawaiian friend. We will go in costume." Terza glanced at Moheenie's large orange tote. "I assume your costume is already in the bag?"

Moheenie grinned. "Yes. I packed it this morning, just in case."

Terza patted Moheenie's shoulder. "What am I going to do with you?"

Moheenie wrapped her arms around Terza. "Be my best friend as always."

Terza returned her hug. "Forever and a day."

CHAPTER SIX

Cameras, Cameras, and More Cameras

Sunday

The alarm clock jolted Terza from a deep slumber. She still felt exhausted and yearned to camp under the covers all day. But even in a sleepy daze, she remembered how attending church always uplifted her spirits. With her eyes barely open, Terza crawled out of bed and stumbled into the bathroom. Olive decided to sleep in.

Dressed in gray slacks and a white shirt, Terza regarded her image in the floor-length mirror on her closet door. *I look like I am going to work.* Terza fiddled with her massive curls by pulling them up and then letting them fall. She decided that loose hair made her look less like a waitress. "Down it is."

Terza moved to the kitchen and selected a premade green smoothie from her refrigerator. Coffee would have to wait. She twisted the metal cap while keeping an eye on the entrance to the kitchen, knowing Olive would hear the sound and be rounding the corner any second.

"There you are, my beauty." Terza bent to scratch Olive's neck. "Would you like breakfast before I leave?"

Olive stood in front of the empty crystal bowl and waited.

Surprised that her cat sat motionless, instead of pushing at the dish, Terza opened the pantry and withdrew the dry cat food. Olive began eating before Terza finished pouring the nuggets.

"Wow, you are one hungry kitty. I was expecting you to complain about not getting wet food."

Olive continued eating while Terza filled her water.

"You can have a treat tonight." Terza reached down and rubbed the length of Olive's back. Only then did Olive finally react. "What is that?" Terza laughed. "Do I hear purring?" She gave Olive one last rub and then stood. Terza grabbed her purse, phone, and keys before heading for the front door. "See you later, Olive. Ciao, ciao!"

Olive's furry face remained planted in her bowl.

After church, Terza drove straight home, parked in her underground garage, and walked directly to the local coffee lounge. She smiled to see her favorite barista working behind the counter.

"Hi, Romano." Terza waved and took her place in line. Two guests stood in front of her.

Romano's bright eyes glinted as he shot Terza a smile. "Good morning! I'll be right with you." He continued to serve the next duo of customers until Terza stood directly in front of him. Romano had already prepared her usual order of a grande Americano.

"You are amazing. Thank you."

"The pleasure is all mine." Romano bowed. "So, how was your Halloween? Did you go to any wild parties?"

"Oh sure!" Terza rolled her eyes. "We catered a wild *build your own pizza party* for several families. It was a joint block party."

"Did you at least dress up?"

"Kind of." Terza crinkled her nose. "I went as a chef."

Romano laughed. "Oh, that's original!"

"Did you dress up?"

"Of course." Looking proud, he placed his hands on each hip. "I went as Scooby Doo."

"Who?"

"You're not a big cartoon watcher, are you?"

Terza shook her head. "No, not really."

"If I remember correctly, you didn't even know about Pebbles Flintstone."

Terza shrugged. "What can I say?"

"Would you like something to eat?"

"Come to think about it"—Terza handed a ten-dollar bill to the cashier—"I'll have a blueberry scone please."

Terza accepted her change and dropped a dollar into the tip jar. She watched Romano use tongs to grasp a blueberry scone from the glass pastry case. "Would you like it warmed?"

"No thank you."

Romano slid the scone into a small paper bag and handed it to Terza. "Enjoy. Wave when you would like a refill."

"You're an angel."

Romano smiled and then greeted the next customer as Terza carried her coffee and scone to an outside table. Although it was autumn, a time for there to be a chill in the air, the weather remained warm.

Terza lifted the coffee lid and dunked a small piece of her scone into the hot liquid. She saturated the pastry and quickly popped it into her mouth before it could drop to the bottom of her cup. When she finished her scone, Terza lingered over her coffee and contemplated making some phone calls. First, she called her mother and was transferred into voicemail. Terza left a *good morning, happy Sunday* message before disconnecting. She then tumbled the phone between her fingers as she considered her next call. When ready, she extracted a business card from her purse and dialed the number.

"This is Carnegie."

Terza could hear a tearful crack in Carnegie's voice. "Carnegie, it's Terza Tiepolo. I know you and Sloan were very close. Did anyone call you?"

"Oh, Terza, how sweet of you. Yes, Brady called me yesterday. He rushed to be with Joshua and has been calling all of Sloan's friends." Carnegie began sobbing. "I just can't believe she's gone. Our beautiful Sloan!"

Terza felt a pain in her heart. "I am very sorry, Carnegie."

"I understand you found her."

"Yes, I found Sloan at the bottom of the stairs when I went over to pick up the espresso machine."

"Was she breathing?" Carnegie sniffled.

"No." Terza spoke softly. "She had already passed."

"Could you tell what happened? Was it an accident?"

"Unfortunately I don't know anything. Did Sloan have any enemies?" Terza asked.

"Not our Sloanie," Carnegie answered. "Well, except for the prejudiced neighbor."

"What neighbor?"

"Oh, don't mind me. I just hate it when people think their *you know what* doesn't stink. Sloan was always very sweet to everyone. But this one neighbor treated her like a leper. I truly believe she was prejudiced."

"Do you think she would go so far as murder?" Terza asked.

"Oh my gosh!" Carnegie screeched. "Do you think Sloan was murdered?"

Terza realized she had to tone it down. "No, of course not, Carnegie. It was probably just a horrible accident." *Should I ask Carnegie which neighbor? I better not.* "May I bring you anything?" Terza tried to change the subject. "I can bring dinner for you and your family tonight."

"How kind of you to offer. Thank you, Terza, but I'll be fine."

Terza bit her lower lip. "I am really sorry."

"Thank you very much."

"Okay, well goodbye, Carnegie."

"Goodbye."

After disconnecting, Terza looked up to the white puffy clouds and stretched the limits of her brain. *The neighbor. I must find out about that neighbor.* She wanted to knock on each door surrounding the Kamoze's residence but dared not go it alone. Terza hesitated before texting Moheenie.

Terza typed:

What are you up to today?

Moheenie responded:

Nothing. Ranger picked up a shift.

Terza typed:

Do you want to play detective?

Moheenie fired back:

I thought you'd never ask!

Terza typed:

Pick you up in 30. Jeans and tennies.

Moheenie responded:

I'll be in the lobby.

Terza drained the last of her coffee, quickly cleaned up her mess, and raced home. She changed into a faded pair of jeans, a loose-fitting T-shirt, and her tennis shoes. Twenty minutes later, she drove out of her parking garage and made the right-hand turn toward Moheenie's building. Terza pulled next to the red curb and saw Moheenie wave from behind the plate-glass window.

Moheenie exited the front door, crossed the pavement, and opened the passenger's door. "Hey, Tee! What do you have planned for us?"

"We are looking for cameras."

Moheenie's eyes narrowed into a *what are you up to now* look. "Lead the way." She buckled her seatbelt.

Terza drove to the area surrounding the Kamoze's home and then steered into the parking lot of the Palm Tree Inn. When they exited the car, Terza pointed to the camera on top of the lobby overhang. "Camera number one."

Moheenie looked up and nodded.

"Let's walk up and down the street so we can check for others."

While they walked through the inn's parking lot, Terza told Moheenie about her conversation with Carnegie, and Carnegie's mention of the unpleasant neighbor. "That's why we're looking for cameras. I would like to see if anyone stopped by Sloan's house on Saturday morning."

"Or what time each person left."

"Exactly, Mo."

The duo passed two houses on their way, each situated on opposite sides of the street. The neighborhood was an older one in San Diego, with the original style of no sidewalks. The lack of footpaths, combined with the narrow street, created a parking conundrum. Property residents were forced to either park in their garages or on their driveways, as the neighborhood mostly prohibited street parking.

Standing next to Moheenie across the street from the Kamoze's home, Terza inspected the houses. "Only the first house on this side of the street has a camera."

Moheenie followed Terza's gaze before looking to the other side. "I don't see one on that house to the left of Joshua, do you?"

Terza turned her head. "Not that I can see, but the overgrown vegetation is blocking my view to the front door. That lot must be at least half an acre."

"You're right. It's the only house directly to the west."

Terza looked back toward the first house they passed. "If *that* camera does work, we may be able to see who walked from the Palm Tree Inn."

Moheenie's head bobbed. "Agreed, but we first have to gain access to the footage. How are we going to make it happen?"

"I have no idea at this point." Terza stepped forward. "Let's keep moving."

As they walked by the front yard directly across the street from the Kamoze's house, Terza noticed a camera mounted above the porch light. She motioned with her chin.

"I see it." They continued walking until Moheenie reached a hand out to stop Terza. "Don't look directly at her, but there is a woman standing at the window across the street."

Terza kept her head still. "Which house?"

"The one right next door. I also think there's a camera."

Terza crouched down and pretended to tie her tennis shoe. When she stood, Terza allowed her peripheral vision to capture their spectator. "Okay, I see her, but I cannot get a good enough look at the front door."

"Do you think that's the mean neighbor?"

"It might be." Terza stretched her arms high. "Carnegie didn't elaborate on where she lived. Let's stay on this side."

Terza and Moheenie covered the distance of five more houses until they decided to cross the street. Two of the five houses had front-door cameras. They then walked in front of the yards leading toward the Kamoze's house. As the duo neared the home next door to the nosey neighbor, a gray-haired woman waved to them from the porch. She was comfortably dressed in a pink warm-up suit. The woman zipped her sweatshirt as they approached. "Good morning. How are you two lovely ladies this fine day?"

Terza smiled warmly. She sensed the woman was eager for conversation. "Hello, I am Terza, and this is my friend Moheenie."

"Well hello. What fun names you have." She chuckled. "You may call me Marilyn, as in Monroe."

Terza and Moheenie both laughed.

"Is that your name or just what you like to be called?" Moheenie asked.

"It's my name." Marilyn's smile filled her lined face. "Well, Marilyn, but not Monroe. It's a great way to get people to remember your name."

"You are so right." Terza touched her forehead, guessing Marilyn to be in her late seventies. "Half the time I hear a name and then forget it just a second later."

"Me, too!" Moheenie agreed. "But Marilyn, I now think I will remember your name forever."

"Then job well done. Tell me, dears, are you selling something?"

"Oh no, we are just looking around the neighborhood." Terza decided to take a risk and seek Marilyn's help. "You see"—she lowered her voice—"I found Sloan Kamoze on Saturday morning. Did you know she died?"

"Oh yes, the poor dear." Marilyn placed a wrinkled palm over her chest. "I am sorry for her family, and for you as well. How sad you must feel."

"I do." Terza glanced to the sidewalk. "Moheenie and I catered her surprise birthday party Friday evening. We only met her the one time, but Sloan seemed very kind."

Moheenie nodded. "I instantly liked her."

"Joshua and Sloan are the sweetest neighbors." Marilyn gestured with her chin. "Of course you would never know that by speaking with *you know who* next door."

"Do you mean the lady we saw standing in the window?" Moheenie asked.

Marilyn stepped off of her front porch, walked a few steps along the cement pathway, and then turned to look into her neighbor's plate-glass window. "That's her." She motioned with a single wave. "I know she sees me, but of course she pretends I do not exist."

"Why is that?" Terza watched Marilyn return to her porch.

"Who knows?" Marilyn shrugged her small shoulders. "Belinda Benson thinks she is superior to everyone. Her parents left her the house, which she could never have afforded on her own. And yet she snubs her nose at everyone."

"Could she be the neighbor we heard that didn't care for Sloan?" Terza asked.

"Of course! Belinda was horrified when Joshua and Sloan moved next door. She said their type would bring down the neighborhood."

Moheenie's dark eyes narrowed. "That's horrible!"

Marilyn nodded. "I felt so badly for both of them. Sloan tried hard to win Belinda over but finally gave up."

Terza lowered her voice. "Do you think Belinda Benson is capable of murder?"

"Oh my! Was Sloan murdered?" Marilyn's voice quavered. "Should I be worried? Is there a killer on the loose?"

Terza instantly regretted her question. "No, please don't worry. I am extremely sorry. I should not have asked you that question."

A frenzied look filled Marilyn's pale green eyes. "Is that what you really suspect?"

"Don't mind us." Moheenie's chuckle sounded forced. "We are avid mystery fanatics. I'm sure it was just a terrible accident."

Fortunately Marilyn seemed to exhale her concerns. Terza took a chance at a follow-up statement. "It would be very helpful to view some of the neighborhood recordings. You know from the various cameras your neighbors have installed."

"Do you mean those crazy doorbells?" Marilyn rolled her eyes.

"Yes, those," Moheenie answered. "Plus the other security ones we saw mounted on some of the homes."

"You need to talk with Ian then." Marilyn pointed to the house across the street. "He has several cameras and is a wiz at anything electronic. Ian comes to our rescue when my husband, Lawrence and I have problems with any of the new gadgets."

Terza looked longingly at Ian's closed front door. "That would be wonderful. Do you think he would speak with us?"

"Of course he would!"

Moheenie followed Terza's gaze. "I wonder if he's home."

"Ian is always home. Come on!" Marilyn took off on a brisk walk toward the street. Terza and Moheenie exchanged amused glances as they watched Marilyn's nurse-style shoes marching in front of them. When Marilyn reached the asphalt road, she hurriedly checked for vehicles and then glanced back at them. "Catch up!"

Terza and Moheenie raced forward and were side by side by the time Marilyn pressed Ian's doorbell.

Seconds later the dark-stained wooden door opened widely. A thirty something, semi-good-looking man stood smiling at Marilyn. Terza suspected he might clean up well, but on this particular morning, Marilyn's neighbor appeared a bit groggy. He stood barefoot, wearing blue jeans and a loose-fitting flannel shirt with rolled sleeves. His scruffy blond hair needed a trim, and he definitely needed a shave.

"Good morning, Marilyn." Ian spoke with amusement shining in his blue eyes.

"Good morning, Ian. My, my, you look like you just woke up."

Ian grunted. "I almost did."

"Don't tell me you were up all night playing those video games again?"

"It *is* kind of my job." He grinned, glancing at Moheenie before locking eyes with Terza. "Now who do we have here?"

At just over five feet Marilyn appeared to stand taller as she introduced her new friends. "This is Terza." She pointed, then pivoted. "And this is Moheenie."

Ian extended his palm first to Terza. "It's nice meeting you, Terza." He then moved his hand to Moheenie. "Moheenie, it is a pleasure meeting you, as well. How can I help you two?"

"I will let them explain," Marilyn told Ian. "Lawrence is waiting for me, so I better be going." Marilyn looked up to Ian's six-foot frame. "Now be nice."

Ian grinned. "I'm always nice." He watched Marilyn walk away before returning his attention to them. "You've piqued my curiosity."

Moheenie looked to Terza who took the lead. "First Ian, we are sorry to bother you."

"It's no problem. Marilyn and Lawrence are a hoot. I never mind helping them. Are you friends?"

"No, we just met her this morning." Terza briefly told Ian about catering Sloan's birthday party, leaving their espresso machine, and then finding Sloan the following morning. She continued by explaining their idea to view any potential videos.

Ian rocked his head. "Smart plan. I haven't heard from the police yet."

"I'm sure you will," Moheenie told him. "This all just happened yesterday."

"You said the party was on Friday night?" Ian rubbed at his chin stubble.

"Yes, and I found Sloan around nine-thirty Saturday morning."

"Hence all of the police activity," Ian commented.

"You were home then?" Moheenie asked.

"Yes, I am pretty much always home. I work out of the house."

"What is it that you do?" Terza quickly sucked air between her teeth. "If it's okay for me to ask."

"Don't worry. It's okay. In simple terms, I'm a software engineer. I specialize in video games but also complete a lot of freelance work. It is a cushy job, except for the hours. I work with companies on the other side of the globe. Often times, I'm up half the night."

"I'm glad we didn't wake you," Moheenie said.

"So am I." He grinned and pulled a phone from his back pocket. "Whose email should I use for the videos?"

"You can send them to our company email." Terza removed a business card from her T-shirt pocket. She printed her number on the back side and extended the card. "Our email address is listed here, and I put my cell on the back."

"Macaroni on Wheels." Ian's baby blues looked directly into Terza's eyes. "Are you a good cook?"

"I can hold my own." Terza's eyes connected with his.

"Ha! She's a great cook," Moheenie added.

"What do you like?" Terza asked him.

"Food. I like any kind of food as long as I don't have to cook it."

"Then we will owe you a specially cooked meal." Terza glanced at Moheenie. "Right, Mo?"

Moheenie nodded. "Absolutely!"

Terza returned her focus to Ian. "As a thank you, Macaroni on Wheels will cater a dinner for you. Just say the word."

"It's a deal."

"Thank you very much," Terza said.

"Yes, thank you for your time," Moheenie added.

"Hopefully I can help. It was nice meeting you both. I'll be in touch."

After the goodbyes ended, Terza and Moheenie crossed back toward Marilyn's home. They instantly noticed that Belinda Benson still stood at her plate-glass window.

Moheenie groaned. "Doesn't she have anything to do?"

"Apparently not."

The ladies decided to end their camera hunting and wait for whichever videos Ian would send. Moheenie spoke as they walked along the street in front of the Kamoze's house. "It doesn't look like anyone is home."

They continued walking toward the lone house before the Palm Tree Inn, stopping directly in front of a chain-link fence. It was covered with decades of overgrown ivy. When they attempted to peek through the rare openings, the mature trees prevented a clear view to the house.

"What do you think about this property?" Terza squinted through a tiny gap in the ivy. "It could be a great place to hide."

Moheenie shook her head. "Not really. The fence is too high." Moheenie held up her hand to measure. "It's at least five feet tall."

Terza examined the fence then stepped back for a better view of the house. "You're right. Plus, even if there is a camera, the home is situated far at the rear."

Moheenie peeked through another gap. "I don't think this property has anything we can use."

Terza pivoted to face the house across the street. "I think that camera will be our only lead when it comes to this house."

"I agree. Do you want to knock on the door?"

"We better not." Terza shook her head. "Let's wait and see what Ian gives us."

"Good call. Are you ready to head back then?"

"I'm ready if you are. What time is Ranger coming home?"

"Not until this evening. He took a double shift today."

Terza looked to her friend. "Then how would you like to come to family dinner? You know we dine early. You could always eat and leave."

"Oh, thank you, Tee, but I have steaks marinating. Ranger and I are going to grill tonight."

"Yum! A steak sounds good. I need to grill more often. Did my father hook you up with the meat?"

"Of course he did." Moheenie grinned. "How can I be best friends with you and not go to my favorite butcher when we're in the mood for steak?"

Terza laughed. "Plus, if you ever purchased meat at a regular grocery store, my papa would never forgive you!"

"Exactly. Tell me, are you going over extra early to your parent's house?"

"Not really." Terza narrowed her eyes. "Why? Are you thinking what I'm thinking?"

"That would be a yes, if you're thinking we have time to work on our murder board."

"Come on then," Terza called as she broke into a soft jog.

"I'm right behind you!"

CHAPTER SEVEN

Murder Board

Back at the Macaroni on Wheels kitchen, Terza removed a white dry-erase board from between her two refrigerators and placed the blank board on top of their expansive kitchen island. It was an identical whiteboard to the one hanging on the wall. At the beginning of each work week Terza printed their catering events on what they referred to as their *catering board*. It looked the same, but the board resting on the kitchen counter served a very different purpose. Terza and Moheenie secretly used it as their *murder board* and a way to keep track of any evidence.

"This is all very sad." Moheenie opened a drawer under the counter and withdrew a black dry erase marker.

"I know. Sloan was so sweet." Terza accepted the marker and hovered it above the blank board. "If Joshua did kill his two wives, we have to make sure he never does it again."

"You need to write that down. As much as I like him, I think Joshua should be first on the list."

Terza printed Joshua Kamoze's name on the top left side. She looked up to Moheenie. "Is Belinda Benson next?"

"No." Moheenie stretched out the word. "I think Ruby Slippers should be next."

Terza nodded. "Agreed." She printed Ruby Kamoze's name on the second column. On top of the third column, she printed

Belinda Benson's name, and glanced at Moheenie. "Do we only have three suspects?"

"Right now we do."

"Okay, let's discuss motive." Terza tapped the marker to her forehead. "What is Joshua's motive?"

Moheenie grunted. "How about psycho serial killer?"

"Maybe I should save that one for Ruby Slippers."

"You're right." Moheenie lifted her eyes to the ceiling. "Greed. I think Joshua's motive might be greed."

Terza angled her head. "Walk me through it."

"Greed doesn't always have to be about money." Moheenie locked eyes with Terza. "But at this point, we don't know if either of Joshua's wives did have money."

"I think Sloan's family came from money."

"Maybe, but Joshua's greed could come from wanting control. He was greedy in the fact that everything had to be his way."

Terza considered Moheenie's theory. "If your thinking is correct, maybe he married Yvette and then wasn't happy when she needed more independence."

Moheenie nodded. "The same could be true for Sloan. Maybe she didn't kowtow to his every need."

"Come to think of it, a surprise party has an element of control."

"You are right about that, Tee. Most people throw a surprise party out of love and joy. But in a way, Joshua might have been orchestrating each and every step."

"For double reasons." Terza held up two fingers.

"Explain."

"First, he wanted to show dominance and control. He planned the party, and Sloan had better like it."

"She seemed to have fun," Moheenie added.

"Yes, but do we really know what happened when the lights went out? Maybe Sloan doesn't like surprise parties. Maybe she didn't show the kind of appreciation Joshua expected."

Moheenie's brows arched. "So he killed her?"

The kitchen went quiet as Terza processed Moheenie's comment. The thought of Joshua pushing his wife down the stairs brought a lump to Terza's throat. She wiped a lone tear from her cheek.

Moheenie exhaled forcefully. "This is all very upsetting, but we can't lose our focus. Tell me about the second reason."

Terza rested her elbows on the counter. "Joshua may have planned the party just for show."

"Do you mean the murder was premeditated? Joshua was planning on killing Sloan the entire time?"

"That is exactly what I mean. After murdering Yvette, maybe Joshua thrived on the attention. You know, all the sympathy he received. Maybe he needed another fix."

"If that is true, then Joshua Kamoze is one sick man."

Terza held the marker. "So what do I write?"

"Write *greed* first and then *power*."

Terza wrote both words. "We can add more later. Should I write *psycho serial killer* under Ruby Slippers?"

Moheenie chuckled. "Maybe. Let me think."

Terza waited while they considered a potential motive.

"Jealousy!" Both Terza and Moheenie shouted at once.

"It must be correct since we each thought of it," Moheenie said.

"Jealousy it is." Terza printed the single word. "Now what are some possible motives for Belinda Benson?"

"I'm not sure what to call a bigot. Maybe rage?"

"Hmm." Terza drummed her fingers on the counter. "Anger, Rage, Resentment. But are they motives or feelings?"

"I think a little of both. Rage for another person could be a motive for murder."

"Good point. Let me write that down." Terza printed motive words under Belinda Benson's name. First she wrote the word, *anger*, followed by the words, *rage* and *resentment*. She looked up at Moheenie. "Can you think of any others?"

"That covers it right now. We definitely need more information."

"We're just getting started. We should think of this kind of like a puzzle, Mo. We have just sorted the end pieces, and now it's time to begin creating the border."

"I agree, Terza. Hopefully the videos will be a great help." Moheenie changed her focus to their catering board and then back at Terza. "It's blank! It's never blank. Don't we have any catering jobs?"

Terza laughed. "Of course we do, I just haven't printed our schedule for the week. Have no fear, my friend. The board will be nice and full before we see each other again on Tuesday morning."

Moheenie wrapped an arm around Terza's neck. "Well, don't work too hard tomorrow. You need a day off."

"Don't worry, I won't." Terza returned their murder board to its hiding place between the refrigerators, being careful not to smudge the black markings. "Are you ready to head out?"

"Ready." Moheenie switched off the overhead kitchen lights.

Terza drove Moheenie the short distance home and then returned to her own condominium. She still had a couple of hours to spare before family dinner. *Just enough time for some online research.*

CHAPTER EIGHT

Family Dinner

Laughter spilled through the open window and out to the sidewalk as Terza stopped in front of her family home. She stood at the waist-high wrought iron fence and inserted her key into the gate lock. The front door instantly opened, and Charley jumped onto the cement steps before Terza had time to turn the knob.

"You're late!"

Terza opened the gate and joined six-year-old Charley at the front step. "I am?" She checked her phone, then looked at her. "I do say that you, Charley Tiepolo, must have been early. It's not even four o'clock yet."

Charley's button nose crinkled. "Everyone else is here."

"Are you sure about that?" Terza lowered her face to look Charley in the eyes. "Is Auntie Angeline here?"

"Yep."

Terza smiled as Charley's mother, Rain stepped up behind her daughter. "Charley, please say *yes* instead of *yep*."

"Y-es," Charlie turned the one syllable word into two. "Auntie Angeline is already here."

Terza stood to hug Rain. "Why is everyone so early?"

"I can only speak for us. Do you know what night it is?"

"Oh." Terza playfully knocked her own head. "It's spaghetti and meatball night!"

Rain's green eyes sparkled. "Yes, it is. The kiddos wanted to come over first thing this morning."

Terza scrutinized Rain's board-straight, shoulder-length hair. The dramatic cut featured fluctuating blunt levels similar to stairsteps. Terza fingered several of the thick strands. "Your haircut is fabulous, Rain! It's like a piece of art." When Terza released Rain's hair the strands fell perfectly into place. "Plus, the color is amazing! It makes your beautiful green eyes simply come alive."

Rain's smile increased. "Thanks, Terza! It's called blaze red. According to the packaging, the color is a fiery mixture of reds, pinks, and oranges."

Terza took a closer look. "I'd say the packaging is correct." She turned her focus to Charley. "What do you think about your mommy's hair?"

Charley's lower lip pushed forward. "I wish I could color my hair." Charley smiled expectantly at her mother.

"Oh, don't give me that face." Rain chuckled. "You know when your father and I will allow you to color your hair."

Charley pretended not to remember.

"When is that?" Terza asked Rain.

"Charley can color her hair when she is old enough to get married."

"That's right. I forgot. When am I old enough to get married, Mom?"

"When you are old enough to color your hair," Rain answered logically.

Terza could almost see the question marks circulating above Charley's head. "Come on, little one." She captured Charley's small hand. "Let's go say hello to your Grandmama."

Rain whispered into Terza's ear. "Thanks for the save."

"Anytime."

Damiano met Terza and Charley as they entered the front door. "Hi, sis!" He greeted her with a bear hug. "What, no date tonight?"

"Not tonight, but I can beat you at bocce ball all by myself." She winked at Charley. "Girls against the boys. Isn't that right, Charley?"

"Auntie Tee and me against Daddy and Caleb."

Damiano tousled the top of Charley's golden curls. "That's right, kiddo."

When they moved toward the dining room, Angeline walked up. "Hi, Tee." She wrapped an arm around Terza's waist. "How's it going?"

"Okay." Terza released Charley's hand and guided Angeline back toward the front door. While busy listening to Charley, Damiano failed to notice them, and Rain had already left for the kitchen area. "Do Mom and Papa know?"

Angeline turned her head. "No, and I didn't see any point in telling them. Sloan seemed so nice. This is really sad."

Terza breathed deeply. "Tell me about it. I'm still having a hard time believing it's true."

"Knowing you the way I do, I bet you already have some suspicions."

Terza pretended to lock her mouth closed.

"You had better be careful, little sister."

"I always am."

"I'm serious, Terza. Do not get involved. Please let the police do their jobs."

"I will. I will." Terza pulled on Angeline's arm. "Come on. I need to say hi to Mom before she gets suspicious."

Terza walked around the kitchen counter and straight to her mother. Benedette stood stirring a massive pot of marinara sauce with meatballs. "Hello, my love. How are you this afternoon?"

Terza leaned in to kiss her mother's cheek. "Hi, Mom, I'm good." She inhaled. "That smells amazing."

"Charley and Caleb came early just because it is spaghetti and meatball night."

"I heard that." Terza looked around. "Where is Caleb?"

"Do you see your father?" Benedette looked amused.

Terza laughed. "I do not. Are they still playing around with that old truck?"

"Your father found several authentic parts," Rain said. "He couldn't wait to show Caleb."

Terza rolled her eyes. "Do you think they will ever drive it?"

"Probably not for years." Benedette continued stirring. "Every part takes a long time to locate because the truck is so old. Your father insists that each detail is as authentic as the original."

"Caleb will probably have his license by the time the truck is finished." Terza chuckled. "What can I do to help?"

"We are almost ready. Please ask your father to wash up and come in for dinner."

"I'll go with you." Rain followed Terza out the back door. "Caleb's hands are probably covered in grease."

Terza and Rain stepped down from the patio area and out into the Tiepolo's backyard. The large rear yard made up for the postage-stamp-sized front yard. There was room for a cement patio area filled with welcoming furniture, an herb and vegetable garden for Benedette, and plenty of space for their three vehicles. A two-car garage could be accessed between the buildings through the alley, and Ezio had built an oversized single-car garage for his work area. Only Ezio's black work boots were visible when they approached.

Rain gasped audibly. "Caleb Tiepolo, are you completely under that truck?"

Ezio immediately slid from beneath, with Caleb emerging second. "The truck is very secure." Ezio's eyes connected with Rain's. Caleb wrapped his tiny arms around Ezio's leg and looked warily at his mother.

"He is only four years old, Papa."

"I would *never* endanger my grandson, Rain. Come and look."

Ezio gently led Rain to each of the four truck sections where it rested on bolted blocks of wood. "These blocks are bolted to each other and to the floor. They cannot move."

Rain's shoulders appeared to relax.

Ezio then placed both palms on the hood and attempted to push the truck. "You can try, too, if you like."

"No, that's okay." Rain sighed. "I believe you."

"Then can I go back under?"

"It's time for spaghetti and meatballs, Caleb!" Terza said.

"Yippee!" Caleb ran toward the house.

"Not so fast, mister!" Rain shouted. "Get back here."

"Come here so we can get cleaned up for dinner," Ezio told Caleb.

Caleb returned and stood still while Ezio unzipped his blue, long-sleeved coverall. Ezio unzipped his own matching coverall, and the two stepped out at the same time. Rain and Terza shared a smile as they watched Caleb mimic his grandfather's moves.

"Isn't his work outfit cute?" Rain asked.

Terza nodded. "Did Mom make it?"

"Yes, she cut down one of Papa's."

Terza laughed. "That must have been a lot of cutting!"

"I think Caleb likes putting on his matching outfit more than he likes the truck."

"I don't know. It may be a bit of both." Terza called out to her father who was busy scrubbing at the garage sink. "We'll see you inside."

"Do you need any help, Caleb?"

Standing on a stool next to his grandfather, he glanced back. "No, thanks, Mom."

Ezio looked at Rain with a fatherly grin. "We've got this."

Back inside the house, Terza joined her mother at the sink. A cloud of steam billowed from the freshly drained spaghetti noodles. "Shall I check on the garlic bread?"

"Yes, please do. I can already smell it starting to burn."

Terza opened the oven and peeked inside. "No, it's perfect." She slid her hands into two potholders and withdrew both baking sheets from the oven. Terza used tongs to lift the bread slices, dropping them into a large basket. She then covered the bread with a green-striped cloth napkin and placed the basket onto the kitchen counter. Benedette and Terza turned when the back door opened.

"Just in time." Benedette smiled at her husband, then looked at little Caleb. "Are you ready for spaghetti and meatballs?"

"Yes, please, Grandmama. I love spaghetti and meatballs."

Damiano joined them in the kitchen, lifting his son into the air. "Do you like *my* spaghetti and meatballs?" He flew Caleb to his place at the dining room table.

"You're silly, Daddy." Charley giggled. "Nobody likes your spaghetti and meatballs."

Damiano placed a hand dramatically over his heart. "I'm crushed. How can you not like my cooking?"

"The answer is simple, my sweet husband." Rain touched his shoulder. "You can't cook."

Damiano looked at Terza. "How come you got all the cooking talent?"

"I didn't get it all." Terza shrugged. "Ange isn't half bad."

Angeline grunted. "Is that supposed to be a compliment?"

"Of course it is. You can hold your own in the kitchen."

Ezio stood behind his wife's chair and pulled it out for her. He then returned to his place at the end and held out his hands. "Are we ready?" Ezio took the hand of his wife to the right and Terza's to his left. When all of the palms were connected, he began. "Dear Lord. Thank you for my beautiful family, and thank you for blessing us with this meal we are about to eat. Please bless this food in your Holy Name. Amen."

A chorus of Amen's sounded, followed by the typical delayed response from Caleb. "Amen."

"Great job, Caleb." Rain looked to Charley. "You did wonderfully, too. I'm proud of you both."

Charley's smile lit up the table. "Thanks, Mom!"

Rain helped Charley while Damiano served Caleb, and the other Tiepolo family members served themselves. The noise of clattering dishes instantly ceased after each took their first bite.

"Oh my." Terza smacked her lips. "Your sauce is absolutely amazing, Mom."

"Thank you, my love."

"No matter how hard I try, my marinara sauce never tastes this good. I follow your recipe step by step. What do you do that I don't?"

"I added a touch of nutmeg this time."

"It must be Mom's love." Damiano winked at his mother.

"Ha!" Angeline laughed. "Are you still trying to be the favorite child?"

Damiano held his hands out expressively. "There is no need to try. I have always been Mom's favorite." He looked directly at his mother. "Haven't I?"

"Speaking of favorites," Ezio interrupted. He focused on Angeline. "Did you call your mother this morning?"

"Yes, she did," Benedette answered. "I talked with both Angeline and Damiano first thing."

Terza raised her palm. "I left a message."

Benedette smiled at her youngest daughter. "Yes, thank you. It was very sweet."

"Who read their Bible?" Ezio looked around the table.

Many hands went up. Ezio focused on Caleb. "Did you read your Bible today?"

"Yes, Grandpapa. I went to Sunday School."

"Good for you, Caleb."

Charley's hand shot into the air. "Me, too, Grandpapa."

"Good girl."

"Since each one of you called your mother, and everyone read their Bibles, you are all my favorites."

Damiano shook his head. "No, no. You cannot have more than one favorite."

"I can if I want." Ezio crossed his arms. "I am the father, and I make the rules."

"Ha! Ha!" Terza giggled. "You are such an old softy."

Ezio glanced her way and smiled. "Mind your manners."

"By the way, Terza…" Damiano changed the subject. "When do we get to meet Nico Suave?"

"You know that's not his name. Besides, I don't think it's going to happen."

"Why not, honey?"

Terza shrugged. "I don't know, Mom." She glared at her brother. "Thanks a lot, Dom."

"What did I say?" Feigning innocence, his dark brown eyes sparkled with mischief as he opened his mouth for another verbal pitch. Damiano looked at his wife and rapidly snapped it closed.

"Would you please behave? How many children do I have?"

"Two, Mommy." Charley raised two fingers.

"One, two." Caleb mimicked his sister.

Rain winked at Damiano. "Sometimes I think the answer is three."

After dinner everyone pitched in to clear the table, load the dishwasher, and handwash the pans. Benedette stopped the organized commotion to ask, "Would you like dessert before or after bocce ball?"

Terza looked to her brother. "After?"

Damiano nodded. "Yes, after bocce ball. Are you ready to walk over?"

"Ready as ever." Terza reached for Charley's petite hand. "Are you prepared to beat the boys?"

Charley stretched to appear taller. "I'm ready, Auntie Tee."

"Are you ready little man?" Damiano asked Caleb.

"Ready, Daddy."

Damiano lifted Caleb up and over his head, and the little boy settled in comfortably on top of his father's shoulders. Damiano looked at Rain. "Are you playing or watching?"

"I'll watch tonight."

"Me, too," Angeline agreed. "We can let the kiddos take over the court."

"Then I'm coming, too." Benedette reached for Ezio's hand. "Come on, honey. Let's walk over together."

Terza watched her father as he squeezed his wife's hand before placing a loving arm around the small of her back. "Let's go, Tiepolo's!"

The bocce ball game was less competitive than usual, and the simulated tournament conveniently ended in a tie, with each team winning two games. After dessert and coffee, Terza headed home with plans to be in bed early. She needed ample sleep for the busy day ahead.

CHAPTER NINE

Medical Examiner and More

Monday

For the first time in weeks, Terza awoke before the buzz of her alarm clock. She fed Olive, had her morning coffee while reading her Bible, and gave her mother a quick call. Terza took a brisk shower, stepped into her jeans, and selected a black long-sleeved T-shirt. After pulling her hair into a high ponytail, she was out the door before 8:00 a.m. Unfortunately, her rapid pace instantly stalled when Terza's Fiat slowed behind a wall of Monday morning rush-hour traffic. "Darn!" Terza slapped the steering wheel. She had hoped to catch the Medical Examiner before he got too involved in his busy day.

The typical twenty-minute drive took Terza almost an hour. She parked her car in the building's parking lot, then entered the three-story green stucco building. *It's been over four months*. Terza wondered if the receptionist would be the same. As she walked up to the desk, Terza saw the familiar woman who still had a *what could you possibly want* expression on her unfriendly looking face.

"May I help you?"

"Yes, thank you. Do you recognize me?" Terza struggled to sound sweet.

"No."

Terza's smile barely curled. "My name is Terza Tiepolo and I'm here to see Doctor Radovan."

"Do you have an appointment?"

"No, I do not, but I think he will see me." *This lady is still like a warden!*

The receptionist hesitated while Terza worried.

"He does know me." Terza's voice squeaked.

After sighing obnoxiously the receptionist finally lifted the telephone receiver and pressed three buttons. "Doctor Radovan, a Terza Tiepolo is here to see you. She does *not* have an appointment." Terza watched as the receptionist's snotty expression changed to a look of surprise. The receptionist carefully returned the receiver to its cradle as if stalling for time. She then looked directly at Terza. "You may go in."

"Thank you." Terza refrained from an *I told you so* and smiled instead. She walked quickly to open the first door and then made her way along the corridor. The familiar looking peach-and-green tiles appeared to be freshly mopped. Terza turned toward the Medical Examiner's office and took a deep breath before passing through the double doors. She knew what to expect. Without hesitating, Terza pushed her way through the doors and walked directly to the desk containing a tin of balm. She nodded hello to the Medical Examiner as she undid the top, acquired some balm with her finger, and dabbed it under her nostrils. Terza breathed in the menthol while walking to meet Jacob Radovan by his row of microscopes.

"Hello, Doctor Radovan. It is nice to see you."

The white-haired doctor met Terza halfway. "It is nice to see you, too, Number Three. Ha! Two, Three, get it?" As his custom, Jacob Radovan frequently laughed at his own jokes.

Terza smiled. "I get it."

"You are becoming quite the expert with my menthol. Maybe I should give you a job."

"Thanks, but no thanks. I could not work around dead bodies all day."

When the double doors again pushed open, Terza could only see the back of someone with long, straight black hair. The height and weight reminded her of Moheenie.

"Speaking of assistants. Here comes one of the best ever!"

The female turned to face them, holding two paper cups. She smiled and extended the one in her left hand to Dr. Radovan. "One extra hot coffee latte with two packets of raw sugar."

Terza formulated a mental note in case she needed a bribe in the future.

Radovan accepted the coffee and sipped a sample taste. "Thank you, Akemi. It is perfect!" He extended an arm toward Terza.

"Terza Tiepolo, I would like you to meet Akemi Tanaka, my esteemed assistant. Akemi, this is Number Three, as I call her."

Looking puzzled, Akemi fixed her brown eyes upon Terza. "Number three?"

Radovan's sea green eye's sparkled. "How many languages do you speak Akemi?"

Akemi looked toward the ceiling as she obviously counted. "I speak five fluently."

"Do you speak Italian or Spanish?"

Akemi rotated her head. "Sorry, but neither."

"Terza in Italian means third," Radovan told her. "So since Terza's name means third, I call her Number Three!" Radovan laughed heartily as Terza and Akemi shared a smile.

"Do you get it?" Radovan pressed.

"Yes, yes I get it." Akemi returned her focus to Terza. "How do you know Doctor Radovan?"

"Number Three helped us solve a murder!" Radovan answered. He rested his eyes on Terza. "Are you here to see one of our bodies?"

Terza grimaced. "Do you have more than one?"

"Of course we do! The weekend just passed so we typically take receipt of two or three bodies." Radovan spoke objectively. "Today we have four."

"That's horrible."

"That's life." Radovan chuckled under his breath. "Ha! Or that's death!" He looked around. "Get it?"

"We get it," Terza and Akemi spoke in harmony.

"I am here to ask you about a woman named Sloan Kamoze."

"We have three women," Akemi answered. "Would you like me to check the tags, Doctor Radovan?"

"She is, or was, a beautiful African American woman," Terza offered. "She just turned thirty."

"Ah yes." Radovan sounded a great deal more compassionate. "She is on my lab table as we speak. You may take a look."

Using both hands, Terza pumped the air in front of her chest. "No, no. Thank you for the offer though. There is something I wanted to ask."

"Ask away Number Three."

"Could she have been suffocated?"

Radovan tilted his head in thought and then walked over to his desk. As usual, his pockets jingled with an assortment of coins, keys, or both. He leaned over the desk, pushed on his mouse to awaken his monitor, and read. "Blunt force trauma." His eyes remained glued to the screen.

"Really?" Terza moved closer. "That is definitely the *only* cause?"

Radovan glanced Terza's way. "I have learned to trust your instincts Number Three. Tell me what you are thinking."

"I found Sloan Kamoze."

"I am very sorry. Were you close friends?"

"No, we just met. I catered her surprise birthday party. When I found Sloan's body, I noticed that one of the sofa throw pillows was upside down."

"Why would that be an issue?" Akemi asked.

"From what I can gather, Sloan was an immaculate housekeeper. The area rugs still had vacuum lines, and the sofa pillows were perfectly plumped."

"Except for one," Radovan added.

"Yes, except one." Terza took out her phone and scrolled through her photographs. She stepped between Radovan and Akemi. "Here, let me show you."

Terza began by showing them the video she had taken. Radovan had her pause it several times as he scrutinized the entire crime scene. She then enlarged each pertinent photo and passed her phone back and forth between the Medical Examiner and his assistant.

Radovan's glasses nearly touched the screen of Terza's phone as he analyzed one of the photographs. "Yes, you can tell the carpeting was disturbed in the area leading to the sofa pillow." He looked up and over his tortoise shell reading glasses. In the light, Terza could see a number of smudges on the lenses. *It's a wonder he can see at all.*

"Can you tell that the pillow is upside down?" Terza asked.

Radovan pushed his glasses up to the bridge of his nose and turned his attention back to the photographs. After several moments his head began to nod. "Yes, yes, Number Three. Good call! You can tell by the fringe."

"Wouldn't that be an easy mistake?" Akemi asked. "Perhaps our victim was in a hurry and never finished fixing the pillows."

"That can't be. All of the sofa pillows, with the one exception, were perfectly positioned, and the area rug had distinct vacuum marks. Therefore, it is obvious that the pillows were plumped before the rug was vacuumed."

Akemi nodded. "I can't argue with that logic."

"I also agree." Radovan continued analyzing the photographs. "The cause of death did look like blunt force trauma, but now I will need to complete an additional examination of the body. Have you spoken with the detective on the case?"

"No, not yet."

Radovan visibly rolled his eyes. "Well, it is not Detective Garza, that is for certain. Are you…" He paused. "Are you seeing one another?"

"Do you mean socially?"

Radovan was quick to respond. "Oh, I am so sorry. You recognizably were hoping for more."

Terza held up her palm. "Wait, wait just a minute. I never even answered your question about whether Detective Garza and I are dating. How can you possibly tell me that I was hoping for more? Maybe we *are* dating."

Radovan crossed both arms and looked at Terza over the rim of his smudged glasses. He stared at her perceptively and finally spoke. "You are not the only one with good intuition."

"Alright, already." Terza flashed a defeated look at Akemi. "Have you met Nicolas Garza?"

"Only once. If I remember correctly, he is very good looking."

"Yes, he is, and he probably knows it. Doctor Radovan is correct." Terza turned her attention to the doctor. "I was hoping we might have another date, but he never called."

"I have not seen much of the detective." Radovan rubbed his chin. "Perhaps he has been away."

"Your guess is as good as mine. Do you know the detective on *this* case?"

Radovan nodded. "Yes, it is Detective Avery Ellington."

"Oh my." Akemi's slender hand shot to her mouth.

Terza returned her attention to Akemi. "Uh oh. What am I missing?"

"Be careful," Radovan politely warned his assistant. "We must treat all of our colleagues with respect."

"You knew I was hiding something about Nico, I mean Detective Garza, and now I know you're hiding something about Ellington. Please, please give me some insight. I might have to talk with him."

Radovan first glanced up at the ceiling and then toward Akemi. He hesitated before speaking. "I can tell you that Detective Ellington can be a bit proper."

"Ha!" Akemi almost spit out her coffee. "Snobby might be a better word."

"He's a snob?"

Radovan inhaled before speaking. "He is from an Ivy League school, and I think his parents are well-to-do."

"That doesn't mean he has to talk down to everyone he meets," Akemi added.

"I don't think the detective does it on purpose."

Akemi rolled her eyes. "He only wears monogrammed dress shirts, even on hot days."

Radovan raised his palm. "Hold on a second. I have seen the detective in a golf shirt."

Akemi placed a pinky finger to the side of her mouth. "Only high-end, signature golf shirts, with the collar turned up."

"Okay, that's enough." Radovan's tone sounded firm. "It is my fault for starting this. Let's return to the matter at hand. Terza, my second examination should be completed before the end of today. Shall I call you?"

"Yes, please. Thank you, Doctor Radovan."

He handed her a business card. "Please write your number on the back."

Terza carefully printed each digit of her mobile phone number and returned the card to Radovan. "Thank you again. You are very kind."

"I am kind?" His shoulders shook with laughter. "I do believe you originally thought I was mean."

Terza cringed. "I did, didn't I? But no, now you are just my favorite mad scientist."

Akemi studied the doctor's face. "He does look like a mad scientist, doesn't he?"

Radovan's chest puffed. "And I do so with pride. Now you must go, Number Three. We have much work to do."

Terza reached her hand toward Akemi. "It was nice meeting you, Akemi."

Akemi shook Terza's hand while saying, "It was nice meeting you, as well, Terza. I hope to see you again."

Terza walked closer to Radovan, raised on her tiptoes, and kissed the doctor's cheek. "Goodbye, Number One."

Radovan smiled, and a hint of pink filled his cheeks. "Goodbye, Number Three."

Back in her car, Terza sat quietly to plan the balance of her day. She knew the shopping centers had just opened, and fortunately she would pass by the Fashion Valley Mall on her way home. *Shopping was meant to be.*

Gone was the rush-hour traffic as Terza drove five miles south to her preferred mall. Almost every store imaginable could be found at Fashion Valley. Since it was a Monday morning, the near-empty lot also gave her lots of options. Terza decided to park on the third level at the Northwest end of the mall, directly across from her favorite clothing store.

When she entered the store, party dresses appeared to be the focal point of each department. The holiday season was just around the corner. As Terza circled the football-field-sized floor, she waited for something to stand out and catch her eye. When she saw a flash of red in a perfect shade, Terza walked straight for the rack of dresses. She checked the tags for a size four, then took the lone item into the dressing room. If it fit the way she hoped, this dress would be perfect.

Feeling elated, Terza exited the dressing room, paid the clerk, and took the escalator down to the store's coffee bar. She stood off to the side and called Moheenie.

"Hi, Tee."

"Mo, I need your help."

"Did you see the Medical Examiner?"

"Yes, but I'll tell you about that later." Terza repositioned the garment bag draped over her arm. "I need your help with a dress."

"Okay, what's up?"

"I just found this amazing dress! It is a vibrant red, off-the-shoulder neckline with three quarter length sleeves. The waist is super-fitted, and the skirt is a wide flair, almost like a skating skirt. Moheenie, it is drop-dead gorgeous!"

"You are going to be drop-dead gorgeous! I know how good you look in red. Conner will probably propose before the night is over. So what's the problem?"

"Shoes are the problem. I think this color red will go perfectly with my strappy red shoes, but I have to check. If they do match, are they dressy enough for semiformal?"

"Do you mean the ones with rhinestones?"

"Yes." Terza sat on one of the small bistro chairs. "Good, I'm glad you remember."

"Terza, those are super dressy."

"Is it okay that they are open toe?"

"Of course it's okay," Moheenie assured.

Terza blew out a breath of air. "Thank goodness. Now I don't have to go shoe shopping."

Moheenie chuckled. "But shoe shopping is ever so fun!"

"I know. But I'd rather not spend any extra money right now, especially this close to Christmas."

"I hear you."

"Okay, talk later."

"Bye, Tee."

"Ciao, ciao."

Terza moved to the counter and ordered an Americano coffee. She carried her dress and cup to an outside table, ready to sit, relax, and reflect on her new purchase. But before Terza took the first sip, her phone rang. The screen read *Conner Reeves*.

"Hi there."

"Hello, gorgeous. I need your advice about clothes."

Terza's mouth formed a slight smile. Conner's comment sounded noticeably similar to the one she just spoke to Moheenie. "I'm all yours. What can I do to help?"

"This semiformal business is causing me problems, and believe it or not, Mando took me shopping yesterday."

Terza whistled. "That *is* hard to believe. Did you buy anything?"

"He convinced me to buy a suit!"

"Wow! You bought a suit? I'm impressed."

"Yes, but shouldn't I be wearing a tuxedo?" Conner sounded concerned. "I was thinking of renting one."

"No, a tuxedo is formal. A suit should be just perfect. What color is it?"

"Gray, but I don't know, Terza. Rico is wearing a tux."

"Who is Rico?"

"The groom."

"Conner, you are such a goof! Of course the groom is wearing a tuxedo. That doesn't mean you have to wear one, too. Is Rico having any groomsmen?"

"Yes. He really wanted Mando and me to be in the wedding, but Rico's family is huge. To be honest, I am glad we're not."

"Weddings are such fun." Terza envisioned the dress hidden beneath her garment bag.

"Weddings are fun when you are not in them."

"But what if you're the groom? You will have no choice then."

"If a certain wild-haired Italian girl would pay me more attention, I just might not mind being a groom."

"I see." The gears in Terza's mind started spinning. "Is that a proposal?"

"Not yet," he teased.

Terza felt a tinge of disappointment when she heard the laughter in his tone. *Do I want Conner to propose? Or do I just want to be married?*

"Oh, sorry, Terza," Conner's voice interrupted her thoughts. "Something's up. I've got to go."

"Okay, we can talk later. Ciao."

"Bye."

Conner's rapid end to their call made Terza feel a bit uneasy. She knew he worked in a dangerous profession, and love him or not, Terza thought of Conner as a best friend. She then considered Nico and the fact that his job could also be dangerous. *Dangerous jobs, dangerous men. Is that what attracts me?*

The time barely neared noon, so Terza decided to spend a little while at her catering company. She finished her coffee, returned to her car, and drove to Macaroni on Wheels. After parking next to the company van, she unlocked her front office. A business card had been slipped between the yellow painted door and the white door jam. The front looked similar to Nico's detective card. However, this particular card belonged to Avery H. Ellington, III. Terza analyzed the front and then flipped the card to view the back. Five words were carefully printed: *Please contact me right away.*

"Interesting," Terza said out loud as she unlocked her office. She dropped the card on her desk, pulled out her phone, and tumbled it from hand to hand. Terza wanted to speak with Nico before calling Ellington. *Should I call him? Text him?* As if looking for a sign, Terza stared out her front window. The main street in Little Italy seemed quieter than normal, even for a Monday afternoon. Terza surmised that the area residents were away at their workplaces, and the typical tourist activity was still a day away. After the cruise ships docked on Tuesdays, the streets tended to be busier than on the weekends. Terza watched a few people walk by before returning her attention to the waiting phone. She decided to send a text:

Hi, Nico. I hope you are doing well. When you have a moment I would like to talk with you.

She pressed send and waited for her phone to ring. After an hour of attempting to make a dent in her paperwork, Terza finally decided to prepare a large pot of chicken noodle soup. She needed the comfort of both preparing and enjoying the soup, and she knew the leftovers would be perfect for the chilly days to come.

Terza seasoned and browned the chicken pieces in a large stock pot and then retrieved them from the pan. She added chopped onions, celery, and carrots and sautéed the trio until softened. Terza added the minced garlic and lots of spices before returning the chicken to the pot. She poured several quarts of homemade chicken stock and turned up the heat. While waiting for the chicken to cook, Terza filled one sink with hot soapy water and washed the dishes. She was rinsing when her phone finally rang. Nicolas Garza's name flashed on the screen.

"Hello."

"Hi, Terza. It's Nico."

"Hi, Nico. Thank you for calling. I really need to talk with you about Detective Ellington."

"Terza, you can't be messing around with him. Ellington considers you a suspect."

"A suspect?" Terza shrieked. "Nico, you know that can't be true."

"Look, Terza," his voice sounded stern. "I do know that, but Ellington doesn't give a rip about what I think, and it's his case. Did he come to see you?"

Terza felt defeated. "He left a card, asking me to call."

"Then you better make it quick," Nico warned. "Call him before he comes back, or it won't be pretty."

Shock rippled through Terza's body. How could she possibly be a suspect? Terza also could not believe how callous Nico sounded. She called him for help and now felt abandoned. "Okay," she finally said. "I'll call him. Thanks, Nico." Terza ended the call.

She checked the chicken in her soup and, using tongs, removed it from the broth. In culinary school she learned not to make the mistake of overboiling the chicken. After the chicken pieces cooled, she would shred them and then return the chicken to the soup once the vegetables were cooked.

Before calling Ellington Terza first needed a friend. She dialed Moheenie.

"Hi, Tee. What are you doing?"

"Making chicken noodle soup."

"Oh no! What's wrong?"

"I do not always make chicken noodle soup when something is wrong." Terza scratched her head. "Do I?"

"Yes, you do. Now spill it."

Terza obliged by telling Moheenie about Ellington's business card and her subsequent conversation with the extremely unfriendly Nicolas Garza.

"I think Nico did it on purpose," Moheenie offered.

"How do you figure that?"

"Nico knows you, and he knows how inquisitive you are. How many times did you step on his toes during the McCool investigation?"

Terza remained quiet.

"Tell me the truth. Did Nico ever get upset at you for interfering?"

"Yes, he did," Terza said quietly.

"Okay then, you are making my point. Nico probably knows that this new detective will be hard on you. Who knows? Maybe he would even arrest you for interfering!"

"He wouldn't. Would he?"

"We don't know, Tee, but Nico knows him. I think Nico is just trying to protect you."

Terza sighed loudly. "I hope so. He really hurt my feelings, Mo."

"Oh, honey, don't let him get you down. He's a guy, and you know how clueless they can be."

"Thanks, Mo. I know." Terza glanced at her stock pot of soup. "I better go and finish up."

"When are you going to call Ellington?" Moheenie asked.

"Soon. I want to call him before he tries to contact me again."

After ending their call, Terza retrieved a ladle, fished for a carrot slice, and tested the orange vegetable by taking a small bite. She then tasted the broth, added some additional spices, and turned down the heat. Before shredding the chicken, Terza decided to call the detective. She dialed the number from his card.

"Detective Avery Ellington."

"Detective Ellington, this is Terza Tiepolo. You wanted me to call."

"Yes, Ms. Tiepolo. I would like you to please come to the station. Are you able to do so now?"

Terza looked at her cooked chicken pieces before answering. "How long will you need me?"

"Probably an hour or so," Ellington answered.

"If it's no more than an hour, I can leave here in about fifteen minutes. If you need more than an hour, I will have to come later."

"An hour should do it."

"Are you at the main station downtown?"

"Yes, just park in the lot and give the desk sergeant your name."

"Okay, I will see you soon."

When Ellington disconnected the call without further pleasantries, Terza quickly shredded the cooked chicken and added it to the waiting soup. She turned off the gas and covered the pot with a tight lid. "It should be fine," she spoke aloud.

Terza then went to her office bathroom mirror and analyzed her outfit. She still wore the same denim jeans and black long-sleeved T-shirt. *I wonder if tennis shoes are appropriate for an interrogation?* Deciding that she didn't care what Ellington thought about her, or her attire, Terza grabbed her phone, purse, and keys. She locked up and drove straight to the downtown police station.

CHAPTER TEN

Avery Ellington – THE THIRD!

White lines of empty spaces decorated the police station's parking lot, giving Terza her choice of at least twenty spots. It seemed odd to see just one other car. *Perhaps this lot is only for guests.*

She exited her Fiat, set the lock, and walked up to the building. Side by side glass doors opened automatically as she neared. Terza entered the vacant lobby and stepped up to the desk. A lone male officer dressed in uniform greeted her.

"How may I help you?"

Terza read the name of Rader on his block style name tag.

"I have an appointment with Detective Ellington."

"The third?" Rader asked.

Terza could not tell if the officer was joking, asking her a question, or what. "Uh yes," her words stumbled.

"Please have a seat. I'll tell him you're here."

Did she hear him laugh? It was easy to sense that Ellington may be the joke of the department, but Terza knew this interview was not a laughing matter. Moments later Ellington entered the lobby, and as expected, he wore dress slacks and a long-sleeved monogramed shirt. Terza noticed how the fine green lines of his dress shirt matched the muted green color of his expensive-looking trousers. The color went well with his light brown hair and hazel eyes. He wore shiny loafers, obviously made from high quality leather. The only symbol of his detective status came from the badge attached to his matching belt.

"Ms. Tiepolo," he greeted her formally. "I am Detective Avery Ellington, the third."

Did he really just say the third? No wonder he gets teased. Terza stood. "Nice to meet you, Detective." She extended her palm to him.

His reluctance to accept it almost made Terza withdraw her offer. As Terza's hand slowly retreated, his hand suddenly locked onto hers. "Yes, it is nice to make your acquaintance." Ellington instantly dropped Terza's hand and said. "Please follow me."

Knowing that she might lose it, Terza was careful not to make eye contact with the desk officer, Rader. Instead, she kept her head lowered and followed Ellington through a single door and down the hallway. Terza wondered if she might see Nico as they passed by several offices. Unfortunately, all of them were empty. They finally came to a bullpen-style area which was also empty. Ellington guided her to a plain wooden table along the far wall. "Please take a seat."

Terza selected the nearest of the two chairs and waited while Ellington settled in the other. She felt relieved not to be in some sort of interrogation room. Terza noted the numerous cameras mounted on the drop ceiling.

"Let's get started." He reached for a yellow ruled legal pad. Ellington first asked Terza questions he already knew, like name, address, phone number, and so on. Terza felt ready to provide her rank and serial number if they existed.

Ellington then focused on Terza's catering company, how she was hired for the Kamoze job, and her involvement with Sloan Kamoze.

Terza sighed loudly. "How many times do I have to tell you? I never met Sloan until the night of the party. I never even spoke with Sloan before that night."

"And yet you felt comfortable walking into her house," Ellington pressed.

Terza placed both palms on the table. "Only because she was expecting me."

"Do you typically leave a mess for the host after you cater an event?"

Terza silently counted to ten before answering. She was ready to punch this idiot. Akemi was right. *Not only is Ellington a snob, but he is also a snot!* "Listen." Terza clipped her words. "No, we do not typically leave anything behind. I pride myself on leaving a home cleaner than when we arrived. But Sloan insisted. She is"—Terza's voice cracked with emotion—"she *was* such a nice person. She seemed concerned that Moheenie and I had worked so hard to make her birthday special." Terza looked to her bag on the table. "May I get my bottle of water?"

Ellington nodded.

After taking a few small sips, Terza continued. "Since Sloan insisted we finish the following day, I conceded by leaving our espresso machine. It takes a while for it to cool down, so that seemed like the best solution."

"Did you get the feeling she was trying to get rid of you?" Ellington asked.

"No, of course I didn't! Sloan was just trying to be nice. Have you never experienced that concept?"

Instead of responding, Ellington just glared.

Terza momentarily thought of apologizing, but opted for silence.

Ellington finally resumed. "Let's move on to the crime scene. Detective Garza may have appreciated your help, but I don't need it."

Terza shot him a death stare. "I wasn't offering."

"I understand you have a video."

Terza quickly decided against denying it. "I do. It's on my phone."

"That was wrong of you," Ellington scolded. "Please hand me your phone."

Terza unlocked her phone and slid it slowly across the table. Without asking permission, Ellington scrolled through her videos, apparently searching for the correct date. He turned the screen. "Is this it?"

She leaned in. "Yes, that's the one."

"Did you take any other videos?"

"No, just photos."

"We'll get to those next." Ellington used Terza's phone to email her video to him, and then he pushed the play button. "Why did you shoot a close up of the carpet?"

"I thought you didn't want my help."

His brows lifted. "Curiosity."

Killed the cat. "Okay." Terza launched into her theory. Ellington listened, and Terza suspected it was more intently than he wanted her to know.

When she finished, he looked directly at her. "Did you make any copies of this video?"

Terza met his eyes. "No, no copies." I only uploaded it to my tablet, she thought.

"Then do I have your permission to delete it?"

"Sure." Terza shrugged. "Go ahead."

After Ellington deleted the video, he clicked on several of her crime scene photos. *Delete away.* Terza had also previously uploaded the photographs.

"I see your photos are focusing on the carpet once again," he commented.

"Yes, as I already explained. Please feel free to delete the photos, too."

"Did you make any copies?" Ellington asked.

"No, I did not."

Once again, Ellington emailed the photos to himself before deleting them. He then abruptly stood and handed Terza her phone. "Okay, that will be all for now."

Terza forced a smile. "Thank you."

"Follow me out."

Ellington led the way through the same corridor, and Terza once again checked the offices for any sign of Nico.

Glad the interview was over, and disappointed at the lack of Nico sighting, Terza returned to the Macaroni on Wheels kitchen and her waiting chicken noodle soup. She needed it now more than ever.

CHAPTER ELEVEN

Videos, Videos, and More Videos

Tuesday

Deep within her dream, Terza heard loud roars and stood face-to-face with a male lion. She wasn't afraid, just mesmerized at the animal's beauty. The sound confused Terza, but the lion's mouth remained closed. There was a push on her chest, followed by several more, and she finally opened one eye. "Olive, what are you doing?"

Olive continued pressing her front paws into Terza's chest, while vocalizing her presence with noisy moans.

Terza sat, leaning against her pillow, and pulled Olive near. "What is the matter? Are you hungry?" Terza stroked Olive's back. Olive then brushed her face against Terza's palm, a definitive sign of complete starvation.

"Oh my, aren't you the dramatic one?" Terza slid out of bed and walked directly toward her kitchen. "First your wailing made me dream of lions, and then you woke me up right in the middle!"

Olive paid no attention to Terza's ramblings. Instead she sat directly in front of her bowl without moving her head. Only Olive's eyes followed Terza's movements.

"Why are you so hungry?" Terza looked down at her cat. When Olive remained still, Terza took it as a sign to speed up the process. She opened the refrigerator and withdrew the rest of Olive's wet food. Terza then retrieved a clean crystal bowl and mixed the wet food with a little dry. "You are in for a treat this morning, my beauty." Terza reached down to exchange the bowls. "I added some of your favorite." Olive's purring while she ate was all the appreciation Terza needed.

She returned to the refrigerator. "Now I'm the famished one! Hmm." Terza stared at the limited selection. "A smoothie is not going to cut it." She filled the kettle, turned on the burner, and dialed her mom.

"*Buon giorno*, my love. How are you this morning?"

"*Buon giorno*, Mom. I'm famished. Olive woke up starving, and I think it rubbed off on me."

"It's only a little after seven. Don't you have time for breakfast?"

"Of course I have time, but I'm just being lazy. I was hoping for one of Papa's breakfast sandwiches."

"Ezio," Terza heard her mother call out. "Can you go to the Mercato a little early?"

"Sure. What for?" Ezio responded.

"Mom, no. I haven't even had my coffee yet."

"Terza is hungry," Benedette spoke to her husband. "She wants a breakfast sandwich."

"Mom, please give Papa the phone."

"*Buon giorno*, my little gnocchi," Ezio said. "Did you call your mother this morning?"

"Papa! I just called her. We are on the phone right now."

Ezio laughed heartily. "Did you read your Bible this morning?"

"Not yet. I just woke up. I'm making my coffee and plan to read when we hang up."

"Then *you* are my favorite daughter," he announced proudly.

Terza laughed along with her father. "Why thank you."

"Now what time would you like your breakfast sandwich?"

"When you come in, Papa. There is no need to open early. Nine is fine."

"You are in luck, my little gnocchi. I am expecting a delivery this morning, so I will be in by eight."

"Then you are going to beat me. I haven't even showered."

"Tell you what. Come by when you're ready, and then I will begin your breakfast masterpiece."

Terza chuckled. "I will, Papa, and thank you. May I speak with Mom?"

"Of course. Ciao!"

"Ciao."

Moments later Benedette spoke. "Did you place your order?"

"I did." Terza glanced toward her kettle at the sound of it whistling. She leaned over to turn off the gas burner. "I have to go now, but I wanted to say goodbye."

"Arrivederci, my love. Have a beautiful day."

"You, too, Mama. Ciao, ciao."

Terza ended her call and finished preparing her coffee. With mug in hand, Terza opened the sliding glass door of her fourth-floor balcony and positioned her coffee on a petite patio table. She then brought her Bible from her nightstand and sat in one of two patio chairs. Olive jumped onto Terza's lap and settled in comfortably.

By half past eight, Terza had showered, dressed in jeans and a red T-shirt, and now stood in front of her full-length mirror. She brushed her long, curly hair into a ponytail and fiddled to secure it with a red band. Terza smiled as she watched Olive watch her in the bedroom mirror. "We have the same coloring, my beauty. My hair is dark brown, and you have gorgeous dark brown fur."

Olive purred energetically.

"You are fortunate though. Your fur is perfectly smooth, while my hair is always a wild mess!" Terza reached down to caress Olive for one last goodbye. "Have a wonderful day. Ciao!"

Ready for a full day of work, Terza walked into the Macaroni on Wheels catering kitchen and then straight through the adjoining door to the Tiepolo Mercato. She could see her father talking to one of the vendors.

Ezio looked up and waved his hand. "I'll be finished shortly."

"No hurry, Papa. I just wanted you to know that I'm here."

Terza transferred the calendar notes from her computer tablet to their white catering board like she did each Tuesday morning. This week, their catering jobs took place on Wednesday, Thursday, Friday, and on Saturday morning. As Terza began printing with her black dry erase marker, Ezio opened their adjoining door.

"Is Moheenie coming in today?"

Terza looked up to their cat kitchen clock. "Yes, she should be here any minute. It's almost nine, and Mo comes in by then."

"Do you think she would also like a breakfast sandwich?"

Terza reached for her phone. "Good idea. Let me ask her." Terza sent Moheenie a quick text. Seconds later, Terza's phone chimed. She smiled and locked eyes with her father. "It's a yes with lots of happy face emojis. Moheenie must be hungry, too!"

Ezio smiled. "Two Tiepolo Mercato breakfast sandwich specials coming right up." As he closed one door, Moheenie opened the other. She entered through their back door leading into the kitchen. "Hi, Tee. Thanks for the text. I'm starving!"

"Me, too. I wonder why we're all so hungry this morning?"

"Who else is hungry?"

"Olive. She must have been meowing pretty loudly because I was dreaming of a lion."

"How funny." Moheenie giggled. "I can't imagine cute little Olive sounding like a lion."

Terza turned her head. "No, she doesn't really. Maybe it was the loud growling of my stomach, and that *I'm* as hungry as a lion. Either way, Papa is working on our breakfast right now."

"Your father is so nice!"

"We are both blessed with amazing dads." Terza finished writing the last few words and then carefully returned the whiteboard to the wall.

Moheenie stepped closer. "It looks like a full week."

"That it does. As you can see, we are free to cook all day today."

Moheenie smiled. "I enjoy cooking days, don't you?"

"Yes, I do. We get to cook, talk about fun stuff, and listen to tunes."

"Without any pressure."

Terza nodded. "That's for sure. Now, Wednesday should be fun. Do you remember the co-ed bridal shower we catered downtown?"

"Do you mean the one this past summer? I think we served lasagna?"

"That's the one. The office manager wants us to duplicate the shower menu, with two additions. She wants us to bring champagne and wine."

"Oh." Moheenie pumped a brow. "And what are they celebrating?"

"I believe one of the owners is retiring."

"What about dessert? Are we making any?"

"No. Last time they had a bridal shower cake, and this time they are having a retirement cake. Other than the alcohol, the menu will be exact. We are making an antipasto salad, both beef and chicken lasagna, and, of course, garlic bread."

"That should be easy."

"Knock, knock." Ezio, holding two wrapped sandwiches, joined them in the kitchen. He placed them on the counter and moved to give Moheenie a hug.

"Thank you very much, Mister Tie. I love your sandwiches."

Ezio grinned. "Anything for my two favorite girls."

Terza hugged her father and kissed him on the cheek. "Thanks, Papa. You're the best!"

"Enjoy!" Ezio winked. "Back to work."

Terza and Moheenie rapidly opened the sandwich wrapping and savored their first bite.

"Yum." Moheenie leaned in for a second bite.

"Double yum!"

Moheenie's attention returned to the catering whiteboard. "Are we catering another executive meeting on Thursday?"

Terza nodded while she finished chewing. "It's our same clients. They obviously like us. This will be the fourth meeting we've catered for them, and, as usual, they are only ordering Salumi E Formaggi with bread, olive oil, and balsamic. I think they just like the meat and cheese board for something to snack on while they talk. I'll go next door later this afternoon. My papa always knows what selection is best."

They continued to munch on their sandwiches while discussing the various catering jobs. Moheenie glanced at the whiteboard and then raised an eyebrow to Terza. "Friday's menu looks interesting."

"Ha! Let's see, we are serving macaroni and cheese, regular and gluten-free, parmesan-crusted chicken strips on skewers, an assortment of finger sandwiches, a fruit platter, and a veggie platter. Now, can you guess our client?"

"Are we catering a children's party?"

"Yes, in a way. We get to roll our catering carts just up the street to the local elementary school. They had a contest, and the winning classroom receives a special lunch."

"What fun!" Moheenie clapped. "How many students are there?"

"Twenty-three students and two teachers. I only hope we have everything covered. I spoke at length with the teacher about any food allergies. The only special request was to have a gluten-free selection."

Moheenie nodded. "That's easy. What if we use bowtie pasta for the gluten-free macaroni and cheese?"

"Great idea, Mo. Later today we can check with my parents. I'm pretty sure they have a good selection of gluten-free pasta on hand."

"What's this I see on Saturday, *Miss* Terza? I thought you were taking off for the wedding?"

Terza chuckled. "What did I write for the catering job name?"

"Now, that's confusing as well. You just wrote *Tiepolo Mercato.*"

"It's because we are helping my pops, and don't worry, we should be done by noon."

"Perfect. That will leave plenty of time for you to get glammed up! How are we helping?"

"Believe it or not, we are making two, five-foot-long sandwiches. It was a special order for a college football tailgate party." Terza knocked on the concrete island. "Do you remember my father's friend, Jasper? He's the one who made this amazing counter."

"I do. He is really sweet. I remember that we've catered a few events for him."

Terza nodded. "That we did."

"Are the sandwiches for Jasper?"

"No, but Jasper came to the rescue again. He cut down two boards, made especially to fit the sandwiches. They are six feet long and a foot wide."

Moheenie spread her arms in order to measure the counter. "I forgot exactly how long this island is, but I know it's more than five feet."

"It's nine feet, to be exact."

"No wonder your pop wants to make the sandwiches here. I'm glad." Moheenie placed a hand to her heart. "He is such fun to work beside."

"Yes, I'm happy we can help. My parents always do so much for me. I'm constantly going next door to the Mercato, and they rarely charge. My mom always tells me not to worry about it, and she promises we will go over the accounting each month. But most of the time, she claims to have lost any record of my purchases."

"Anytime we can help them out just say the word. I'm game."

"Thank you, Mo. I knew I could count on you." Terza looked up to the catering board. "So that's our week. Shall we begin making the lasagnas?"

Moheenie reached for her red-and-white striped apron. "Yes, indeed. Let's get cooking."

Terza removed a second apron from the kitchen hook and tied it around her waist. Both chefs moved in perfect synchronization as they began their initial prep work. When Terza's phone chimed, her left hand was holding a sizeable onion in place, while she rapidly sliced through the layers with a large butcher knife. Within seconds, she had a pile of diced onion on her cutting board. Terza wiped her palms on a cloth towel, and clicked on her text.

Check your email. You owe me two dinners. Ian

"Mo, it's Ian! He says we owe him two dinners." Terza raced into the front office and pressed the power button of her computer.

Moheenie followed her. "Why not use your tablet?"

"My monitor is larger. I have a feeling this is going to be good." After her computer powered up, Terza clicked on her email and read the encrypted message from Ian:

Hi Terza,

As you can see, I was able to locate several videos. Please keep this between us.

Thanks!

Ian

Terza opened the first video and selected play.

"This is the video from the Palm Tree Inn." Terza screeched. "How is this possible?"

Moheenie shook her head. "Ian must have hacked into their closed-circuit system."

They watched the video and noticed several vehicles pulling in and out of the hotel parking lot. A few visitors entered the lobby, and several also exited. Neither of them recognized any of the visitors or their vehicles.

"What type of car does Ruby Slippers drive?" Moheenie asked.

Terza shrugged. "I have no idea, but maybe Conner can tell us." She pointed to the screen. "Do you see the cars parked along the back of the lot?"

"Yes, I do, but it's hard to tell the make or model."

Terza checked the time frame on the video. It began at 8:00 a.m. on Saturday, October 31st and ended at 9:30 a.m. on the same day. She looked up to Moheenie, who was sitting on the side return of the desk. "We have an hour and a half of footage here. Later today we can watch it more closely, but let's move on."

"I agree."

Terza clicked on the next video and pushed play. They could tell the recording was from the camera mounted above the porch light, across from the Kamoze's house.

"It looks so far away." Moheenie squinted at the video.

Terza leaned closer to her monitor. "At least you can see Joshua's house. Maybe I can zoom in." Terza clicked on the image and was able to enlarge it. She pointed to the screen. "Can you see the side of the Kamoze's house?"

"Not really." Moheenie drew closer. "I can see the driveway, but nothing to the left of it. Someone could have walked by the large lot between Joshua's house and the Palm Tree Inn."

"There are more recordings, and we still need to take a better look at the hotel video. Let's keep going." Terza sped through the second recording, until a person entered one of the frames. She instantly pressed the pause button and zoomed onto the image.

Moheenie inched forward on the desk. "Is that Belinda Benson?"

"I do believe it is. Let's advance it frame by frame and see where she goes."

"What time was this taken?" Moheenie asked.

Terza clicked on the video. "It appears to be nine in the morning, shortly before I arrived."

"Then Belinda Benson could be the killer."

"She certainly could." Terza clicked each frame until Belinda was out of view. The video showed Belinda walking up the Kamoze's driveway. "She must have gone to the side kitchen door."

"Yes and no. We see her walk up the driveway, but then she is out of view. Belinda could have walked back and then turned right toward the Palm Tree Inn."

Terza sighed loudly. "Darn, I wish we had a better angle." She glanced at Moheenie. "Why do you think she went up the driveway in the first place?"

Moheenie shrugged. "Who knows? Why don't you fast forward and see if she returns?"

"Good idea." Terza advanced the video. Less than ten minutes passed before Belinda walked back into the frame.

"Whatever she was doing I think it would be hard to murder someone in under ten minutes."

"I don't know, Mo. It doesn't take long to push someone down the stairs."

"Yes, but she first had to knock on the door, go upstairs to find Sloan, and then push her down. It doesn't make sense."

Terza considered Moheenie's timeline. "I agree, but it also doesn't make sense for Belinda to be snooping around the side of the house."

"Maybe you should play it again in real time."

The two watched the video as Belinda walked along the street directly in front of the Kamoze's home, pause momentarily, and then turned up their driveway.

"She heard something," Terza announced. "You can tell by the way her head angled."

"Yes, she did. So what if Belinda heard the murderer?"

"Oh, good thought, Mo. But that doesn't rule her out as the actual killer. What if she heard Sloan and then went up the driveway? Maybe they got into a confrontation."

"That still gives Belinda less than ten minutes to kill Sloan, drag her into the house, and place her at the bottom of the stairs."

Terza drummed her fingers on the desk. "It is possible."

"Yes, it's possible, but is it probable?"

Terza chuckled. "That sounds like one of the questions in our murder mystery book club." She clicked on another video. "Shall we check the final one?"

Moheenie's head bobbed vigorously.

The last video was taken from the camera mounted on the Benson house. It clearly showed Belinda leaving her home and returning ten minutes later. Terza paid close attention to the look on Belinda's face as she walked toward her doorbell camera. "She doesn't look traumatized. Wouldn't you think Belinda would show signs of stress if she just committed a murder?"

Moheenie grunted. "Not if she's a cold-blooded killer."

"Make up your mind, Moheenie. First, I'm the one who thinks Belinda did it, and then you talk me out of it. Now you think she did it?"

"I just don't know. I am trying to consider every possible angle."

"We need to take time and review the Palm Tree Inn video. Maybe we can look at it later when we finish up."

"Let's see how much we get accomplished." Moheenie hopped off the desk. "I promised Ranger a home-cooked meal this evening, so unfortunately I can't stay late."

"No problem, Mo. I completely understand. I'll rejoin you in a minute. Let me send Ian an email."

"Please thank him from me, too."

"Will do." Terza closed all of the videos and replied to Ian's email.

Dear Ian,

Thank you very much! Moheenie and I cannot believe all of the footage you sent us. We are extremely grateful! Please let me know what you would like for dinner. I can bring you one freshly homemade dinner this week and another one next week. If you prefer, I can also bring both meals at the same time, and you can freeze any leftovers. The choice is yours. What would you like us to cook for you?

Thank you again!

Terza and Moheenie

P.S. You can email, call, or text.

CHAPTER TWELVE

LOTS OF LASAGNA

After sending the email to Ian, Terza returned to her pile of chopped onions. She retrieved the extra-large pot they used for making marinara sauce and placed it upon the burner. When it was nice and hot, Terza drew olive oil circles in the bottom of the pan and dropped in the onions. They instantly began to sizzle.

Fueled by their breakfast sandwich, and a desire to return to the videos, Terza and Moheenie both worked at a rapid pace. When Terza's phone rang, she checked to see the name. *Ian.*

"Hi, Ian. Thank you! Thank you!"

"No problem. It was easy." Ian laughed. "Wait, I take it back! It was really difficult, and I worked extra hard for my dinner."

"Don't worry, I'll make you two dinners no matter what. What would you like?"

"What is your speciality?" Ian asked.

"Anything Italian," Terza answered. "But seriously, please let me know what you would prefer. We definitely owe you."

"Lasagna is one of my favorites, but I'm sure it's a lot of trouble."

Terza caught Moheenie's eye. "Lasagna is no trouble at all. Do you seriously want lasagna?"

Moheenie and Terza shared a smile. They both knew it would be simple to prepare an additional pan.

"Yes, I'm sure it will be better than the frozen ones I buy."

"Well, I hope so!" Terza chuckled. "Do you prefer ground beef or chicken?"

"Beef," Ian spoke with confidence. "Plus, I have never heard of chicken lasagna. Is it really a thing?"

"Yes, it is. Chicken lasagna is delicious. We can prepare a pan of each, if you like."

"No, just one is perfect. Thank you, Terza."

"Seriously, I'm the one to be thanking you. Now what would you like for your second meal?"

"Really, one pan of lasagna is all the thanks I need. You don't owe me two dinners."

"Yes, we do! Tell you what. If you are going to be home this evening, I can drop your dinner off around five-ish. We can talk about your second selection then."

"That sounds good to me, Terza. See you around five." He paused. "Ish."

Terza chuckled softly. "See you then." She disconnected her call and grinned at Moheenie. "Ian wants lasagna, and we are already making lasagna. It's kind of ideal, don't you think?"

"I would say so. An extra pan of lasagna is easy."

"Yes, but let's do it up right for him." Terza looked out the kitchen window in thought. "Why don't we make two large pans of lasagna? Ian said it was his favorite. We can cook one, and I will take it to him while it is nice and hot. Let's freeze the second pan, and we can give him cooking instructions."

"Good call, Tee. I like that idea. We should also make Ian a salad and some garlic bread."

"Yes, that's perfect."

Moheenie angled her head. "I wonder if he eats dessert."

Terza shrugged. "I have no idea, but let's bring him some chocolate cannoli. I need to make a batch anyway, especially since the retirement party is at the same office building as last time."

"I don't understand." Moheenie's eyes narrowed. "Why are you making cannoli if they didn't order dessert?"

Terza flashed a devious smile. "Do you remember when we parked in the loading zone, and I went to speak with the guard?"

"Kind of, but nothing specific. Go on."

"When I asked him if we could park and just unload, he basically gave us enough time to take everything upstairs."

Moheenie nodded. "I remember that we put the lasagnas in the oven here at **MOW** and then returned for them so they would be nice and hot."

"Exactly. Since it worked perfectly, I plan to use the same strategy."

"What does that have to do with cannoli?" Moheenie rested an elbow on the counter.

"We are going to need a place to park just like before." Terza chuckled. "I thought a bribe just might solve the problem."

Moheenie grinned. "Are you talking about a chocolate cannoli kind of bribe?"

"I am. It turned out that the guard's mother used to make cannoli every Sunday, and of course, chocolate is his favorite!"

"Wow! That's a fantastic idea, Tee."

"Last time, I didn't even have to ask if we could leave our van in the loading zone. The guard called out to me when I was walking away. He told me to leave the van, and he would watch it."

"Good call. Hopefully the same guard will be on duty."

"I hope so, but now we really have to get moving. We have two extra lasagnas to make **and** a double batch of chocolate cannoli."

Moheenie glanced up at their cat wall clock. "We can do it."

"I like your confidence, but we need a tiny bit of help. I'll be right back." Terza walked through their adjoining door to the Tiepolo Mercato. Her father was busy helping several customers behind the butcher counter, and her mother stood waiting behind the cash register. She stepped closer. "Hi, Mom."

"*Buon giorno*, my love." Benedette smiled. "You seem rushed."

"I am, and I'm sorry. We are extra busy right now, and I could use Papa's help."

Benedette looked over at her husband. "He shouldn't be too long. Shall I call you when he is finished?"

Terza sighed. "No. Do you mind giving him a message?"

"Of course not. How can I help?"

"Thank you." Terza instantly relaxed. "Please tell Papa that I am making a Salumi E Formaggi board for the same executive meeting as I do each month. He will know."

"How many people are you feeding?"

"Six, or maybe seven total." Terza extended her hand across the low counter. "Thank you very much."

Benedette squeezed Terza's hand. "It is my pleasure. Now go."

"Yes, ma'am!" Terza quickly returned to her catering kitchen.

"That was fast," Moheenie said.

"Thank goodness, Mo. My papa was busy, so I asked my mom to give him a message. He always tells me which meats and cheeses to select anyway."

Terza took a moment to assess their progress and decided to prepare the four meat lasagnas, while Moheenie prepared the two pans of chicken lasagna. By 2:00 p.m., Terza commenced the chocolate cannoli preparation, and Moheenie worked on enough antipasto salad for Ian.

Moheenie also prepared the garlic bread, placed it upon a foil tray, and wrote out the baking instructions. "Would you like me to write out instructions for the lasagna Ian is going to freeze?"

"Yes, please."

Their kitchen door opened, and Ezio walked in holding six white packages.

Terza rushed to wrap her arms around his waist. "Papa, you are a lifesaver!" She took the packages and placed them into one of her two refrigerators. "Thank you!"

Ezio rubbed his stomach. "It smells like Heaven in here."

Terza smiled at her father. "I would love to feed you, but nothing is ready yet."

"These look amazing." Ezio maneuvered closer to the chocolate cannoli.

"And yes, there is one with your name on it. I promise to bring it over before you leave for the day."

Ezio scrunched his forehead and looked sideways at Terza.

"What? No good?" Terza then promptly slapped her forehead. "Oh, I get it! You don't want mom to know."

Ezio grinned comically. "What can I say?"

"Would you like to come back in about an hour?"

"I'll be counting the minutes." Ezio hugged Terza goodbye and winked at Moheenie. "See you ladies soon!"

Terza called out just as her father reached the door. "Papa, please don't be late. I have to leave by four-thirty."

"Got it."

Within the one-hour period, Terza and Moheenie finished preparing the four lasagnas for the retirement party, one of Ian's lasagnas was baking in the oven, and they had already placed the second one in the freezer. Ezio returned in time to enjoy his chocolate cannoli while they finished cleaning for the day. At 4:15 p.m., Terza wrapped Ian's meals for delivery.

"Darn." Moheenie moaned. "We didn't get a chance to look at the videos again."

"I know. I can either watch them later this evening or wait for tomorrow when you come in."

"No, go ahead and start without me. You can catch me up in the morning."

"Will do." Terza glanced into the large cooking pot on the stove. "I can't believe we still have some leftover marinara sauce. Maybe I should make a quick plate of pasta when I return from Ian's house. I can eat while I watch the video."

"That sounds like a fantastic idea, Tee."

Terza's heart warmed as she watched Moheenie rotate her Hawaiian heirloom wedding band. Her ring had been custom-made in the royal heritage-style jewelry of gold and black leaves.

"Earth to Terza."

Terza lifted her eyes to Moheenie's face.

"Where did you go, and why are you smiling?"

"I was back at your wedding in Hawaii. It was such a wonderful time."

"Only the best day ever!" Moheenie shared Terza's smile. "What made you think of our wedding day?"

"Watching you turn your ring. It brought me back, that's all."

Moheenie glanced at her ring. "Your wedding will be just as much fun."

Terza nodded. "I'm sure it will. But *where* will it be? That is the question."

"Do you want a destination wedding like we had?"

"Hawaii was more like a hometown wedding for you. If I remember correctly, at least half of your relatives still live on the islands."

"And the other half live on the ninth island!"

Terza narrowed her eyes. "You mean Las Vegas, right? I forgot why they call it the ninth island."

"It's because so many people from Hawaii have either moved or travel there frequently for a visit." Moheenie removed her apron. "Now, back to planning your wedding."

"Ha! I think there's plenty of time for that." Terza chuckled. "I need to find a groom first!"

"Good point."

"See you in the morning. Say hi to Ranger for me."

"I will. Call me later if you want."

Terza turned her head. "No, I'll wait until tomorrow. Enjoy your evening together."

After Moheenie left, Terza drove off with Ian's dinner packed securely in the trunk of her Fiat. She arrived shortly past 5:00 p.m. and knocked softly on his front door. Moments later, the door opened, and Ian appeared looking more vibrant than before. His blonde hair still needed a trim but was combed neatly. This time Ian wore canvass slip-on loafers, along with jeans and another flannel shirt. Terza noticed his clean shave.

"Hi, Terza." Ian greeted her with a warm smile. "Come on in." His blue eyes appeared both alive and a bit inviting as he stepped aside.

Terza returned his smile. "Thank you." She pointed to her car. "I actually could use your help."

Ian followed her gaze. "Oh, of course."

They walked side by side and stopped at Terza's trunk. She opened it and withdrew two large foil trays of lasagna. Ian held out his hands.

"Here, you take these, and I can handle the rest."

"This looks like a lot of food."

Terza laughed. "It's not as much as you think. Take it into the kitchen, and I'll meet you there."

Ian saluted. "Yes, ma'am."

When Terza met up with Ian in the kitchen, she reviewed the reheating instructions Moheenie had carefully printed for the cooked lasagna. She also offered to slice the pan into sections for him to enjoy.

"Thanks, Terza, but I can manage. I can't believe you also made antipasto salad and garlic bread! What a treat."

"I still cannot believe how many videos you were able to send." She opened one of the smaller bags and withdrew a box. "Do you eat dessert?"

Ian's eyes bulged. "Are you kidding?" He watched her open the lid. "Chocolate cannoli? Okay, I am officially spoiled!"

"You deserve to be. Moheenie and I are extremely grateful." Terza went over the instructions for the frozen lasagna and made sure Ian had ample room in his freezer. Before leaving, Terza once again thanked him, and asked. "By the way, how can you possibly procure all of these videos, especially the one from the Palm Tree Inn?"

"It's all right there for the taking." Ian lifted his palms. "That's the problem with Wi-Fi connections."

"But don't people use passwords on their Wi-Fi?"

"There is always a back door. Tell me, do you have an in-home security system?"

"No, but it is only because I live on the top floor of a condo project. I do have a deadbolt."

"What about any type of nanny cams? Many people have cameras set up for both children and their pets."

"I have a gorgeous Siamese cat named Olive, but no cameras." Terza laughed. "Although it would be interesting to see all of the trouble she gets into when I'm gone."

"If you do get a camera, please remember to turn it off when you're home."

A shiver raced up Terza's spine. "Are you serious?"

"I am *very* serious. Tell you what. Install a camera, give me your address, and then leave it on. I can walk by your building and locate your signal. Then, I will call and tell you exactly what you are doing when we talk."

Terza's hand shot to her opened mouth. "Ian, that is horrible! I didn't know something like that was possible."

"It's sad to say, but it is true. If I wanted, I could spy on many of my neighbors. But I have no desire."

"*You* don't, but just think of how many creeps are out there!"

"Exactly." Ian nodded. "That's why I'm cautioning you to be careful."

"Wow! I will be very careful." Terza held out her palm. "Thank you for everything, Ian."

Ian accepted her hand and placed his second one over hers. "Thank you, Terza. It was nice meeting both you and Moheenie." He then lifted the large tray of lasagna. "Plus, I think I got the better end of this bargain."

"You better wait until you taste it!"

"I'm sure it's delicious." Ian moved toward the door. "Come on, I'll show you out."

Ian walked Terza to her car and waited on the porch until she backed out of the driveway. She waved goodbye before driving forward. Fortunately there would be plenty of video viewing time. So not to feel rushed, Terza stopped by her house to feed Olive. She then returned to the Macaroni on Wheels kitchen to make herself a serving of pasta with marinara sauce.

CHAPTER THIRTEEN

CONNER TO THE RESCUE

Video time! Terza's plate of marinara-covered pasta had a generous dusting of freshly grated parmesan cheese, a glass of Chianti sat waiting for the first sip, and the Palm Tree Inn video was cued and ready for viewing. Terza used her computer mouse to push play.

Between sips of her wine, and mouthfuls of twirled capellini, Terza closely watched the hotel parking lot video. Approximately thirty minutes into the recording, she noticed a silver-gray compact car exit the driveway farthest from the lobby. It seemed odd, as she did not remember watching anyone walk to the car. The driver was too far away to detect any features, and Terza could not tell whether the person was male or female. She rewound the video and specifically scanned for the possible driver, but not a single guest exited the lobby and walked toward the car. Terza surmised that the driver either left the lobby before the recording or made it to the far end of the parking lot without being seen. Focused on the latter, Terza carefully inspected the perimeter of the parking lot. It appeared that foot traffic could easily access the lot from the restaurant next door. She made a mental note to drive by the area for further examination.

Terza moved on to the recording from the camera directly across from the Kamoze's home. She watched it from the beginning, without seeing any sign of Joshua or his vehicle. "You are still my number one suspect," Terza spoke softly. Joshua could have moved his vehicle well before the video started. His first wife was found dead at the bottom of the stairs, and now Sloan had also died at the bottom of the stairs. Terza stared at her computer screen and then leaned forward to look closely at the front windows. *Joshua, were you in there murdering Sloan?* She needed some answers and decided to call Conner.

"Hey, lovely lady," Conner said. "How are you this evening?"

"I'm doing great. What are you up to?"

"Unfortunately I'm still at work. There never seems to be enough time in the day for all of the paperwork required by this crazy job of mine."

"You're still at *work*?"

"Oh no, Terza. You want something!"

"Just one little something."

"Your *one little something* usually leads to another little something. Am I right?"

"You could be." Terza struggled not to laugh.

"You will owe me, Tiepolo," Conner told her.

"What do you have in mind?"

"Well, we are already going out Saturday night."

"Yes, we are," Terza prompted.

"And I do love kissing those luscious lips of yours—"

"Hang on a second," Terza interrupted. "I'm not going to be trading for any sexual favors."

"Sexual favors? I'm talking about a kiss!"

"I'm a good girl, so be nice."

"And that is why you're so special. Now tell me what I can do."

"Please keep in mind that I'm not asking you about anything current," Terza explained. "This is a previous matter that has been closed. Anyone has the ability to look it up."

Conner started laughing.

"What is so funny?"

"You crack me up, Tiepolo. If anyone can look it up, why are you calling me?"

"Well…" Terza stalled.

"Well, what?"

"It would be hard, but I'm sure I could find the information somewhere."

"Go on. I will keep in mind that this is a closed matter. Why are you telling me that?"

"Because maybe it is easier for you to give me information on a closed matter rather than one that is open," Terza explained.

"I shouldn't be giving you any information at all," Conner told her.

"Okay, I get it. Just listen. There was a woman named Yvette Kamoze—"

"How do you spell her name?"

After she spelled Yvette Kamoze's first and last name, Terza continued, "She lived in Los Angeles and was married to Joshua Kamoze. Yvette Kamoze was found dead in her Los Angeles home."

"What year was this?"

"I have no idea," Terza answered.

"Anything else?"

She hesitated. "Is it hard to find out what type of car a person drives?"

"It's not hard for me." Conner chuckled. "But it may be hard for you."

"Seriously, Conner, does it take a lot of time?"

"Is the subject vehicle registered in California?"

"I think so. The person lives in Los Angeles."

"Are you asking me to find out what type of vehicle Joshua Kamoze drives?"

"No, his sister Ruby Kamoze. Joshua drives a blue SUV."

"If Yvette Kamoze is already deceased, and you know what type of vehicle her husband drives, why do you care about his sister?" Conner pressed.

"I just do."

"Terza Tiepolo, are you investigating another murder?"

"How could I be? Yvette Kamoze potentially died years ago."

"That is *not* an answer," Conner told her.

"Okay, okay, I'll tell you. Joshua's current wife, Sloan, died this last Saturday morning. I found her dead at the bottom of the stairs."

"Terza, I am *not* kidding!" Conner spoke firmly. "You had better be careful."

"I will. I promise."

"Let me get this straight," Conner continued. "Yvette Kamoze, the previous wife of Joshua Kamoze, was found dead?"

"Yes."

"Did she die at the bottom of the stairs?"

"That is correct."

"And his current wife also died the same way?"

"Pretty suspicious, isn't it?"

"It is very suspicious," Conner agreed. "Joshua was obviously found not guilty. Did the police ever suspect him?"

"I don't know, Conner. That's what I'm hoping you can find out. It's an old case. There must be some information in your records."

Conner sighed audibly. "We have a problem though. If I look this up for you, I know you will remain involved. And that scares me, Terza. I don't want you getting hurt."

"If you don't look it up for me, I am still going to investigate. You will just be making my job easier."

"What am I going to do with you?"

Terza smiled into the phone. "Take me to the wedding on Saturday."

"I'll get back to you in an hour." Conner paused. "And what does the sister have to do with all of this?"

Terza considered telling Conner about the videos but instantly changed her mind. "I just want to know. It's no big deal."

"Are you investigating the sister, as well?" Conner asked.

"That would be a yes." Terza's voice squeaked.

Conner sighed, loudly, a second time. "I'll call you back."

"Thanks, Conner," Terza said, before realizing he had already disconnected their call. She finished eating her pasta and then decided to make herself an affogato. Terza prepared two shots of espresso before locating a small container of vanilla gelato in her freezer. After placing one scoop of the gelato into a glass mug, she poured the espresso on top. Terza used a teaspoon to capture a mixture of the ice-cold gelato and the hot liquid. "Yum!"

Terza's phone rang shortly after she finished cleaning her catering kitchen. "Hi, Conner," she said sweetly.

He laughed. "No need to butter me up. I already have the information."

"I'm all ears."

"Let's start with the small item. Ruby Kamoze drives a two door Honda Civic."

"Is it silver-gray?" Terza asked.

"The color is just listed as silver on the DMV records, and I'm not even going to ask how you knew. Now about Yvette Kamoze. Her death was ruled an accident. Joshua Kamoze was originally a person of interest, but his alibi checked out, and he was cleared."

"Were there any other suspects?"

"It doesn't look like it, but my access is limited. From what I can tell, Joshua's alibi was confirmed by the location of his mobile phone."

"That doesn't prove a thing." Terza's thoughts raced with possible ideas. "He could have simply left his phone wherever he was supposed to be."

"I agree. Plus, it looks very suspicious that his second wife died the same way."

"Conner, do you think the San Diego detectives will look into Joshua?"

"I'm sure they will. At least, they should. It is too much of a coincidence not to consider him a suspect. They will probably also speak with the detectives who handled the Los Angeles case."

Terza nodded. "I hope they do."

"Terza, you do know the police were able to solve murders before you came along, right?"

"Stop teasing me, Conner."

"I'm just asking you to please be careful. There are a couple of things at play here."

"What do you mean exactly?"

"Didn't you tell me that you found Sloan Kamoze's body?"

"I did," Terza confirmed.

"And is there a possibility Joshua murdered his wife?"

"Yes, most definitely!"

"Then first, you may be considered a person of interest in Sloan's death. If you do not stay out of the way, the detectives could make it hard on you. Second, Joshua may be a murderer. If he thinks the police are after him, Joshua may try and pin it on you."

Terza grunted. "There's no way, Conner. I was the one who found Sloan and then reported it."

"Yes, Terza. You don't know how people react when they feel trapped. I am warning you to please be careful."

Terza relented. "I understand, and I will keep my distance."

"Do you promise me?"

"Yes, I promise. Now what time are you picking me up on Saturday?"

"How about five-fifteen? The wedding begins at six."

"Five-fifteen is perfect. Shall I wait outside?"

"No, you shall not," Conner told her. "I will come to your door like a perfect gentleman."

"But Conner, there is never any place to park. Tell you what. Text me when you arrive, and you can wait for me at the curb."

"May-be." He stretched out the word. "I'll see what the parking situation is like when I get there."

"Okay, thanks again, Conner. I better get home."

"You're not going to walk, are you?"

"Conner, you are way too cautious. It is barely six blocks, but I do have my car tonight."

"Good thing. Sleep tight and I'll see you Saturday."

"Ciao."

After ending her call, Terza took another look at the Palm Tree Inn video. She was unable to zoom in on the silver gray vehicle and could not tell the make. Terza thought about calling Ian to see if he could zoom in but held that thought for another day. Instead, she pressed pause to freeze the frame, took a photo with her phone, and then enlarged the image. Unfortunately, the closer Terza got to the driver, the blurrier the photo became. She still could not tell if the driver was male or female. Terza focused on the side angle of the front hood, but the brand symbol could not be seen. She needed to look at the body styles for Honda Civics or get a better angle of the image on her screen. The latter seemed the least likely. A trip to her local Honda dealer might be in order.

"Another day," Terza said out loud.

CHAPTER FOURTEEN

CATERING COMES FIRST

Wednesday

By the time Terza made her way to Macaroni on Wheels, she had already fed Olive and read her Bible. Since she also called her mother while walking to her catering company, Terza took note that she was her father's favorite. In reality, she knew he loved all of his children equally and just enjoyed his amusing game.

Moheenie entered shortly thereafter. "Good morning, Tee. I bet you have news for me."

"I do." Terza smiled. "But first, how was your evening?"

"It was nice. Ranger and I enjoyed a relaxing dinner together. I kept my phone on just in case you decided to call, but all was quiet."

"I didn't want to bother you, and I knew it could wait. Let's finish preparing the antipasto salad while I catch you up."

"What time shall we begin cooking the lasagna?" Moheenie secured her apron.

Terza reached for the second apron. "Right about eleven."

The duo worked together in harmony as Terza told Moheenie about her discovery of the silver car on the Palm Tree Inn video. She talked about her subsequent conversation with Conner. "I took a photo of the car but cannot tell the make or model."

"Do you think it could belong to Ruby Slippers?" Moheenie asked.

"Yes, of course I do. After the luncheon today I think we should go to one of the Honda dealers."

"I agree." Moheenie separated the salami slices. "But let's find one that sells both new and used vehicles. If it is a Honda Civic in the video, it may be an older model."

"Good idea, Mo. After that, I think we should go to the Palm Tree Inn and scope out the parking lot."

Moheenie nodded. "We need to see if someone could park at the hotel and sneak to the Kamoze's house without being seen on any of the videos."

"I almost think we should try a test run. What if I give Ian the exact time and see if he can locate a recording of us?"

"That's brilliant!" Moheenie's eyes widened. "Oh, by the way, how did he like his lasagna?"

"He loved it. Ian sent us a text last night to say thank you and let us know how much he enjoyed our cooking."

Moheenie smiled. "That is always nice to hear."

Terza's head bobbed. "It never gets old."

At 10:40 a.m. Terza turned on their double oven, and at 11:00 a.m. she placed one large foil pan filled with lasagna on each of the four racks. She and Moheenie then quickly changed into their casual catering uniforms. As typical for a non-formal catering event, they wore tan khaki pants and black golf-style shirts with the Macaroni on Wheels logo. Moheenie brushed her straight jet-black hair into a high ponytail, while Terza attempted to also brush through the length of her dark brown hair.

Terza moaned. "Why does it take me twice as long to make a ponytail?"

"Because you have a gorgeous head of curls." Moheenie fingered Terza's hair. "And I am jealous!"

"Please. Even my cute little niece, Charley, wants straight hair like you."

"I remember." Moheenie finished her hair with a black ribbon. "I also remember what you told Charley: girls with straight hair will try and curl it, while girls with curly hair will use a straightener."

Staring into their bathroom mirror, Terza looked at Moheenie standing behind her. "Did I really say that?"

"Yes, you did, and it's true."

"It certainly is." She finished securing her ponytail and finally lowered her hands. "We have to move. Let's load the van and get this party started!"

When everything, with the exception of the lasagna, was packed securely in the catering van, Moheenie locked their back kitchen door and climbed into the passenger's seat. Terza turned the ignition and drove the short distance to their destination. She parked in the office building's loading zone, got out, and rushed to see which parking guard was working. As she briskly walked toward the guard station a familiar face smiled back at her.

"I was hoping to see you." Terza flashed him a smile.

"How's my favorite cannoli lady doing today?"

"Just fine, thank you. How are you?"

"I got up, and I'm still breathing." The elderly guard laughed. "I call that a good day." He gestured to her van. "Don't worry about moving after you unload. Those amazing chocolate cannoli gave you parking privileges for life."

"Why, thank you! You are too kind. I take it you liked my cannoli?"

His smile grew larger. "Don't tell Mama." He pointed skyward. "She's in Heaven," he whispered, "but she can still hear me. They were the best I have ever tasted."

"Then wait here." Terza winked. "I have a surprise for you."

"I'll be waiting," he called as Terza returned to her van.

Terza retrieved the chocolate cannoli and handed the box to the anxiously waiting guard. "I hope these are as good as last time."

"I'm sure they will be." He peeked into the box. "Thank you very much."

"You're welcome. It's my pleasure. Thank you for being so kind about the parking."

"It's the least I can do."

Terza flashed a warm smile and rushed to finish helping Moheenie unload. Together they filled their rolling cart and headed for the elevators. When they reached the office suite, Terza and Moheenie greeted their contact before guiding the cart toward the miniature kitchen area. "You better drive back for the lasagnas, Tee. I've got this."

"Are you sure?"

"Yes, it feels like old times."

Terza left to retrieve the freshly cooked lasagna. When she returned, Moheenie had just finished pouring the champagne and wine.

"How are we doing, Mo?"

"So far so good. Everyone seems excited about having wine and champagne. I have a feeling they are going to close the office early today."

"Or late!" Terza laughed. "They will all probably stay and talk shop but definitely not go back to work. Shall we serve the antipasto salads?"

"Yes, the timing is perfect. Last time I served a plate to each person and then left the remainder on the table."

"I think that's the best idea. Then they can select an extra portion of their favorite goodies."

While Terza began plating the antipasto salads, Moheenie left to bring a huge basket of garlic bread into the conference room.

She returned to the kitchen laughing. "Once again I almost got attacked. These people certainly do like their garlic bread!"

"That is *always* the case." Terza joined Moheenie's laughter. "Tell me, is it safe to serve the salad?"

"Oh yes, they are happy campers. A little alcohol and lots of garlic bread. They probably won't even notice when we come in with the antipasto!"

After they completed serving the salad course, Moheenie and Terza lingered in the kitchen area. Each one took turns peeking at the progress. When the first person was done with his salad, Terza began to slice the lasagna. They then entered the conference room with two of each type.

Both lasagnas turned out to be hits, with the meat lasagna taking the early lead. After hearing several comments on the chicken lasagna, Terza and Moheenie cut into the second tray. It rapidly became the favorite.

Next came the retirement cake, followed by speeches. Terza sliced through the chocolate layers while listening to the retiree's coworkers' praise and comically roast their colleague. When Moheenie finished serving the cake, they returned to the office kitchen.

"What a successful party!" Terza separated the trash from the recyclables.

"And such fun speeches. Our guest of honor was well-liked."

"Yes, he was."

After they finished cleaning up, Moheenie and Terza rolled their catering carts toward the row of elevators. Terza looked to Moheenie. "Do you still feel like hitting the Honda dealer, or are you too tired?"

"I'm good to go. I just don't feel like dealing with any car salespeople right now."

Terza pressed the down button. "Okay then. Let's make up something."

"Like what?" Moheenie's eyes narrowed.

"I don't know." Terza chuckled. "We can make it up on the fly."

The doors opened, and they rolled their carts into an empty elevator car. Terza checked her watch. "It's just three o'clock. No wonder it's so quiet."

"Do you want to change first?" Moheenie asked.

"Yes. Let's unload the van, get changed, and if you don't mind, we can take your car."

"I don't mind at all. I'll check for dealerships on the way back to *MOW*."

Dressed in jeans and T-shirts, Terza and Moheenie walked onto the Honda dealership lot filled with used, or so-called *pre-owned*, vehicles. A fleshy man, dressed in navy blue slacks, a light blue long-sleeved shirt, and navy tie watched them walk onto the lot. He bounced on his toes, almost as if revving his engine, and jogged toward them.

"Here he comes," Terza whispered to Moheenie.

"Welcome," the salesman practically shouted. "How are you lovely ladies today?"

His smile looked phony, and Terza instantly noticed the poor attempt of combing over his bald spot.

"Just fine," Moheenie spoke quietly.

Ignoring Terza, the man zoomed in on Moheenie. "Are you looking to buy a car? Perhaps two cars, you know, one for each?" In an eerie way, he spoke through constantly smiling lips.

Terza took the lead. "Thank you, but we actually have a crazy kind of request."

"Crazy? I like crazy." His voice boomed. "What can I do for you?"

You can stop acting so weird. "Don't tell anyone." Terza lowered her voice. "We are kind of spying on my boyfriend."

He winked. "I get your meaning."

Terza refrained from rolling her eyes. "Anyway, we were hoping to just look around your lot of used cars."

"Do you mean *pre-owned*?"

Terza quickly corrected herself. "Yes, of course. I have a photo, and we would like to compare it to your pre-owned cars."

The salesman moved closer and reached out his hand. "Would you like to show me? Maybe I can help?

Terza clenched her phone. "No, thank you."

"Do you mind if we just look around?" Moheenie asked sweetly.

When the salesman seemed suddenly distracted, Terza followed his gaze and saw a vehicle parking near the front office. "Sure. Help yourselves," the man mumbled, rapidly walking away.

Moheenie chuckled. "Saved by another potential buyer!"

"Thank goodness. He would probably sell more cars if he just acted natural."

Moheenie's laugher now roared. "Maybe that *is* natural for him!"

"Maybe." Terza surveyed the lot. "Let's start at the far end and work our way forward." She opened her phone gallery and selected the car photo. "I only have this side view."

As Terza and Moheenie approached each car, they took turns looking at the photo and then back to the vehicle next to them. They shook their heads when they failed to find a match and moved on to the next car.

After covering three additional rows, Moheenie asked to see Terza's phone. She inspected the photo and then turned her attention to a specific black car. "Terza, this may be the same model. What do you think?"

Terza reached for her phone to examine the photograph. She brought her hand to the car. "This side trim looks exact, doesn't it?"

Moheenie nodded. "I think so. With the exception of the color, I think this car is the same model as the one in your photo." She walked to the front and read from the window sticker. "It is a two thousand fifteen Honda Civic," Moheenie announced. "What year does Ruby Slippers drive?"

"I'll text Conner." Terza's thumbs bounced along her keyboard:

Hi, Conner,
What year is Ruby Kamoze's Honda Civic?
Please and thank you.

Conner replied via text:

2015

A second text came through:

What are you up to?

Terza replied:

About 5'3" last time I measured.

Conner ended with a smiling emoji.

Terza grinned and looked up from her phone. "Ruby Slippers drives a two thousand fifteen Honda Civic!"

"Terza." Moheenie grabbed her elbow. "She could have parked at the Palm Tree Inn, snuck back to the Kamoze's house, and killed Sloan!"

Terza blew out a large breath of air. "What if she also murdered Yvette?"

"You're right! We need to tell someone."

"Who are we going to tell?"

"Nico. Perhaps he can look into Yvette's death. There could be a connection."

"I don't know, Mo. It's not even his case. We should probably investigate a little more on our end first."

Moheenie creased her brow "But what can we do?"

"Let's go to the Palm Tree Inn and try to sneak back to the Kamoze's house. I can then call Ian and see if we were successful."

"Shall we try it now?"

Terza checked her phone. "It's getting late and will probably be dark before we finish. Maybe we should go first thing tomorrow morning."

"How does our catering day look for tomorrow?"

"We have the afternoon board meeting." Terza mentally calculated. "It will take us less than an hour to prep, so that's no big deal. I would also like to make the macaroni and cheese for the school luncheon on Friday, but everything else can wait. Can you pick me up right at eight in the morning?"

"I can do that, and I like your thought pattern. By the time we scope out the Palm Tree Inn parking lot, we will be moving toward the Kamoze's house about the same time as the killer."

"If the killer wasn't already in the house," Terza warned.

"Meaning Joshua?"

"Exactly."

When Terza arrived home, she served Olive a dish of her favorite wet food and then prepared a large Cobb salad for herself. Before sitting at the table, she dropped a grocery-sized, brown paper sack onto the dining room floor. Terza watched Olive play while she munched on her salad. Olive would race in, push the bag around the floor, and then race out. Sometimes Olive seemed to be stuck, but Terza imagined that was half the fun. Later, she searched for a good mystery show, and the two snuggled together on the sofa. Before retreating to bed, Terza set her alarm for 6:00 a.m.

CHAPTER FIFTEEN

A Couple of Spies

Thursday

The ringing of Terza's alarm came much too early. Even Olive looked at the clanging clock with contempt. When Terza dragged herself from the warm bed, Olive was quick to nestle into the relinquished site.

Terza prepared a quick breakfast of orange juice, banana, and toast. She read her Bible while eating and then turned on the kettle for coffee. Olive finally decided to join Terza in the kitchen when the loud whistle sounded.

"Good morning, my beauty." Terza glanced down as Olive zigzagged through Terza's calves. "Breakfast was served nearly an hour ago."

Olive purred her response before sinking her head into the crystal bowl.

With coffee mug in hand, Terza called her mother.

The telephone rang several times before her mother answered. "*Buon giorno*, my love."

"*Buon giorno*, Mom. How are you this morning?"

"I feel fantastic. Your father and I already went for a long walk. You know how much he adores Little Italy in the morning. We are enjoying our coffee together before heading to the Mercato."

"I'm just having my coffee, too. Moheenie is picking me up at eight."

"I thought you typically walk to the Macaroni store?"

"Mom, you are so funny! It is called Macaroni on Wheels, not the *Macaroni store*. Plus we just call it *MOW*."

"But you call Moheenie, *Mo*. Isn't that confusing?"

"Not really. Plus it is more like *MOW,* as in now."

Benedette laughed. "I'll stick with the Macaroni store. Is Moheenie picking you up for a special reason?"

"No, not really. We just have errands to run." *Like investigating a murder.*

"Hang on a second," Benedette told Terza. "Your father has a question."

"Hello, my little gnocchi."

"Hi, Papa. How are you this morning?"

"Healthy as a horse! Your mom has me on a new exercise routine. We walked the entire Little Italy this morning."

"And how many times did you stop to say hello to all of your cronies?"

Ezio laughed. "Just a few. Now tell me, did you read your Bible this morning?"

"I did, Papa."

"Then you are my favorite! Here's your mom."

"Your father is such a character."

"That he is. Have a wonderful day, Mom. I love you!"

"I love you, too. Arrivederci."

"Ciao, ciao."

Terza ended her call and sent Moheenie a text:

What are we wearing?

Moheenie responded:

Spy wear.

Terza knew that meant they were dressing in all black clothes. Last time she wore black yoga pants and a black hoodie. This time would be the same.

When Moheenie arrived to pick her up, Terza smiled at their matching outfits. "Do yoga pants really denote spy wear?"

Moheenie giggled. "They do to us! Buckle up. We are on a mission."

Their so-called *mission* slowed to a stop as they ran into a wall of commuter traffic.

"We should take the back roads," Terza suggested.

"I agree. Aren't you glad we don't have to deal with this traffic on a daily basis?"

"More than glad. I'm ecstatic!"

Moheenie guided her Jeep Rubicon off the freeway ramp and turned right at the stop sign. She drove through the Old Town portion of San Diego, then selected a winding road leading to the Presidio Park neighborhood. Once they arrived, she parked her Jeep in the Palm Tree Inn lot.

"Let's do this." Terza jumped down.

Moheenie locked her car and studied the parking lot. "Where did you originally see the Honda Civic parked?"

"I'll show you." Terza walked to the far end and stopped in front of an empty space. "Right here."

They both looked around. The parking lot for the breakfast restaurant abutted the Palm Tree Inn lot, with only a low concrete barrier separating the two. One could easily park at the Inn and step over to the restaurant. A green hedge, at least six feet tall, extended the full length of both lots. It served as a divider between the frontage road and the parking areas.

"Why don't you move your Jeep to this exact spot?" Terza pointed to the asphalt. "I'll wait on the other side of the hedge, hidden from the Palm Tree Inn cameras. When you get out, stay low, and try to sneak around the hedge. I'm hoping your Jeep will block the camera's view."

"Got it." Moheenie left to retrieve her Jeep.

While Terza waited behind the hedge cover she made a mental note of the time. Her phone read 8:27 a.m. Moments later Moheenie joined her.

"Good job, Mo. Now let's stay close to the hedge and see if we can make it to the other side of the street without being recorded."

When the spy duo reached the last portion of the hedge they had a decision to make. If they turned right, the sidewalk would lead them directly to the Palm Tree Inn lobby. If they crossed the street to the other side, the Inn camera may be able to capture their image.

"I think we need to turn left, away from the Inn." Moheenie pointed. "Let's cross the street out of the camera's view."

"I agree. But do you really think Ruby Slippers would know to do all of this?"

"I do, Terza, especially if she truly is a cold-blooded killer."

They walked to the far end, crossed the street, and hugged the perimeter of the corner house. As they rounded the bend, they moved along the dense vegetation of the only property to the west of the Kamoze's home. Terza and Moheenie stopped when they drew near the end of the fence.

"We need to duck." Terza motioned with her head. "I think the camera across the street may capture us."

Moheenie lowered her frame and made a sharp left. At this point, she crouched along the hedge separating the Kamoze's house from the neighboring half acre. Terza did the same until they were standing in front of Joshua's side kitchen door.

"I hope Joshua isn't home," Terza whispered. "I didn't even think about that."

"Let's go back," Moheenie mouthed. "We can talk in the car."

After retracing their steps they got into the Jeep and breathed deeply.

"We did it!" Terza clapped Moheenie's shoulder. "I can't believe I failed to consider Joshua. What if he saw us?"

"I don't think he was home. It didn't look like any lights were on in the kitchen."

"He could have been at work," Terza suggested.

"So soon? I bet he went to stay with his parents in Los Angeles."

Terza nodded. "Good point. Speaking of work, shall we get to it?"

"I don't know." Moheenie rubbed her stomach. "That breakfast place sure smells good."

Terza's smile brightened. "Are you thinking pancakes?"

"Or a waffle." Moheenie grinned.

Terza opened the car door and hopped down. "Count me in!"

They stepped across the low barrier and headed straight for the restaurant. After placing their order, Terza texted Ian:

Any chance I can ask for another favor?

Moments later he responded:

You can ask two favors. Your lasagna was short of amazing!

Terza's eyes moved from her screen to Moheenie. "Ian says yes. He thought our lasagna was amazing."

"It is!" She sipped her coffee while Terza typed:

We did a test run this morning from 8:15 a.m. to 8:45 a.m. Can you please show us the videos from the Palm Tree Inn, and the one across from the Kamoze's house, for just that 30-minute window?

Ian responded:

Sure thing. You should have stopped by.

Terza replied:

Thank you very much. Moheenie and I are having breakfast at the Pancake Place if you would like to join us.

Ian responded:

I am stuck on a conference call so can only text right now. Thanks for the invite. I'll be in touch.

Terza thanked him a second time just before their breakfast arrived. Moheenie ordered a waffle, which she split in two to share with Terza. Four pancakes were delivered to Terza, who took off the top two to share with Moheenie. They each reached for a slice of bacon.

"Yum, yum." Moheenie bit into the thick bacon. "I adore breakfast."

Terza reached for the syrup. "Me, too."

As they enjoyed their food, and the company of being best friends, Terza and Moheenie planned the balance of their day. It looked to be a busy one.

Back in the Macaroni on Wheels kitchen, they set out to prepare the regular and gluten-free macaroni and cheese dishes. Terza also decided to prep the parmesan-crusted chicken strips in advance. "Tomorrow we can bake everything. We should begin with the mac and cheese as it needs to set. The chicken strips take less than twenty minutes. We can add the wooden skewers the minute they come out of the oven."

Moheenie glanced up at their catering board. "Would you like me to start on the food for the executive meeting?"

"That would be perfect." Terza's phone chimed. "Maybe it's Ian with our videos." She reached down and read the screen. "It's a text from Nico. He wants me to call him when I have a minute."

"That's odd." Moheenie's eyes narrowed. "Why didn't he just call you?"

"I don't know. What do you think he wants?"

Moheenie made a whooshing sound. "Your guess is as good as mine."

"Should I call him now?" Terza felt anxious.

"Not yet." Moheenie shook her head. "Wait at least fifteen minutes or more."

"I hate this," Terza whined. "I wonder what he wants."

"You'll find out soon enough."

Terza kept busy by making a list of the exact times they needed to cook each dish for tomorrow. She started from when they wanted the students to have their lunch celebration and worked backwards. When she finished, Moheenie granted her permission to call Nico.

"Hi, Terza," Nico spoke softly.

"Can you talk?"

"Yes, but hang on. Let me close the door."

Terza waited through the sound of a door closing.

"Okay," Nico said. "Radovan wanted your phone number, but I thought I should ask you first."

Terza wondered why Nico sounded so formal. "Of course. Thanks for checking, but I already gave him my number once. He must have misplaced it, so yes, please, give it to him again. Should I call there?"

"No, I'll call him. He asked for your number so let's keep it simple."

"Okay." Terza hoped their conversation would continue. "How have you been?"

"Good." Nico's one word answer sounded routine. "Busy," he added.

"I'll let you go then." Terza didn't want to end the call but was uncertain what to say next.

"Bye."

"Ciao," Terza responded. She stared at her phone until Moheenie finally broke the silence.

"Well?" Moheenie asked.

Terza rolled her eyes. "That man! He sounded so..."

"He sounded what?"

"I don't know." Terza shrugged. "He just didn't sound very friendly."

"What did Nico want?"

"Jacob Radovan was looking for my phone number, so he called Nico. Before giving it out, Nico wanted to check with me first."

"Well, that was nice," Moheenie suggested.

"Yes, it was, but he could at least ask how I am doing."

"Maybe he was busy, Tee."

"That's what Nico said." Terza moaned. "He said he was fine and busy."

"Don't read anything into it. There could be something going on right now. You just don't know."

"You're right." Terza exhaled loudly. "I need to focus on work. We should be leaving soon."

"And change out of our spy clothes!" Moheenie smiled. "We are wearing our casual uniforms, aren't we?"

"Yes, the dress ones are only for dinner parties. After tomorrow though, we need to do some laundry."

Together they finished preparing the Salumi E Formaggi board, sliced several fresh baguettes, and filled the olive oil and balsamic vinegar bottles. Moheenie offered to drive since everything could easily fit into the rear seat of her Jeep. "There's no point taking the van."

"Thanks, Mo, but then you will have to bring me back here."

"Or I can take you directly home." Moheenie changed into her khaki slacks. "It's only a few blocks either way."

Terza finished changing. "Okay, if you're sure. I love riding in your Jeep. It makes me feel like we're back in the islands."

Moheenie chuckled. "I fell in love with Jeep Wranglers when we lived in Hawaii. Then Ranger talked me into getting this Rubicon. He says it is a step up."

Terza grinned. "It's the perfect transportation for an island girl!"

Ian sent Terza a text while Moheenie drove to the downtown office building. Terza read it out loud:

I sent the two videos via email. Talk soon!

Terza thanked him and looked to Moheenie. "What do you think? Should we check out the videos after we drop off the food?"

"I would love to, Tee, but it's getting late. Ranger is always starving after a long lifeguard shift."

"I completely understand, plus we started early today. I'll probably watch it on my tablet at home. Most likely Olive is starving, too."

They delivered the executive meeting snacks and then returned to the Jeep. Terza and Moheenie looked at each other with exhausted eyes but perked up when Terza's phone announced a call from the medical examiner.

"It must be Radovan!" Terza quickly answered. "Hello."

"Is this Number Three?"

"Hi, Doctor Radovan. Yes, it's me, Terza."

"How are you my dear?"

"I'm fine, thank you. How are you?"

"Being careful not to wake the dead!" He laughed at his own joke. "Get it?"

Terza smiled knowingly. "I get it." She looked to Moheenie who was anxiously waiting to hear something.

"I have some news for you." He paused. "It is probably better not to tell Detective Ellington though."

"I understand," Terza said.

"I was going to call you sooner, but I wanted to get all of the facts first. Now do you recall seeing the pillow in a state of disarray?"

"I do," Terza told him. "Did you find something?"

"A fiber," Doctor Radovan said. "I found a tiny little fiber in our victim's nose. I ran a test, and the fiber matches one of the colors in the pillow."

"Oh my goodness! Does that mean Sloan Kamoze was smothered to death?"

"It is a possibility she was smothered, but not to death. Since our victim was obviously also cleaning the house, she could have inhaled the fiber when she fluffed the pillows."

"I'm confused," Terza told him. "Sloan may have been smothered, but not to death. What do you mean?"

Jacob Radovan cleared his throat. "The official cause of death was blunt-force trauma. There are numerous contusions on various parts of the body that lead me to believe she tumbled down the stairs."

"Could she have been pushed?"

"Most definitely," Radovan answered. "However, I cannot confirm this to be true."

"Then why is the fiber important to your findings?"

"Because it could point to a homicide rather than an accident," Radovan explained. After a brief pause, Radovan continued. "Due to the lack of the classical asphyxia signs, such as petechial hemorrhages, we can tell that our victim did not die from suffocation."

"Okay," Terza stuttered, not understanding.

"Let me explain."

"Please do."

"Let us imagine that our victim was pushed down the stairs. The murderer then approaches the body, uncertain whether she is still alive. Are you with me?" Radovan asked.

A light seemed to pop on in Terza's brain. "Yes! So, the murderer panics, races to the sofa for a cushion, and smothers Sloan."

"You've got it. But she was already dead, so none of the classical asphyxia signs appear on the body."

"You're good, Doctor Radovan. I'm impressed!"

"Why thank you, Number Three. By the way, did Detective Garza call you?"

Terza thought for a moment and then chuckled. "Oh, I get it. I specifically remembered giving you my telephone number, and you are not one to misplace things."

"Ha!" Radovan laughed. "Please tell that to my wife."

"You pretended to lose my number in hopes that Nico and I would reconnect."

"Did it work?" Radovan asked exuberantly.

"No, in fact, he was kind of rude."

Radovan made a clicking sound with his tongue. "I don't know about the young men these days. Maybe I will have a talk with him."

"Oh no, please don't!" Terza quickly said. "If things are meant to be, it will happen when the time is right."

"Number Three, you are a wise woman. Now I am going to contact the medical examiner in Los Angeles. I think we need to talk about the first potential victim."

"Do you seriously think Yvette Kamoze could have been murdered?" Terza asked.

"If this turns out to be a homicide, and not an accident, then yes, I do."

"Wow, thank you, Doctor Radovan. I really appreciate you letting me in on this."

"Of course," he told her. "After you brought me that wonderful bovine bone in the McCool case, I'd say you deserve to remain in the loop."

"Well, I won't tell Detective Ellington."

"That is a very smart decision. I'll be in touch. Goodbye, Number Three."

"Goodbye, Number One." Terza ended the call and turned her full attention to Moheenie. "Did you catch any of that?"

"Quite a bit." Moheenie nodded. "Fortunately, he talks loudly."

"I wanted to put the call on speaker, but I didn't think I should."

"No, we're good. I missed a little about the smothering. It was not the cause of death?"

"No. The cause of death was blunt force trauma." Terza took the time to review the doctor's explanation. "Did you hear that he is going to contact Los Angeles?"

"Yes, I did, and that's fantastic. Maybe Joshua really did murder his first wife."

"But how do we prove it?" Terza chewed on her lower lip.

"I have no idea."

Moheenie first drove to Macaroni on Wheels so they could unload their catering supplies, and then she dropped Terza off in front of her condominium. "Call me if you see anything interesting on the video Ian sent."

"I will." Terza stood at the driver's side window. "Have a wonderful evening with Ranger. Tell him hello."

Moheenie waved and beeped her horn twice as she drove away.

By the time the elevator reached Terza's floor, she felt like skipping dinner and going straight to bed. She walked along the interior hallway, unlocked her front door, and beckoned for Olive.

"Mommy's home," Terza called. "I'm all alone!"

As typical, Terza knew Olive was waiting until positive there were no intruders in her domain. The only time Terza's cat appeared quickly was when Olive desperately needed nourishment.

"Are you here?" Terza locked her door. She tossed her bag and phone on the dining room table and went into the kitchen. Terza smiled as she remembered her leftover chicken noodle soup. Just as she ladled a generous serving into a stainless-steel soup pan, Olive meowed loudly. Terza turned on the stove and crouched down.

There you are!" She lifted Olive into her arms. "I missed you."

Olive's thunderous purring warmed Terza's soul. She rocked from side to side and rubbed her cheek along Olive's velvety fur. Enjoying the comfort, Terza closed her eyes and allowed the busy day to fade from her thoughts. "Let's have dinner."

She returned Olive to the tiled kitchen floor. While Terza moved around the kitchen Olive encircled her legs. The dance continued until Terza filled Olive's crystal bowl with her favorite food. Terza loaded her own bowl with the steaming chicken noodle soup and took it to the kitchen counter. While eating, she opened Ian's email on her computer tablet and loaded the videos.

Terza's eyes remained focused on the thirty-plus-minute video. Not wanting to miss a second, she pressed pause before capturing each spoonful of her comfort food. She observed Moheenie's black Jeep Rubicon drive onto the Palm Tree Inn parking lot and watched as they walked around exploring the area. Terza also saw her image exit the frame when she left the lot. The video revealed the rear right angle of Moheenie's Jeep and the right passenger's side. The complete left driver's side was beyond the camera's view. Terza did not see Moheenie exit her car, nor did she observe them again beyond her initial sighting. It would have been easy for someone to park at the far end of the Palm Tree Inn lot and make their way to the Kamoze's home without appearing in any of the recordings along the street. If Joshua did not murder his wife, Ruby Slippers could have. Terza and Moheenie needed to update their murder board.

CHAPTER SIXTEEN

Friday

Making a mental note to call her mother while walking to Macaroni on Wheels, Terza sped up her typical morning routine. She woke up late and had less than an hour to have coffee and breakfast, take a shower, feed Olive, and read her Bible. Fortunately Terza knew God loved her no matter what.

By 8:15 a.m., Terza was talking and speed walking. Fifteen minutes later, she stood at the kitchen island writing on their murder board. When her phone rang, she glanced at the screen. Terza's stomach fluttered at the sight of Nico's name.

"Good morning, Nico."

"Do you have a minute?"

Terza instantly tensed. *Oh no, now what did I do wrong?* "Yes, of course."

"I wanted to apologize for yesterday." Nico's tone sounded heartfelt.

Terza's shoulders relaxed.

"I didn't mean to sound curt," he explained.

"It's not a problem, Nico. I completely understand. You have a stressful job."

"Did Doctor Radovan ever call you?"

"Yes, he did, and thank you for giving him my number."

"It was my pleasure."

Terza noticed how Nico seemed to be stalling. She waited quietly for him to continue.

"So," he finally said. "Did he also tell you about the fiber?"

"Oh, my goodness, he told you, too?"

Nico laughed. "Of course he did. The doctor and I go way back."

"But I thought it was Detective Ellington's case."

"It is, but his partner is having surgery, so Ellington decided to keep me in the loop."

"I'm sorry," Terza offered. "I hope it is nothing serious."

"It isn't. I don't have many details, but I think it's just a routine outpatient procedure. He should be back at work within the next couple of weeks."

"That's good to hear. I'm curious…" Terza hesitated. "Is it okay that you know Doctor Radovan shared with me? He told me specifically not to tell Detective Ellington."

"Who Jacob Radovan shares information with is none of my business. He knows I'm cool with it. He also knows Avery Ellington, the third, and probably just wants to keep the peace."

"So what do you think about the fiber?"

"It definitely opens up some other possibilities. I am interested to hear what the Medical Examiner in Los Angeles is going to say."

"I did make a tiny discovery," Terza spoke softly.

"Uh oh. Have you been investigating on your own?"

"Well… maybe just a little."

"Go ahead and tell me."

She exhaled loudly as if preparing for a speech. "This is between us?"

"Yes," Nico answered, and then added, "at least for now."

"When Moheenie and I first met Ruby Slippers, I mean Ruby Kamoze, Joshua's sister—"

"You call her Ruby Slippers?"

"That is an entirely different story. I'll tell you later."

"Okay, go on."

"The Kamoze's house is located on an older street that doesn't have any sidewalks. Parking is very limited, and Joshua's sister, Ruby, mentioned that she sometimes parks at the Palm Tree Inn."

"Near Presidio Park, right?"

"That's correct. Now we found out that Ruby owns a Honda Civic," Terza continued.

"You obviously didn't just see her driving the car. Do I *even* want to know how you found out?"

"No, you definitely do not. On the morning of Sloan's death, a silver Honda Civic was parked at the Palm Tree Inn for almost an hour."

"There are a lot of silver Honda Civics on the road. How can you be certain this particular vehicle belongs to Ruby Kamoze?"

"We can't be sure it is Ruby's car, but we are positive it's the exact same model. We also did a test, and it is possible for someone to exit the Honda Civic in the exact place it was parked and then sneak to and from the Kamoze's home, all without being seen."

"Do you mean you weren't picked up by video cameras?"

"Yes, the Palm Tree Inn has a video camera, and there are several doorbell and front porch cameras along the street. None of the recordings captured our images when Moheenie and I completed the test."

Nico let out a groan. "I don't know whether to be impressed or angry."

"Don't be angry," Terza pleaded.

"How could you have possibly gotten a hold of all those videos?"

"Nico, I can't tell you that. I don't want to get anyone in trouble."

"Then you better not share this information with Ellington. He may force your hand."

"I get it." Terza's panic rose. "Please, do not tell him either."

"Don't worry, I won't."

"If Ruby Kamoze is involved, I don't want her to get away with it. Do you think Detective Ellington will check for any cameras in the area?"

"He already has," Nico told her. "I am pretty sure we have everything you have, and at least we obtained it legally."

"I didn't do anything illegal," Terza insisted. "At least I don't *think* it was against the law."

"I'm not hearing this," Nico bemoaned.

"Have you watched the videos?"

"Not yet, but now I'm going to make it a priority."

"What about her phone?" Terza asked. "Can't you track the location of Ruby's phone to see if she was really on her way back to Los Angeles?"

"Yes, with a warrant."

"Do you have one?"

Nico grunted. "You know I can't tell you that."

"What about your investigation of Joshua? Is there anything you *can* share?"

"Hum," Nico stalled. "Okay, I'll give you this. We know that Joshua left his house a little before eight. He was supposed to have a meeting in his office at eight-thirty."

"Yes, I remember Sloan telling me that. Did the meeting get cancelled?"

"It was supposed to be a staff meeting, but one of the owners called it off. Joshua originally told us he never left the office until the police arrived later that morning, but then he remembered leaving for the local coffee shop."

"I bet you have a recording."

"We do. He left the office shortly after arriving and didn't return for nearly two hours."

"Was he at the coffee shop the entire time?" Terza asked.

"No, that's our concern. Of course, the lobby recordings tell us the exact time he entered and exited the building, and there are also cameras in the coffee shop. But Joshua ordered his coffee and left immediately. He took it *to go*."

"He was gone for almost two hours, and then he lied about it?" Terza pressed. "How could he forget something like that?"

"Joshua's excuse was that he simply forgot. He told us about the party and how busy he had been the entire week before. Once it was over, he was finally able to relax."

"That kind of makes sense, but not really. Where did Joshua go after he picked up his coffee?"

"We don't know. He walked to the downtown park area, and we lost him."

"What about *his* phone? Are you able to share any information with me?"

"We didn't need a warrant as he freely volunteered his mobile data," Nico told her. "And maybe a little too quickly for my taste. We were able to determine that Joshua's mobile was on his desk the entire time."

"Oh, that's convenient!" Terza shrieked. "No wonder he gave you permission."

"It does look suspicious. He could have easily taken a taxi back to his home."

"Or even a rideshare service."

"That would be easy to track," Nico said. "More so than a cab. Plus it is hard without a phone."

"Maybe he just flagged down a car with a rideshare sticker and paid cash."

"That's a possibility. We're checking all angles."

"Well I don't think Joshua would have taken a taxi to his house. That would be too easy to trace."

"Maybe he took one to the Palm Tree Inn," Nico suggested.

"Then I would have seen him in the video."

Nico laughed. "That's right. You are ahead of us in the surveillance department."

"You're funny. Seriously though, there are lots of hotels around the area of the Palm Tree Inn. Joshua could have picked any of them and slipped back home."

"You're right about that. Well, I better go. It looks like I have my work cut out for me today."

"Thank you for calling. I really appreciate your trust in me."

"Thank you for accepting my apology. *Grazie*," he finished in Italian.

"*Prego*," Terza also spoke in Italian. "You're welcome."

When the call finally ended, Terza's smile grew from ear to ear. Moments later, Moheenie walked in.

"Terza Tiepolo, your face is glowing. What happened?"

Terza circled her arms above her head and danced around the kitchen. "I just talked to Detective Nicolas Garza! He called to apologize for being so short with me yesterday."

Moheenie raised her hands for two high fives. Terza slapped palms before gripping Moheenie's hands. "We talked, Mo!"

"I guess so!" Moheenie grinned. "That's a good first step."

"Yes, it is. Hopefully he will call again, but I'm happy with this for now. Plus, he shared news about the case!" Terza moved to their white murder board and lifted the dry erase marker.

Moheenie stepped up to the counter. "I thought Nico wasn't on the case?"

"I guess he is now."

"Then share!" Their eyes connected. "What did he say?"

"He talked mostly about Joshua." Terza recounted the information Nico shared regarding Joshua's cancelled meeting and then leaving the office for two hours. "So where are we?" Terza rolled the marker between her thumb and forefinger.

"Write that Joshua had opportunity." Moheenie pointed to Joshua's column. "We know he had motive, but we now know he could have returned to the house. It is very odd that

Joshua left his office for such a long time and also that he left his phone."

"You're right. It makes no sense." Terza printed on the white board and looked up. "What about Ruby Slippers?"

"She also had opportunity. The Honda Civic parked at the Palm Tree Inn could belong to her."

Terza printed the words *Honda Civic*. "She could have made it from the Palm Tree Inn back to the house. What shall I write?"

"Hidden path from Palm Tree Inn to Kamoze's home," Moheenie suggested.

"That sounds perfect!" Terza printed the phrase under Ruby Slippers' name. "Do we know anything else?"

Moheenie bit her lower lip in thought. "Hmm," she sang out. "What about the fiber?"

"Yes, the fiber, but where should the information go?"

Moheenie studied their murder board. "Maybe right at the top, above the names."

"Good idea. Thanks." When Terza finished printing on the murder board, they stepped back to review the findings. "I wish we could track Ruby's phone."

"Me, too." Moheenie nodded. "Maybe she never even left for Los Angeles."

Terza stared at Joshua's name. "Why do you think Joshua would leave his office for such a long time?"

"I have no idea. It is more than odd."

"You can say that again." Terza carefully slid the whiteboard between their two refrigerators. "Duty calls. Are you ready for the little ones?"

"I think this is going to be one fun day!"

"Yes, indeed. Now, let's get this party started!"

CHAPTER SEVENTEEN

Here Come the Kiddos

Their pace quickened as Terza and Moheenie prepared for the school luncheon. Everything seemed more fun as they baked the chicken strips and heated the macaroni and cheese selections. Moheenie clapped her hands. "I am really looking forward to this!"

"Me, too." Terza smiled. "I just adore being around little ones."

"You get to see Charlie and Caleb every Sunday," Moheenie told her. "I think I'm jealous."

"Don't be. You should just come to family dinner more often."

"That's sweet, Tee. We are booked for the next few Sundays, but maybe after that."

Terza laughed. "You just called me 'sweet tea'!"

"Well, you are sweet, and your nickname is Tee!"

"You're one funny girl, Moheenie Brickman." Terza glanced at the oven. "How does the macaroni and cheese look?"

Moheenie turned on the oven light and peered through the glass. "The tops are almost brown. I'll check it in five more minutes."

"Would you like to help me put the skewers in the chicken strips?"

"Of course." Moheenie lifted one of the popsicle sticks. "They look nice and safe."

"I thought it would be better than sharp, pointed skewers."

"You're right about that. Should we make any dipping sauces?"

"We think alike." Terza finished sliding a stick onto the chicken strip. "I made some ranch sauce and a honey mustard."

"I bet the little ones go for the ranch, and the teachers will prefer the mustard."

Terza nodded. "I think you're right."

When the macaroni and cheese pans were ready, Terza and Moheenie loaded both of their chrome catering carts. They checked and rechecked each item and finally left for the school. Terza rolled her cart out their back kitchen door, with Moheenie following behind. The wheels rumbled along the asphalt parking lot until they reached the smooth sidewalk. Terza made the left turn, pushing her cart up the gradual incline. She held on tightly while calling back to Moheenie. "I forgot about the hill."

"I think we'll be okay, Tee. Good thing we used two carts though. At least they're not very heavy. Put your legs into it!"

When Terza reached the first intersection she rolled her cart down the wheelchair ramp, checked for traffic, and crossed the street. As several small potholes threatened to topple her cart, she squeezed the handle until her knuckles turned white. "Yikes! Maybe we should have driven."

"This asphalt is gruelling!"

After successfully maneuvering the pothole landmines, Terza waited for Moheenie on the opposite sidewalk. They rested momentarily and gawked at the upcoming second hill.

Moheenie groaned. "It looks higher from this side of the street."

"Ha! Just put your legs into it!" Terza motioned with her chin. "You first."

Moheenie laughed. "Okay, but catch me if I come rolling back down!"

Terza watched Moheenie push her cart slowly up the hill. She then exhaled loudly before beginning the trek. Counting her steps seemed to help with her cadence. Finally, she reached Moheenie at the top.

"Not bad." Terza commented. "It looked harder than it really was."

"I think the asphalt road was actually worse."

"I do, too. Let's go to the school office and tell them we're here."

After checking in with the administration, Terza and Moheenie were directed to the special activities room of the school, where the party was to be held. When they walked through the door, everything had been decorated, and the tables were set. The only thing missing was the food.

"How long do you need to set up?" Ms. Radcliff, the principal, asked.

"Less than ten minutes." Terza smiled at the woman, thinking she looked much younger than any principal Terza had in school. "You did an amazing job, Ms. Radcliff. This room looks so festive."

"Why, thank you. Please call me Janie."

Moheenie extended her palm. "It's nice to meet you, Janie. I'm Moheenie. I really like all of the games you set up."

Janie shook Moheenie's hand. "Thank you. We wanted to make it special." Janie's eyes moved to the round school clock high on the far wall. "Okay, ten minutes it is. When I send in the kiddos, watch out! They can be a hungry bunch."

Terza's smile grew. "Don't worry. We'll be ready."

Fifteen minutes later, the children did not simply *enter* the party room. They *blasted* through the door. Terza and Moheenie looked with astonishment as they instantly headed straight for the food. Fortunately, the head teacher took immediate control and had the students first greet their guests. Terza's heart melted when each young child said hello and politely spoke their name. She looked at Moheenie, who also had an ear-to-ear grin. The children then formed two lines, and Terza and Moheenie helped fill their plates. The room went from deafening to almost silent as the little mouths filled with food.

With her plate in hand, the head teacher approached the catering duo. "This is the best macaroni and cheese I have ever tasted!"

"Thank you. I'm glad you like it."

"I see you have both types on your plate," Moheenie commented. "Which did you prefer?"

"Both!" The teacher laughed. "Frankly, I cannot tell the difference."

"Would you like the recipe?" Terza asked. "I am always happy to share."

"May I just call and order a tray full?"

"Of course, you may. It would be our pleasure."

After devouring their lunch, the children were ready for games. Terza and Moheenie started by helping with the games and ended up playing along. When the day finally came to an end, it was much easier walking down the hill with empty carts. They called it quits, and Terza made it home before 4:00 p.m.

Olive seemed content to ignore Terza's early arrival. She opened one eye, checked on her owner, and then stretched out her legs on the sunny window ledge. Determined to pull off the perfect hairstyle for the wedding, Terza knew it required washing and conditioning her hair today. She wanted to wear it down, but not wild. Large rollers would be in order, too.

Terza poured herself a glass of Chianti, lit several candles, and filled her soaking tub with warm water and bubble bath.

She undressed, stepped into the lavender-scented water, and sank below the luxurious warmth. Terza pressed her lids together and allowed any leftover stress to leave her body. As Terza moved her palms through the water, she felt long tendrils from her hair floating by her sides. She remained immersed until the water chilled. Reluctantly Terza finally moved to a sitting position and began washing her hair. She applied conditioner then waited a few minutes before using the handheld shower to rinse.

After wrapping her hair in one towel and using a second to dry off, Terza dressed in her pajamas. She combed out her hair before opening a plastic box of Velcro-style rollers to help control the natural curl. While Terza wrapped the hair sections around the large, multicolored rollers, Olive sauntered into the bathroom. She meowed once, a sign of irritation.

"Don't you meow one time at me, little lady." Terza looked at Olive in the mirror. "I was ready to feed you right when I got home, but you were too busy napping."

Olive purred loudly.

"That's better. I'll feed you in a moment, and we can eat together."

With the last roller secured, Terza prepared Olive a mixture of dry and wet cat food. She then arranged her own Salumi E Formaggi plate, taking it to the dining room table along with the wine remaining in her glass. Terza tossed a paper sack under the table and added her slippers to the pile. If she wanted perfectly manicured fingers and toes for the wedding, Olive needed to stay busy.

Terza first enjoyed the selection of meats and cheeses. She then savored the Chianti while painting her toenails a bright red enamel color. Smiling at the results, Terza moved to her fingertips and spread the vibrant color on each nail. Fortunately Olive vaulted from the paper bag to Terza's slippers and back again, having a hard time deciding on a favorite.

Terza sat back in her seat and propped her feet on a second dining chair to enjoy the show.

CHAPTER EIGHTEEN

Saturday

Terza felt fantastic. She had enjoyed a relaxing evening before going to bed early, and she did not have to meet her father for another two hours. After feeding Olive, Terza turned on the coffee water and called her mother.

"*Buon giorno*, my love," Benedette greeted her daughter.

Terza always looked forward to hearing her mother's voice. "Hi, Mom. Is Papa excited about today?"

"Yes, and he is thrilled about receiving all the help. That was very nice of you and Moheenie."

"Are you kidding? It's the least we can do. You guys always help me with absolutely *everything*. Speaking of helping, you must give me a bill for the food we keep taking from Tiepolo Mercato."

Benedette chuckled. "I'll tell the bookkeeper."

"You *are* the bookkeeper, Mom! I'm serious."

"I will very soon," Benedette told her. "Now tell me, are you looking forward to the wedding?"

"Yes, I am. It should be fun. I'm a bit concerned about the weather though. I really don't want to cover up my gorgeous dress with a coat."

"It is red, correct?"

"Yes, bright red. Why, do you have something that might work?"

"I have a red pashmina that may look perfect. But, if the color is off, I also have a silver one. Would you like me to bring them both this morning?"

"Oh, Mom, that would be fantastic. Thank you. By the way, are you and Papa going to the eleven o'clock service tomorrow?"

"Yes, just like every Sunday. You know how your father loves his routines. He sleeps in late on Sunday mornings, and then we enjoy breakfast together before church. Why do you ask?"

Terza giggled. "Because I may be just like Papa tomorrow. After staying out late for the wedding, there's no way I will be able to make it to the eight o'clock service at my church. I thought it would be nice to join you two."

"That would be lovely. I'll see you in a little while."

"See you soon! Ciao, ciao."

"Arrivederci."

Terza rushed to turn off the flame beneath the blaring kettle. She poured the scalding water over the waiting coffee grounds and inhaled the fragrant aroma. *Freshly brewed coffee. One of life's little pleasures.*

She continued her morning by reading her Bible on the balcony while enjoying her coffee. Terza made a simple breakfast of oatmeal and toast and then dressed in jeans and a T-shirt to help her father with the sandwich making.

Later that afternoon, Terza stood in front of her full-length mirror wearing her high-heeled, red-rhinestone shoes. She pressed her red dress against her chest and flipped the silver pashmina over her left shoulder, with the red one over her right. Terza studied her image. "What do you think, Olive? I personally like the silver. It seems to bring out the bling on my shoes."

Olive seemed more interested in playing with Terza's loose

shoe straps than rendering an opinion on the selection of pashminas.

Terza reached down to pet the back of Olive's neck. "Thanks for the help, my beauty." She then removed her shoes and remembered to carefully close them inside the closet, away from Olive's reach. Terza undressed, wrapped her hair in a terry cloth turban to protect it from the steam, and took a quick bath. She shaved her legs, rinsed off, and used her most luxurious, perfumed lotion.

Dressed in a comfy bathrobe, Terza carefully applied her makeup. Tonight was a night for special, party makeup. Next came her hair, and Terza decided to wear it down, clipped to one side. She bent over at the waist, brushed her hair with vigorous strokes, and flipped it back. Terza smiled when she saw that her curls remained full and shiny. She had successfully managed to reduce the natural frizz. Terza combed her hair to one side and secured it with an invisible band. "Not bad," she spoke to her image.

She quickened her pace after checking the time, changing into her red lace panties and matching strapless bra. Terza next stepped into her vibrant red dress. She sighed with relief when she remembered the side zipper. It was much easier than struggling with one in the back. Terza then added her grandmother's ruby-and-rhinestone earrings, the matching bracelet, and a dramatic ring. "Thank you, Grandmama," she said aloud while looking to Heaven.

Terza slid her manicured feet into the rhinestone shoes and sat on her bedroom chair to buckle the straps around her ankles. She wiggled her red painted toes with delight. She added a few more sprays of her favorite perfume and checked the final image. Before Olive could announce her approval, Terza's phone rang.

"The cherry bomb awaits," Conner said when Terza answered.

"I'll be right down."

"Oh no! I am coming up to escort you, my princess."

"We can split the difference. I'll meet you in the lobby."

"Deal."

As the elevator doors parted, Terza saw Conner looking more handsome than she had ever seen. His blond hair was freshly trimmed and partially spiked on top. When he smiled at her, she felt overwhelmed by the genuine sparkle in his baby blue eyes. Conner wore a finely tailored gray suit with matching leather lace-up shoes. His white dress shirt featured slim gray stripes with a hint of crimson. Conner's matching bowtie made the outfit pop.

"If it isn't the lady in red," Conner said before Terza had a chance to exit the elevator. "Terza, you look absolutely amazing!"

"This old thing?" Terza gave a throaty laugh. She completed a spin and then tapped her foot on the tiled lobby floor. "Do you like my shoes?"

He stepped closer and wrapped both arms around her waist. "I like your shoes." He kissed her on the right cheek. "I like your dress." Conner kissed her left cheek. "I like *you*!" He ended with another kiss on her right cheek. Conner took her hands within his and stepped back. His smile beamed. "Terza Tiepolo, you are breathtaking."

Terza felt her face flush. "Thank you, Conner." She made a point to look up and down his frame. "You're not so bad yourself. Seriously though, you look incredibly handsome. Have I ever seen you in a suit?"

"Probably not. It's all Mando's fault."

"Then I must thank him." Terza reached up to touch one end of his tie. "The red is a nice flair. Plus, it matches my dress."

"And your dress matches my car." Conner laughed. "We just might be the perfect couple."

"I agree." Terza wrapped her arm around Conner's bicep. "Lead the way!"

The striking couple walked arm and arm together, exiting the lobby's glass double doors, and then out to the sidewalk. Conner had parked his classic red Mustang in the front loading zone. He opened the passenger's door for her and extended his hand to help Terza inside. When she accepted his palm, Terza glanced to her right. *Is that Nico?* As she positioned herself in Conner's bucket seat, Terza strained to see farther down the street. At first glimpse, it looked like Nico walking toward her. But now, she could only see the back of a man walking away. Terza felt instant guilt as if caught being unfaithful.

Don't be silly. She dismissed the feeling by inhaling the lingering scent of Conner's cologne. Terza turned to watch him slide into the driver's side. She smiled and reached for his palm.

Conner took her hand, brought it to his lips, and kissed the back. "You smell divine."

"I was just thinking the same thing about you."

When they arrived at the church, Conner guided Terza to a seat on the groom's side. He snuggled close to her on the bench-style pew and pointed out several people they would later meet.

"He's cute." Terza watched the groom make his way to the front of the church.

"The groom is Rico, and those are his brothers."

"All six of them?"

"I think so, but maybe one is a cousin. I'm not sure."

Terza nodded while she watched Rico and his groomsmen wait for the wedding to begin. The groom's name of Rico brought Nico's name to her mind. The frustration mounted as she tried to block his face from her inner screen. She was here with Conner. He was a great guy who deserved all of her attention, not just part of it. As if reading her mind, Conner wrapped a strong arm around her shoulder.

"I'm glad you came with me," he whispered.

"I am, too." She leaned her head onto his chest.

Terza straightened when the music signaled the beginning of the wedding. It turned out to be an elegant, black-and-white formal wedding, with the cutest ring bearer wearing a mini tuxedo. The bridesmaids wore solid black, long formal gowns, with one bare shoulder. Terza melted when she watched the precious little flower girl walking down the aisle in a black-and-pink princess dress. She dropped white rose petals along the black satin runner in preparation for the bride.

The wedding march announced the bride, and all of the guests promptly stood. When the bride finally appeared, Terza heard an audible gasp from the audience. The bridal gown, sewn from white satin, looked like it belonged in a royal wedding. As the bride walked elegantly toward her groom, her face was obscured with a satin-trimmed veil. Terza's breath caught in her throat when she saw the magnificent length of the white satin train. She guessed it to be more than ten feet long.

The ceremony touched Terza's heart, and she found tears forming without knowing why. After the groom lovingly kissed his bride, the newlyweds turned to face their guests. Terza could see the ultimate joy in their smiling faces.

"Ladies and gentlemen," the priest announced, "for the very first time, I am pleased to introduce you all to Mr. and Mrs. Enrique Hernandez." The guests cheered loudly as Rico and Daniela first waved and then embraced as they left the church.

Row by row, the guests also exited the church and congregated outside while the wedding party posed for photographs.

Standing on the top of the front church steps, Terza watched an impressive couple walk arm in arm toward them. "Alexandra, Jake, so good to see you." Conner wrapped an arm around Alexandra's waist. "Alex, you look gorgeous!"

"Why thank you," Alexandra replied softly.

Conner extended a palm to Jake. "Jake, you look dashing, too, my friend." He quickly turned to Terza. "Let me introduce you. Terza, these are my good friends, Jake and Alexandra Taylor. This is Terza Tiepolo."

Alexandra held her hand out to Terza. "It is so nice to meet you, Terza."

Terza found herself nearly stunned by Alexandra's beauty. She stood several inches taller than Terza with sun-kissed hair worn in an elegant chignon. Flowing tendrils brushed along the smooth skin of Alexandra's bare neck.

"It is nice to meet you, too." Terza suddenly felt younger than her age. Mesmerized by the liquid brown color of Alexandra's eyes, Terza forced herself to acknowledge Jake. After they exchanged greetings, she returned her focus to Alexandra. "Your dress is spectacular. You could be at the Academy Awards."

Alexandra's soft laugh enhanced her elegance. "You are very sweet. I actually had it made. A client of mine and I traded services." Alexandra turned slowly to reveal the low-cut back. The ankle-length sheath dress was made from a dramatic purple satin with a thigh-high split. A matching length of purple satin enhanced the strapless bodice. Alexandra wore the scarf draped across her neckline with the open ends cascading down her back. Her only jewelry consisted of diamond-and-amethyst earrings, a matching bracelet, and her exquisite wedding ring.

"I am in awe." Terza's lips remained parted. "What do you do?"

"Jake and I own an architectural design firm in Old Town." Alexandra smiled at her husband. "Jake is the architect, and I am the interior designer. My friend, who is trying her hand at fashion design, asked for help with her kitchen remodel." Alexandra smoothed her palm along the side of her dress. "Frankly, I think I got the better end of the deal."

"Your dress *is* fantastic." Conner chuckled. "But we haven't seen her kitchen. You have been known to come up with some great designs yourself."

"Speaking of designs," Alexandra reached her fingertips toward Terza's dress. "Terza, I love your red dress, especially the skirt. Doesn't it remind you a bit of the forties?"

Terza smiled. "It does. I feel like I should be wearing tap shoes."

"Then you better save a dance for me," Jake said. "Alex is wondering if her dress will hinder her dancing."

Alexandra slid an arm through Jake's and leaned closer. "We may be limited to slow songs my dear."

"Fine by me." He kissed the back of her hand.

"Terza is like a designer, too," Conner announced. "You design houses, and she designs food."

Alexandra's eyes widened. "Are you a chef, Terza?"

"Yes, I am. Do you cook?"

"A little, but I'm impressed. I have always admired the talent of true chefs. When did you begin?"

Terza chuckled. "Most likely the day I was born! My mother is an amazing cook, so I kind of grew up in the kitchen. We have a large Italian family where almost everything centers around food."

"They have dinner together every Sunday." Conner looked to Terza and pumped his eyebrows. "Sometimes I even get an invitation."

"Don't worry, you'll get another one soon," Terza told him.

"Do you help with the Sunday dinner?"

Terza turned her head toward Jake. "Not really. My mom is very possessive when it comes to our weekly family dinner. I graduated from culinary school, and my mom still cooks better than me."

"Your mom is a great chef, Terza, but your cooking is through the roof," Conner bragged.

"With compliments like that I just might cook for you more often."

"Then my plan worked."

"Terza, do you ever offer cooking lessons? I've been wanting to take a few classes."

"I've actually been thinking about it, Alexandra. Several people have recently asked me the same thing."

"Maybe you could teach at Macaroni on Wheels," Conner suggested.

Jake looked puzzled. "What is Macaroni on Wheels?"

"It is the name of my catering company. We're located in Little Italy right next door to the Tiepolo Mercato. Do you know it?"

Jake's blue eyes lit up. "No wonder your name sounded familiar. Of course I know the Tiepolo Mercato." He looked to his wife. "Honey, do you remember the amazing submarine sandwiches I sometimes bring for lunch?"

Alexandra nodded. "I know exactly the ones."

"Well, I get them from the Tiepolo Mercato." Jake locked eyes with Terza. "Don't tell me Ezio is your father?"

Terza's smile grew from ear to ear. "The one and only Ezio Tiepolo is definitely my papa. When it comes to Little Italy, I think he is almost famous."

"I'll say. Oh look." Conner pointed to the front of the church. "They're lighting the sparklers. Let's form a line."

Jake, Alexandra, Terza, and Conner stood side by side with lit sparklers in hand. "I was concerned about being cold," Terza told Alexandra.

"Me, too. Fortunately, it's not that bad."

"Especially with the heat from these sparklers." Terza laughed. "I hope they hurry! Mine is getting low."

Rico and Daniela looked like a prince and princess as they emerged from the church, then walked between the rows of sparkling lights. They waved to the crowd before entering the decorated carriage, while Jake and Conner promptly doused the sparklers in the waiting buckets of sand. The four of them watched as the commanding horse trotted away.

"That was fun," Alexandra said to Terza. "And a bit scary."

"Yes, a little of both."

"Shall we?" Conner held out his arm to Terza.

"Our limos are here." Jake took Alexandra's hand.

They shared a limousine, with four other wedding guests, for the short ride from the church to the Grand Hotel. When they arrived at the entrance to the ballroom, Jake and Conner reviewed place cards in search of their table assignments. Terza felt like she had made a friend and hoped they would be sharing a table with Jake and Alexandra.

Their names were listed together along with Conner's partner Armando, and his date Isabella, their supervisor Kevin, and his wife Casey. As cocktail hour commenced in the expansive foyer, Conner grabbed Terza's arm. "Come with me."

Terza moaned. "Now? The hors d'oeuvres are being passed."

"Shush, we'll be quick." Conner directed them to a secluded area in the hotel lobby, away from the entering wedding guests.

"What is it, Conner?"

"I'm stupid, that's what. I can't believe I didn't think to tell you."

"Tell me what?"

"We're sitting with my SAC, my Special Agent in Charge, and big mouth, Mando. I just don't want you to ask how we all know Alexandra and Jake. Especially since we're sitting together."

"How *do* you know them?"

"Let me ask you this. Did you notice anything special about Alexandra?"

"Yes, she's drop-dead gorgeous."

"What about the bride, Daniela?" Conner pressed.

"She's beautiful, too. I don't understand. What are you trying to tell me?"

"Okay, I'm going to make this really quick, and I'm not going to answer any questions." Conner drew in a deep breath. "Daniela's brother, Miguel Santiago, was an assassin in Mexico, and Rico went in undercover to try and bring him down. He met Daniela, and they fell in love."

"Did Daniela know he was undercover?" Terza asked.

Conner looked frustrated. "No, she didn't, and I said no questions."

Terza pretended to zip her lip closed.

"Rico wasn't successful, but by chance we discovered Alexandra, who looks exactly like Daniela." Conner must have noticed Terza's confused look. He paused, and then added, "One day I will show you a close-up photograph of them side by side."

Terza nodded without speaking.

"Alexandra took the place of Daniela to gain access to her brother. She was successful, and Santiago is now serving several life sentences in prison. It wasn't easy, and Alexandra was abducted, until Rico saved her. Do you remember when I told you about my assignment in Mexico?"

Terza once again nodded.

"That was the assignment."

"I have to ask something!" Terza told him firmly. "You cannot just leave it at that!"

Conner tapped his foot. "What do you need to know?"

"Does Alexandra really work for the DEA?"

"No, she was recruited just for this mission."

"Oh my goodness," Terza shrieked softly. "She's beautiful *and* brave. What about Daniela? She married the man responsible for sending her brother to jail?"

"Daniela had no idea who her brother was and what he did. She still loves him but realizes that he got what he deserved."

"What about Alexandra? I don't understand why Daniela would invite her to the wedding."

"Alexandra and Rico became best friends. They spent a lot of time together, and it was Alexandra who convinced Rico to go after Daniela."

"It sounds like a movie, and all so hard to believe." She moved closer to Conner, stretched up, and kissed his cheek. "Thank you for trusting me with this. I know you have to be careful."

"You're a good person to trust. Now, are you ready for those hors d'oeuvres?"

"More than ready." She tugged on his arm. "Let's go."

They returned to the foyer area where everyone was busy talking, laughing, drinking, and enjoying the remarkable selection of hors d'oeuvres. Not one person mentioned their absence. When Armando noticed Terza, he moved to greet her with a generous hug.

"What a stunning lady in red." Armando held both of her hands. "It's good to see you, Terza."

"It's good to see you too, Mando. You look dapper this evening."

"Thank you." Armando bowed.

"And thanks for dressing Conner." Terza winked. "He is styling."

Armando grinned. "Yes, he is. Come meet my date."

"Should I take my time and get to know her?" Terza giggled. "Or is she just a passing fancy?"

Armando shrugged. "The jury is still out."

"You're incorrigible," Terza told him.

"But loveable all the same," Armando added.

Armando introduced Terza to Isabella, who seemed very nice. Terza rejoined Conner just as the doors opened to the reception hall. It looked spectacular with lighting everywhere. String lights encased in white toile draped from the ceiling, where enormous floral centerpieces seemed to float above each dining table. Terza leaned toward the arrangement above their table and inhaled. She lost count of how many white roses the florists must have used. "What a great idea," Terza told Alexandra.

"The flowers are gorgeous," Alexandra remarked, "and yet they're not in the way. How perfect to suspend the arrangements from the ceiling like a chandelier."

"I need to remember this idea for my catering." Terza made a mental note while also admiring the table centerpieces. They consisted of a smaller, but matching, flower arrangement, encircled by tea lights and rose petals. Live potted Ficus trees surrounded the entire ballroom, with white string lights peeking from the branches. Terza noted the remarkable attention to detail and wanted to know more about the bride and her family.

Dancing began after the delicious dinner, which was then followed by a champagne toast and the cake cutting. Terza had a blast and was disappointed when the evening finally ended. Conner drove her home and insisted on escorting Terza to her front door. As she slid her key into the lock, Terza's excitement bubbled over. Perhaps it was the champagne, or the exhilaration of the wedding, but Terza knew she wanted to feel Conner's soft lips connect with hers.

"Thank you for being my plus one." He slipped his palm around her waist. Conner moved closer, fixing Terza with steady blue eyes. "I had a fantastic time, Miss Tiepolo," he whispered.

Terza leaned into his chest. "So did I, Mr. Reeves. Thank you for allowing me to be your date."

Without saying another word, Conner pressed his lips onto hers.

Terza melted at his touch and went weak when he began to explore her mouth with his tongue. She wrapped both arms around his neck, meeting his tongue with hers. The situation proved volatile, and Terza felt her willpower fading.

Conner continued to kiss her, while he unlocked and opened her door. He then lifted her into his arms and guided Terza toward her sofa. Terza realized she must regain control.

"No, no, no," she moaned. "Conner, you have to go."

"I know." Conner carefully placed her upon the sofa and bent down to kiss her forehead. "Goodbye my lady in red. I—" He stopped short from finishing his sentence.

Terza watched Conner walk toward her front door, turn, and blow her a kiss. "Thank you for understanding."

He nodded. "Be sure and lock up."

"I will."

CHAPTER NINETEEN

Mama Knows Best—Or Does She?

Sunday

When Terza finally opened her eyes, she regretted not setting her alarm. She now had less than an hour to shower and get ready for church. Breakfast would have to wait, but she desperately needed coffee. Terza fed Olive, filled the kettle, turned on the stove, and jumped in the shower.

Terza heard a faint whistle as she reached for her towel and then had to rush into the kitchen before she finished drying. The kettle blared when she finally made it to the stove. Olive looked at Terza with stern disapproval.

She gulped her coffee and quickly dressed in brown tweed slacks and a short-sleeved beige sweater. Terza grabbed a banana before racing out the door. By the time she met up with her parents only the banana peel remained.

"Did you just wake up?" Benedette asked.

Terza laughed. "Is it that obvious?" She kissed her mother on each cheek.

"Only to the trained eye."

"Good morning, Papa." Terza wrapped both arms around her father's neck.

"*Buon giorno*, my little gnocchi. I think you look beautiful."

"Terza always looks beautiful," Benedette agreed. "Let's go inside."

As typical, after service ended, the church courtyard filled with people enjoying coffee together. Terza helped herself to a cup, while watching her father mingle with his friends.

"How was the wedding?"

"It was outstanding, Mom, and just like a fairy tale. I could not believe the attention to detail. The wedding itself was beautiful, and the wedding dress looked like something a princess would wear."

"Do you have any photos?" Benedette asked.

"I don't, but I'm sure there will be postings online soon."

"How was the reception?"

"Just as nice as the wedding. I even approved of the food!"

"Now *that* is saying something." Benedette looked sideways at her daughter. "And how was your date?"

Terza rolled her eyes.

"Not good?"

"It was great, and that's the problem." Terza sighed. "Conner looked so handsome, and he treated me like a queen."

"But—"

"We had fun together, we danced, and we even had a delicious good-night kiss."

Benedette smiled. "I'm still waiting."

"When things got a little too passionate, Conner respected my wishes and left. Mom, he is such a good man."

Terza watched her mother smile knowingly.

"And I thought about Nico more than once during the evening."

Benedette nodded.

"It started when Conner picked me up. I think I saw Nico less than a block away. After I got into Conner's car, I looked through the windshield, but the man had already turned around. Part of me wanted to rush over and tell him I wasn't really on a date."

"Are you sure it was him?"

"Not one hundred percent sure, but almost."

"You could always call and ask him. Be bold. What could it hurt?"

Terza shrugged. "Oh, I don't know if that's a good idea."

"Why don't you invite him to family dinner? I believe you mentioned it to him once. That would be a good excuse, and it's not officially a date. It is family dinner, and who doesn't like a good time?"

"Maybe." Terza looked up to the blue sky. "First, I need some breakfast to clear my head."

"Do you want to come over? I can make you something?"

"Thank you, Mom, but there's no way I can do that. I know you already made breakfast for Papa this morning, and you are making family dinner this evening. I am off to Solunto for a quiche."

"Call Nico on your way," Benedette instructed.

"We'll see." Terza kissed her mother goodbye and went in search of her father. After greeting several of his friends, Terza finally left the courtyard.

On her way to the bakery, she suddenly stopped and decided to be bold. Terza searched through the contacts on her phone and pressed Nico's name. Unfortunately the call went to voicemail.

"Hi, Nico. It's Terza. I just left my mother, and she wanted me to invite you to family dinner. Call me when you have a minute." Terza disconnected, slowly dropping her eyes toward the ground. *That sounded stupid.* Wanting to delete the message, she just shook her head and continued on her way.

Terza ordered coffee to enjoy with her quiche and took both to an outside table. While she dined, Terza's phone rested quietly on the patio table. She stared at the screen trying to compel it to ring. Finally a text from Nico appeared:

Did you call?

"Yes, I called," Terza spoke aloud to her phone. "Didn't you listen to your voicemail?" Hoping to have a verbal conversation instead of a written exchange, Terza typed:

Yes, my mom thinks I should invite you to family dinner.

Nico responded:

That's nice of your mom, but what do you think?

Terza felt hopeful. Perhaps he would really join them. She typed:

I would like you to come. Can you make it today around 4:00?

After a long pause, his message read:

Thank you, but I have to work tonight. By the way, you looked very nice in your red dress.

Terza groaned loudly. *That was him!* She typed:

I thought that was you! Where were you going?

Nico responded:

Back to my car. I was thinking about gelato and thought you might join me at Solunto.

Terza couldn't believe her eyes. Nico actually came to see her! She typed:

You went by MOW? I'm sorry I missed you. That would have been nice.

After several long minutes his response finally chimed:

I don't think your date would have appreciated it.

Without thinking Terza rapidly typed:

It wasn't a date, and then backed through the letters. It was a date, and now she was more confused than ever. She thought about how to respond and finally typed:

I would love to have a gelato rain check. Can you make it again?

Nico responded:

I'm not sure. I'll call you. Ciao.

Terza slowly typed:

Ciao.

She blinked several times to stop the tears from forming, as she lowered her phone to the table. Nico's terse-sounding text sent a dagger through her heart. Terza waited until she controlled her tender emotions before calling her mother.

"*Buona sera*, my love," Benedette answered. "Did you invite your friend?"

"Yes, but unfortunately he has to work. It will just be me."

"Perhaps another time."

Terza was instantly comforted as she listened to her mother's soothing voice. "Yes, perhaps. I'll see you in a little while. Ciao."

"Arrivederci."

When the entire Tiepolo family was seated around the dining room table, Ezio offered his hand to Terza on his left and Benedette to the right. They all joined hands while he said a prayer of gratitude to God for their family and the meal.

"Amen!" a chorus sounded, instantly followed by the clamour of plates being filled and the typical brother and sister teasing.

Charlie's eyes ballooned with wonder when Terza shared the events of the wedding, and Damiano taunted his two sisters about their potential future as *old maids*. When Rain, Angeline, and Terza banded together, each threatening to bring up certain events from his past, Damiano quickly apologized and changed the subject.

The family amusement helped Terza disregard her previous exchange with Nico and focus on the wonderful time she had spent with Conner. As usual, the evening ended with a fierce game of bocce ball. The team of Terza, Charley, and Caleb easily beat Damiano and Rain. Terza made a mental note to choose the children as partners, as she realized it ensured her an automatic win.

CHAPTER TWENTY

Confrontation

Monday

The piercing alarm clock shocked Terza awake. Although earlier than normal, she had set her alarm for 6:00 a.m., as she wanted to be on the road by 7:30 a.m. She hoped to beat the Monday morning rush-hour traffic on her way to the medical examiner's office.

Terza hit the snooze button and snuggled with Olive for a few moments before beginning her day. She then prepared a smoothie, fed Olive, and quickly showered. Terza decided to dress a bit more professional than her last meeting with Jacob Radovan and slipped into the clothes she wore yesterday for church. *Who is going to know?*

Terza called her mother while making coffee, then took her mug and Bible to the dining room table. Thoughts of both Conner and Nico wrangled for space in her brain as she struggled to read. Her focus then moved to the murder of Sloan Kamoze. Terza had hoped to receive an update on the death of Joshua's first wife, Yvette, by now. She blinked rapidly, locked her eyes to the page, and completed reading another Psalm before closing her Bible.

Once on the interstate, her Fiat almost reached the maximum speed limit. Traffic seemed light, and Terza smiled at her pre-rush-hour success. She drove onto the lot, parked in a visitor's space, and walked to the neighboring coffee shop.

Shortly thereafter, while holding a cup of hot coffee in each hand, Terza smiled at the disagreeable receptionist. This time, the warden wore a *not-you-again* expression on her face.

"I bet you remember me now." Terza strained to sound extra friendly.

"No. How may I help you?"

You've got to be kidding! Terza thought. "I'm here to see Doctor Radovan. My name is Terza Tiepolo." In her mind she added, *and I know you know who I am!*

The receptionist lifted the receiver, spoke something inaudible, and then returned the handset to its cradle. It seemed like hours before she finally looked up. "You may pass."

"Thank you." Terza rapidly left the reception area. Her heels clicked along the tile flooring until she reached the medical examiner doors. Terza backed in and tried to hold her breath. She nodded to Akemi, Dr. Radovan's assistant, hurriedly lowered the coffee cups to the desk, and fumbled for the menthol. By the time Terza finished rubbing it under her nose she gulped for air. "I don't know how you do this!"

Akemi laughed. "You get used to it."

Radovan approached. "Good morning, Number Three."

"Good morning." Terza lifted one of the coffee cups. "I hope you are still in the mood for coffee." She extended the large paper cup. "I brought you an extra-hot coffee Latte with two packets of raw sugar."

Radovan smiled brightly. "Oh my, aren't you the perceptive one?" He accepted the cup with a smile of gratitude. "Thank you very much."

"It is my pleasure." Terza passed the second cup to Akemi. "I hope they got this right. I asked the barista for what you typically ordered."

"Why thank you." Akemi smiled and accepted the coffee cup. "I'm not as picky as our fearless leader."

Terza chuckled. "I'll say! Black with one sugar?"

Akemi nodded. "That is exactly correct. You are a good detective."

"I am glad you're here, Number Three," Radovan told Terza. "They reopened the case in Los Angeles. From what I understand, Joshua Kamoze is there as we speak."

"Is he under arrest?"

"I do not know that." Radovan lowered his coffee cup to the desk. "This is what I do know." He raised his right index finger. "First, the medical examiner in L.A. took an extensive look at the full report on the death of Yvette Kamoze."

"Did he find anything?"

Without answering, Radovan moved his extended finger to the front of his lips.

Terza accepted the silencing sign and waited for him to continue. He held up a second finger. "Something in that report caused her to reopen the case." Radovan widened his eyes before continuing. "She has not shared her findings with me."

He held up a third finger. "I do know that the detective in charge of the case summoned Joshua Kamoze for an interview. I believe he traveled to Los Angeles today."

Terza waited to make certain Radovan had finished. When positive, she asked, "Do you think the medical examiner will reach out to you?"

"Yes, of course I do." Radovan nodded aggressively. "We will need to compare notes on how the deaths are related."

"Wow." Terza blew out a puff of air. "It looks like Joshua may be guilty of two murders. I just don't understand it. He seemed to adore Sloan."

"I have learned never to jump to conclusions." Radovan reached for his coffee and took another drink.

"I know. Weigh all the evidence first."

Terza thanked Akemi and Radovan before leaving. As she made her way through the empty corridor, Terza's mind analyzed all of the information she now possessed. Joshua Kamoze was definitely her number-one suspect. As much as she liked the man, Terza also knew not to overlook a coincidence. Both of his wives died as a result of blunt force trauma due to falling down the stairs. This fact must be investigated.

But could Ruby Slippers have pushed Yvette and Sloan Kamoze? Was she jealous of their relationship with her brother? She is a wacko, but was she even in town at the time of either death?

Terza's thoughts turned to Belinda Benson, the neighbor. Although they had a recording of her going to the Kamoze's house, Terza had her doubts. She stopped on the tile floor and replayed the scene in her mind. She finally shook her head and whispered, "There is no way she killed Sloan. She didn't have enough time." Terza made a mental note to remove Belinda's name from their murder board. And now there were two.

Back in her Fiat, Terza pressed the contact button on her phone for Moheenie.

"Good morning, Tee."

"Good morning, Mo. What are you doing? You sound out of breath."

"I am. I just finished a run."

"Good for you. What are your plans for the day?" Terza asked.

"You name it. I am doing laundry, house cleaning, and shopping. You know, all of those fun things!"

"Is Ranger at work?"

"Yes, he just left. What's up, Tee?"

"Is Ranger also working tomorrow?"

"Yes." Moheenie extended the word. "Now what are you not telling me?"

"How would you like to work today and take tomorrow off instead?"

"Of course, I'll work at *MOW* today, and I can also work tomorrow, too. I'm sorry. I didn't know we had a job."

"We don't. I have an idea, and also news."

"About the case?"

"Yes, it's about the case, and I can't wait to tell you! How long until you can meet me at the Pancake Place?"

"Thirty minutes or so. I can be showered in fifteen, and head right out."

"Perfect. I'm leaving the medical examiner's office right now. I'll get us a table and see you soon. Don't worry. I will catch you up over breakfast."

Terza guided her car out of the parking lot and onto the freeway heading south. Less than ten minutes later, she took the offramp and drove toward the Pancake Place. *So, Joshua is in Los Angeles and not at home right now.* Not knowing what she hoped to accomplish, Terza turned left before the Pancake Place driveway and passed the Palm Tree Inn to her right. She made a second left onto the street leading up to Joshua's house. Terza slowed as she neared the front, drove less than a block, and circled back. She pulled close to the driveway, stopped her car, and peered through the passenger's window. All appeared normal. She considered getting out but instantly changed her mind. Instead, Terza drove to the Pancake Place parking lot, turned off her engine, and exited the Fiat. As she walked slowly toward the front, Terza surveyed the restaurant roof line, looking for cameras. The only one visible from outside was mounted above the entrance.

The inviting aroma of bacon lingered in the air as she stepped through the front door. Terza requested a table for two and then followed the young woman to a booth by the window. She looked out while sliding onto the bench seat and saw Moheenie's Jeep pull in one of the front spaces. They shared a wave when Moheenie looked up.

Moments later Moheenie slipped across the opposite bench seat. "This is a nice surprise. You know how much I adore breakfast. I feel like we are playing hooky!" She slapped her palms on the table. "Now, you must tell me everything, but start with work. Why are you giving me tomorrow off?"

"It's really no big deal, Mo." Terza scanned the menu. "We simply don't have many catering jobs this week."

Moheenie creased her forehead. "Should I be worried?"

"Absolutely not," Terza answered. "Do you remember last December?"

Moheenie rolled her eyes. "Of course I do. We were slammed."

"Exactly." Terza's head bobbed. "And we are going to be slammed this year, too. Let's take the break when we can get it."

"Okay, I understand. Now tell me about the case."

Terza focused her attention on Moheenie, just as their female server approached. She paused her update so they could each order coffee, a short stack of buttermilk pancakes, and a side of bacon. When the server walked away, Terza finally began. "I went to see Jacob Radovan this morning, and it looks like they reopened Yvette's case."

Moheenie clenched her fist. "I knew it. Joshua killed her, too."

"It is beginning to look that way. In fact, Joshua is in Los Angeles as we speak."

"Maybe he'll finally confess."

"Yes, maybe." Terza watched their server fill both coffee cups. "Thank you," She said before returning her attention to Moheenie. "I was thinking about our current three suspects, and it seems that Belinda Benson is out of the picture."

"I agree." Moheenie poured cream into her coffee. "What about Ruby Slippers?"

"I still have a bad feeling about her." Terza reached for the small pitcher of cream.

"She is weird, but is she a murderer?"

Terza added a teaspoon of sugar to her coffee and stirred. "We just don't know at this point. I say we erase Benson's name and keep the focus on Joshua and his wacky sister."

"I agree. Now, why exactly are we here?" Moheenie locked eyes with Terza and sipped her coffee. "Were you planning on stopping by the Kamoze's house again?"

"No, in fact I drove by on my way here, and all looks quiet." Terza motioned toward the entrance with her chin. "There's a camera on the outside, right above the front door."

Moheenie turned to look behind her.

"You can't see it from here, but I already checked."

Moheenie glanced up to the ceilings. "There are lots of cameras inside the restaurant. Does the one outside look the same as these?"

Terza scrutinized the dome-shaped cameras on the restaurant ceiling. "No, it is just a plain camera pointing toward the parking lot. If someone did park at the Palm Tree Inn, I was hoping to catch sight of them from this angle."

Moheenie nodded. "Good call, Tee."

When their breakfast arrived, they busied themselves spreading butter between the steaming pancakes and pouring maple syrup over the top. Moheenie showered her bacon with pepper, while Terza moved three strips to the side of her plate. She purposefully wanted her bacon slices to rest in the pooling syrup.

"You do know the only way to eat bacon is separate from the pancakes with lots of pepper," Moheenie commented.

"Oh no," Terza teased. "The bacon absolutely must be mixed in with the pancakes and syrup."

Moheenie grinned. "Then why didn't you just order the bacon pancakes? Don't they cook the bacon inside?"

"Yes, but the bacon is never crispy enough. This way makes the perfect bite." She lifted a fork full of pancake and bacon, quickly stuffing them into her mouth before the syrup dripped. Terza's eyes widened. "Yum-oh!"

Moheenie lifted a slice of bacon and loudly crunched on the crispness. "Nothing better than crisp bacon."

The friends laughed together and enjoyed their breakfast while continuing to share their thoughts about the two remaining suspects. When the server brought their check, Terza asked, "Do you know anything about the camera above the front door? I see that it is a different type than the ones in here."

"We used to have a lot of *eat and runs.*" The server crossed her arms.

"Is that like a hit and run?" Moheenie asked.

"Kind of. I've been here over thirty years, and I've seen it all. People would come in, order extra food, wait until we were busy, and then leave without paying the bill."

Terza gasped. "That's horrible!"

"I agree, and so do the owners. After the cameras were installed we had a few incidents but quickly located the suspects. They were staying at the hotels nearby. But the cameras are extremely visible, and word also got out. There have been no incidents in more than three years."

"And what about the camera out front?" Terza pressed.

The server waved her hand at the air. "That old thing is just for show. When the ceiling cameras were mounted, we just let it be."

"So, it doesn't work?"

"Not at all. Who wants to look at a parking lot anyway?"

We do, Terza thought. "Thank you for your time and for the fantastic breakfast."

"My pleasure. Come back soon."

Terza and Moheenie took their bill to the register to pay. As they walked out the front door they both stopped to look up at the disabled camera.

"That's too bad." Moheenie sighed. "From the angle, it might have covered the parking lot."

Terza glanced back. "What about the cameras inside? Do you think any of them would show the parking lot through the glass windows?"

"I don't think so." Moheenie shook her head. "None of them are really close."

"I tend to agree." She directed her attention back to Moheenie. "Now what do we do?"

Moheenie's eyes bulged. "We ask Ruby Slippers what she is doing by your Fiat!"

"What?" Terza's head snapped toward her parking spot. Sure enough, Ruby Slippers was standing right beside Terza's Fiat. Her arms were folded across her chest, and she was defiantly glaring at them. "Let's go!" She marched forward.

"Stay calm," Moheenie warned from behind. "Let's play it cool."

Terza took a breath, instantly resolving to follow Moheenie's lead. They walked up to Ruby Slippers and greeted her with a smile.

"Hi Ruby!" Moheenie called out. "It's so nice to see you."

"Hi Rub–"

Ruby Slippers lashed out at Terza before she had a chance to finish. "Stay out of our business!"

"I'm not in your business," Terza spoke firmly through clenched teeth.

"Don't lie to me. I saw you parked in front of our house."

"It's a free country, and I can park wherever I want. Besides, I was thinking about visiting your brother. I thought it was *his* house and not yours."

"I don't believe you." Ruby sneered. "And what are you doing *here*?"

"We were just having breakfast," Moheenie said lightly.

"I don't believe you either." Ruby almost spit out her words. "I think the two of you are spying on my family." Her eyes narrowed and turned to steel, while the smell of hatred escaped from her pores.

And I think you are nuts, Terza wanted to say. "Why would we spy on your family?"

"You know why!" Ruby accused.

"Do you mean because Joshua's first wife and his second wife died exactly the same way?" Terza immediately wanted to retract her words. She watched Ruby's eyes narrow further into tiny slits. Terza also noticed the white knuckles on Ruby's clenched fists. Her mind raced with thoughts of her next comment, but nothing came to her.

"Let's go." Moheenie guided Terza toward her Jeep.

They got in and sat in silence while Moheenie watched in her rearview mirror. Ruby remained frozen in place right next to Terza's Fiat.

"What is she doing?" Terza whispered.

"Just standing there. She hasn't moved a muscle."

"Well, she better not mess with Cab," Terza said, referring to her Cabernet-colored car.

Moheenie nodded, her eyes glued to the mirror. "Okay, she's walking away. I think she is returning to the house."

Terza exhaled loudly. "My, oh my."

"You can say that again." Moheenie frowned at Terza. "You need to tell Nico. This girl is dangerous. I could see it in her eyes."

Terza considered Moheenie's comment. "I agree. I'll call him when I get home."

"I'm happy to come back to *MOW* with you. After all, I am supposed to be working today. So far, all we've done is to have breakfast."

"And run into a psycho!" Terza grunted. "Seriously though, Mo. Take advantage of this slow period. They don't come very often."

Moheenie saluted. "Whatever you say, boss."

They said their goodbyes, and Terza drove straight home. She had considered spending time at Macaroni on Wheels but decided instead to take a true day off from work. Terza planned to prepare herself a huge chef's salad with all the trimmings. Olive would receive extra attention, and together they could binge-watch one of Terza's favorite shows. She smiled at the thought of a *do-nothing* day.

Terza also considered the best way to contact Nico. She had left a message before, and he sent her a text back. Should she leave another message? Should she send him a text? Should she even bother? *Yes, Nico needs to know*. There was something evil about Ruby Slippers. Terza thought about telling Avery Ellington instead of Nico but quickly dismissed the idea. He would never understand, and blame her for meddling.

After concluding that Nico was the best one to tell, and a phone call would be better than a text, Terza pressed his contact button. The call went straight to voicemail.

"Hi, Nico. It's Terza. I didn't want to bother you, but something happened today. Moheenie and I had a confrontation with Joshua's sister, Ruby. I really thought you should hear about it. Please give me a call when you have a moment."

Terza disconnected and half expected a return call within minutes. She felt positive that Nico would hear her message and immediately come to her rescue. No such luck.

CHAPTER TWENTY-ONE

Still Waiting

Tuesday

The time neared noon, and Terza still had not heard back from Nico. As she worked in her Macaroni on Wheels kitchen Terza was uncertain whether she felt mad or sad. Nico should care that she had a confrontation with Ruby Slippers. The fact that he obviously did *not* care made her mad. But it also saddened her. Terza wanted him to be concerned.

A call from Moheenie finally brought a smile to her face. "Hi, Mo!"

"What are you doing? Please tell me you're not at work."

"Okay, I'm not at work."

"But you *are*, aren't you?" Moheenie pressed.

"You know I always prepare the weekly catering whiteboard on Tuesdays."

"Yes, but you also told me that we didn't have many jobs this week. Now I feel even worse about not coming in to help."

"Don't be silly." Terza smiled into her phone. "I'm hardly doing anything. I gave you the day off so enjoy it."

"You also said I was going to work yesterday instead of today." Moheenie laughed. "The only thing we did was have breakfast!"

"Then you deserve both days! Remember what I said. This Christmas season is going to be brutal."

"Okay." Moheenie sounded doubtful. "I really called to find out about Nico. What did he say about Ruby Slippers?"

Terza grunted. "He never even bothered to return my call."

"Oh, I'm sorry, Tee. That's too bad."

"He probably just doesn't care."

"Or he never got your message. Why don't you text him?"

"No way!" Terza rolled her eyes. "I am done with Nico Garza."

"Don't be too hasty. If he does call, just be sure and hear him out before you hang up."

"Yes, ma'am. See you tomorrow."

Terza stared at the screen after ending her call. She then blinked hard and returned her focus to their catering board. When her phone rang a few minutes later, she suspected Moheenie had forgotten something and was calling back. The name *Nicolas Garza* appeared on her screen.

Anticipation fluttered within her stomach, pushing any feelings of anger away. Just the thought of hearing his voice caused Terza's palms to perspire.

"Hello," she spoke softly.

"Terza, are you alright?" Nico's tone reflected genuine concern. "I just got your message. I thought it was the same voicemail you left me on Sunday. Terza, I am *very* sorry!"

He cares! He really cares.

"Terza, are you there?"

"Yes. I'm here. Thank you for calling me back."

"Of course," Nico assured her. "Please tell me what happened."

Terza shared the story of her encounter with Ruby Slippers and then asked him about Joshua Kamoze. "Did you know they reopened the case on Yvette Kamoze?"

"I did. I take it you received the news from Radovan?"

"Yes, and he also told me that Joshua was called back to Los Angeles. Have you heard anything?"

"No, nothing yet."

Terza rubbed her chin. "I wonder what Ruby is doing here in San Diego while Joshua is near where she lives?"

"I don't know. Perhaps he asked her to watch the house?"

"Could be."

"Terza, I'm serious though. You need to be careful."

"I will. I promise."

"Maybe there is something I should tell you." Terza could hear the hesitation in Nico's voice.

"What is it?"

Nico remained quiet for several seconds while Terza waited abnormally patient. He finally spoke. "This stays between us," Nico said firmly. "Got it?"

"I understand."

"We ran a check on Ruby's mobile. Her phone was turned off beginning at eight in the morning on Saturday, the day of Sloan's death. The next tracking we have of her mobile clocked in at three in the afternoon. By then Ruby was at her condominium in Los Angeles."

"I find it interesting that Joshua was away from his mobile and Ruby's was turned off."

"We do, too."

"Could they be in this together?"

"That's one theory, but we are working on several."

"Do you care to share?"

"Not at this time. I did want you to know that Ruby is a possible suspect, and that also makes her potentially dangerous. Please remain vigilant."

"I will," Terza promised. "Thank you for confiding in me."

"We'll talk more later," Nico said. "I've got to go now. Duty calls."

"Ciao," Terza said.

"Ciao."

At least he had called, and his explanation sounded genuine. Terza instantly felt better. She finished the catering whiteboard, then reached for their murder board. She considered each suspect before slowly erasing the column with Belinda Benson's name. *Joshua Kamoze or Ruby Slippers? Which one of you is guilty of murder? Or did you plan this together?* Terza recognized the irrational and almost psychotic behavior of Ruby Slippers, but Joshua seemed normal. And yet, there was nothing normal about two wives dying the exact same way.

CHAPTER TWENTY-TWO

Knight is Shining Armor

Wednesday

"What a beautiful day!" Terza spoke to Olive while standing on her balcony looking out over the Little Italy neighborhood. The temperature felt exceptionally warm for an autumn day, and the sky appeared a glorious blue. She leaned down to caress the back of Olive's head. "Perhaps I am just feeling happy because Nico called." Terza lifted Olive high, placing their faces nose to nose. "What do you think, my beauty? Is this a sign I'm falling in love?"

Olive responded with a wiggle as if to say, "Forget all of the questions. It's time for breakfast!"

Terza lowered her cat to the ground and walked into the kitchen. She filled Olive's crystal bowl before preparing a green smoothie for herself. Later, she enjoyed her morning coffee while reading her Bible out on the balcony. Olive finally joined Terza on the opposite patio chair.

Right before taking her morning shower, Terza checked in with her mother.

"*Buon giorno*, my love."

"*Buon giorno*, Mom. How are you?"

"Your father and I are both feeling great. Isn't it a beautiful day?"

Terza chuckled. "It is. I immediately noticed the day and thought maybe I was falling in love."

"I take it you spoke to the dashing detective?"

"Yes, but nothing personal. At least he returned my call."

"That is progress! Plus, it is a glorious day. I cannot believe the blue sky. It looks like a painting."

"Yes, it does." Terza gazed out the window. "Give Papa my love, and tell him that I read my Bible."

"I will." Benedette laughed. "I'm sure he will say that you are his favorite."

"Good thing! Ciao!"

"Arrivederci."

Terza disconnected and headed straight for the shower. She dressed in her usual jeans and T-shirt work clothes before locking up and walking to Macaroni on Wheels.

Moheenie arrived shortly thereafter, and together they reviewed their catering jobs for the week.

"You were right." Moheenie stepped closer to the whiteboard. "We *are* slow."

"It's kind of nice that our first job is tomorrow. That gives us the entire day to prepare."

"Is it a dinner party?"

Terza's eyes widened. "It's an escape-room party!"

"Are you serious? Do you mean like the escape-room we went to with our book club?"

"I think so." Terza's head bobbed. "I guess the host and hostess ordered it online. They are having a party for eight of their friends. There will be two teams of four, with Mr. and Mrs. Giralt operating as the moderators."

Moheenie clapped her hands together in swift succession. "I am so excited. If all goes well we should host our own escape-room."

"That's a fantastic idea, Mo. Maybe we could set it up in Barnaby's conference room?"

"Oh, my goodness, that would be amazing!" Moheenie's eyes zeroed in on their catering board. "So what are we serving?"

"The Giralt's are giving their guests a choice of Herb and Lemon Risotto with Scallops, or Chicken Parmesan. Mrs. Giralt is going to email me today with the exact count. I am guessing it will be about fifty-fifty, so I already asked my papa to order several pounds of fresh scallops."

"They each sound delicious." Moheenie rubbed her palms together. "Are we making the same salad for both main courses?"

"Yes, I suggested just a simple salad with a lemon vinaigrette dressing."

"I agree. The lemon will accent the scallop dish and brighten the heavy Chicken Parmesan."

"My thoughts exactly."

Moheenie glanced at Terza. "I see you wrote down appetizers. What specifically did the hosts request?"

"They would like three different appetizers. When I gave them the choice, they agreed upon Crispy Polenta Bites, Italian Style Deviled Eggs, and Spicy Frico."

"Spicy Frico is like Parmesan Crisps, correct?"

"Yes, Mo, you are exactly right." Terza moved to their kitchen island. "The party begins early at five, and the Giralt's would like us to serve the appetizers from five until six. They are figuring an hour for the escape room adventure, and then dinner after that at seven."

"This is going to be so much fun!" Moheenie retrieved their work aprons, handing one off to Terza. "All through dinner their guests are going to be talking about the game. What a perfect evening. I didn't see any mention of beverages. Are we having a bar?"

"No, Mr. Giralt is completely in charge of the beverages, with the exception of coffee. We are bringing our espresso machine."

"Do you need Ranger's help?"

Terza shook her head. "I think we'll be fine." She wrapped her apron strings around her waist and tied them in front. "The desserts will already be made, as we are preparing Tiramisu Pudding Cakes. They just have to bake while the guests are enjoying their main courses. We will have plenty of time to prepare the coffee drinks."

Moheenie's eyes grew excited. "Tiramisu Pudding Cakes? Have I ever tried those?"

Terza grinned. "I don't think so. Would you like me to make a few extra?"

"Of course!" Moheenie practically salivated. "Just the name sounds amazing. Who doesn't like tiramisu, and who doesn't like pudding? I can't wait!"

"Don't worry." Terza snickered. "We can start on those first so you can take one home and bake it tonight."

"I'm not so sure that's a good idea. If I take it home, I'll have to share with Ranger," Moheenie whined, while Terza laughed.

"Alright, already. We will make extra, and you can take home two."

Moheenie's smile beamed. "Thanks, boss."

"You do know that you're spoiled," Terza told her.

"I know." Moheenie grinned. "But so are you."

"Yes, I am. Now let's talk about Friday. We are catering another work luncheon."

Moheenie glanced back at the whiteboard. "*MOW* is certainly becoming popular with the downtown office crowd."

"I know, and I'm thrilled. It's nice to work in the afternoon instead of at night."

"What's the occasion this time?"

"I have no idea." Terza bit the bottom of her lip. "It is a law firm and has something to do with celebrating their production. This is really a job for my papa. All they want is a submarine-style sandwich bar. We are making meatball sandwiches, eggplant parmesan sandwiches, and Italian deli sandwiches."

"That sounds kind of fun. Are we serving dessert?"

"Just cookies and cannoli. They wanted everyone to be able to walk around and talk. The office closes right at noon, the same time we are serving lunch. I was told that everyone gets the rest of the day off."

"Hmm." Moheenie angled her head. "An early start to the weekend. Good for them."

"Good for us, too. After we finish on Friday, we're done for the week. If the weather holds we should go SUP boarding together on Saturday."

Moheenie nodded aggressively. "Count me in!" She raised her palm for a high five. "You know how much I adore stand-up paddling."

Terza slapped hands with Moheenie. "Let's get this party started. I'll work on the pudding cakes while you begin the Chicken Parmesan."

Moheenie placed the red-and-white striped apron over her head and pulled her long ponytail free. "Chicken Parmesan, coming right up." She wrapped the apron strings around her back and tied a bow in the front. "How many should I prepare?"

"I think we'll be extra safe with ten servings. That's one for each person. Once we get the exact count, I'm hoping we will have some left over for a second helping. Plus, it's always nice when we can sample our own creations and not have to cook dinner."

Moheenie and Terza worked together with the comfort of close coworkers and even closer long-time friends. Moheenie chopped onions, minced garlic, and used fresh tomatoes for the Chicken Parmesan's marinara sauce. She also prepared extra marinara for Friday's meatball sandwiches.

Terza slowly melted chocolate in preparation for the pudding cakes, while she precisely and separately measured the dry and wet ingredients.

"This is exactly why you are the baker, and I am not." Moheenie stared at Terza. "You look like a scientist measuring out some important discovery."

Terza used a stainless-steel offset spatula to perfectly level the cup of flour. "You have to be exact when baking."

"I know." Moheenie murmured. "That's why I don't like to bake."

When they successfully completed every possible component of the food preparation, Moheenie focused on cleaning the kitchen while Terza placed three Tiramisu Pudding Cakes into the oven to bake. She closed the door, set the timer for thirty minutes, and focused her attention on Moheenie. "Now comes the big question. Are you going to enjoy your dessert here, before dinner, or are you taking it home to appreciate with Ranger?" Terza watched the many expressions on Moheenie's face while she mentally weighed her options. "You are so funny, Mo!"

"It's a hard decision." Moheenie lifted her palms in self-defense. "I can already smell the yummy chocolate baking, and it would be wonderful to enjoy the pudding cake fresh from the oven."

"But then you would spoil your dinner," Terza added.

"Exactly my thoughts. But you also know how much I adore chocolate. Will I be able to wait? Plus, won't they cool down too much?"

"Just the opposite, Mo. What time are you planning to have dinner?"

"It's slow cooker night, so dinner should be ready when I get home. I love the aroma of home-cooked soup when I open our front door."

"Yum. What kind of soup?"

"Chicken Tortilla. It's one of my favorites. You know how slow-cooker meals can all taste the same?"

Terza nodded.

"This soup is different and very special. Plus, it comes out perfectly every time. We top it with grated jalapeño jack cheese, cubed avocado, and tortilla chips."

"Moheenie, I am *so* proud of you! Plus, I need the recipe. It sounds delicious!" Terza checked their vintage, kitchen wall clock. The swinging cat tail kept perfect time, much to her delight. "It's just past four. What time will Ranger be home?"

"Right at five, and he walks in the door starving. We should be eating by five-fifteen."

"Then you're good. The Tiramisu Pudding Cakes will be done shortly, and they have to rest for at least thirty minutes. I will wrap your two in foil, and you can carry them home in one of our hot bags. They will be absolutely perfect by the time you finish dinner."

Moheenie grinned. "Terza, you are an angel! Ranger is going to be thrilled. Thank you very much!"

"Of course. I only hope you think they taste as good as they smell. I tried a new recipe using actual melted chocolate instead of just cocoa powder."

"Won't that make them a bit more like lava cake?"

"That was my goal. But please be honest. In fact, call me right after you are finished. If something went wrong, I will need to make another batch before the party tomorrow evening."

"Sure thing." Moheenie peeked through the oven glass. "But aren't you going to try yours tonight?"

"Yes, but probably not until after you. First, I need to go next door and meet with my father."

"I can stay if you need me."

"No, go home to your husband. We are good here."

After removing the three pudding cakes from the oven, Terza packed two large ramekins for Moheenie to take home.

With keys readily in hand, Moheenie lifted the hot bag. "What time are we starting tomorrow?"

Terza creased her forehead. "Hmm, let me see. How about coming in at noon? Since we're working late, I think noon will be perfect."

"Is that enough time to prepare for the party?"

"Yes, we're practically finished already."

"Then noon it is!" Moheenie beamed. "I just might sleep in." After they said their goodbyes, Moheenie left for the evening.

Terza leaned over the counter to inhale the aroma of the lone pudding cake. It smelled delicious. No time to dawdle. She still had work to do. Terza opened the adjoining door to the Tiepolo Mercato and saw her father restocking a shelf by the cash register.

"Hi, Papa!"

"Hello, my little gnocchi. How was your day?"

"Very busy but productive." Terza smiled. "How was yours?"

"The same." Ezio narrowed his eyes. "Did you read your Bible this morning?"

Terza puffed her chest. "Yes, and I called Mom. Didn't she tell you?"

"Of course, she did." Ezio winked. "You are officially my favorite child."

Terza chuckled. "I'll be sure and brag about this with Ange and Dom," she said, referring to her older siblings. In reality, all three of Ezio's children appreciated their father's enduring commitment to the Lord and treasured the loving way he always treated their mother. As a married man with two children, Damiano strived to also set a good example. Angeline and Terza often spoke about their potential futures. *We need to find a husband as loving as our father*, they would say.

"I have your scallops ready." Ezio walked to the butcher's counter. "They are fresh and beautiful!"

"Thank you, Papa. I am also going to need some of Mom's amazing meatballs, an eggplant if you have one, and deli meats."

"I have everything you need." He circled behind the glass case. "Come with me, and you can help."

Terza scurried to the back of his prized area, a treat that reminded her of their childhood. The three siblings always jumped at the chance to help their father. He would tie a white butcher apron around their tiny frames and give them something that, at the time, seemed important to do. Thinking back, Terza realized their pseudo jobs were not really jobs at all.

"Look at this Branzino I ordered from the Fish Merchant. I am making dinner for your mother this evening."

"It looks exceptionally fresh." Terza leaned closer. "Mom is going to love it. I remember that Branzino is her favorite fish."

"You are welcome to join us. We have plenty."

"Oh, thank you, but I still have a lot of work to do."

Ezio rubbed his stomach area. "You have to eat."

"I have at least one Chicken Parmesan at my disposal." Terza looked out the large plate-glass windows at the front of the Mercato. "I can't believe how dark it is outside."

"I know." Ezio followed her gaze. "It's because we just changed back from daylight savings to standard time. I wish we could pick one and stick with it. Now it seems later than it really is."

"Yes, it does."

"Please be extra careful walking home. You should stay on Little Italy's main street until you have to turn."

"Don't worry, Papa, I will."

Ezio finished wrapping Terza's selections in white butcher's paper and then handed each packet to her for placement in a handled shopping bag.

"Thank you very much." She hugged him first and then kissed his right cheek, his left cheek, and his right a second time. "Ciao, ciao."

"Ciao, ciao!"

Terza returned to Macaroni on Wheels through their adjoining door and quickly settled in front of her computer. She logged into the office email account and searched for one from Jennifer Giralt. After opening the email, Terza reviewed the meal count. She was pleased to read the six orders of the Herb and Lemon Risotto with Scallops, and four orders of the Chicken Parmesan. *Perfect. Now I can keep three.*

Terza spent the next hour finishing company paperwork, a job she enjoyed the least. *If only I could simply cook all day!* When Terza's phone chimed, she read a text from Moheenie:

Tiramisu Pudding Cakes were amazing! Don't change a thing!

Terza responded with several heart emojis. Before leaving for home, she removed the plastic liner from their tall kitchen trash can, secured the top, and walked it out to their large bins in the back alley. A shiver crept up her spine as she crossed the asphalt leading from her rear kitchen door to the dumpster. She glanced at the back window of the Tiepolo Mercato and saw only darkness. Her father had gone home for the evening.

When Terza reached the dumpster, she lifted the lid with one hand and tossed the white trash bag in with the other. She then eased the lid closed, rather than let it slam. But as Terza raised her head, a shadowy movement captured her attention. She focused on the area toward the end of the alley and waited a beat. Although a streetlight illuminated a portion of the concrete driveway, all seemed quiet. Terza finally turned to walk away.

"You couldn't let it go, could you?" Ruby snarled from the darkness.

Terza froze at the sound of Ruby's voice behind her. Her heart hammered as she rotated to face her accuser, her focus instantly shooting to the knife. Ruby's hand gripped a large butcher knife, with Terza entirely vulnerable. She yearned for the bag of trash to at least serve as a shield.

"What do you mean, Ruby?" Terza asked, in the sweetest voice possible. Her brain calculated the approximate six-foot distance between her and Ruby and the eight-foot distance to her back kitchen door. *I'll never make it. My only chance is to stall her and pray someone comes.* "Why are you holding that knife? I don't understand."

Ruby took a step forward, while Terza moved back. The distance between them remained the same, but now Terza was closer to her door. *Maybe we can keep this up.*

"Don't act all innocent with me." Ruby's eyes burned with hatred. "I know your game."

Terza cautiously inched back.

"Stop moving!" Ruby screamed.

Movement. Terza thought she saw movement in the shadows behind Ruby. When she dared to take a quick look, Ruby immediately noticed. As Ruby also stole a glance to her rear, Nico came into view. Terza was instantly relieved.

"Drop the knife, Ruby." Nico's gun was pointed directly at Ruby's chest.

Terza watched in slow motion as Ruby looked with hesitation from Nico to her and back to Nico. Her green eyes darted nervously in their sockets. Taking a chance, Terza stepped back, hoping Ruby would not be dumb enough to try and lash out with Nico ready to fire a shot.

"I said drop it!" Nico shouted his second warning.

Ruby's shoulders finally relaxed, and she allowed the knife to slip from her hands. The sound of steel hitting asphalt seemed to take forever. Detective Avery Ellington suddenly appeared from Terza's right. He kicked the knife away and held onto Ruby as Nico secured the handcuffs.

"Let's go," Ellington said to Ruby, leading her to the waiting police car.

Nico reached Terza's side and wrapped a strong arm around her waist. "You're alright," he assured her. "Let's go inside."

Nico led Terza into the kitchen area and locked the door behind them. He guided her to sit on one of the counter stools and then sat next to her. "Do you need a drink of water?"

Terza turned her head.

"You're fine." He rubbed her back. "Take a deep breath."

Terza obeyed by breathing in deeply and then slowly blowing out. She breathed again. It felt good to know her body was functioning properly.

"How did you know?" Terza stammered.

"That question covers a lot. I need to leave with Detective Ellington right now, but I'll be back."

Terza blinked hard, worried that the hovering tears would breach the surface of her eyes. "I didn't even see him. Ellington, I mean."

Nico smiled. "That's a good thing. Your focus was on me."

"And the knife," Terza murmured. "Thank you for saving me."

"Any time." Nico laughed. "You're worth saving." He looked into her eyes. "That comment was supposed to make you smile."

Terza strained to form a slight smile but never made it happen.

"Tell you what." Nico took Terza's hand. "Let me get Ms. Kamoze booked. I'll come back and take you to dinner."

Terza looked down at her jeans. "Thank you, but not like this. I should go home and change."

"Absolutely not. I don't have my car, so I can't drive you home right now. I need you to sit tight here until I'm finished." He removed the phone from his belt and checked the time. "I should be back by seven-thirty, and then I can take you home to change."

"Do you really feel like going out, Nico?"

"No, but I want you to get something to eat."

"I can cook," Terza suggested.

"Not a chance. You need to relax and have someone wait on you this evening."

Terza's countenance brightened. "It's perfect, Nico. Moheenie and I prepared Chicken Parmesan this afternoon. I have three more than we need for tomorrow evening. All I have to do is bake them. Dinner will be ready by the time you return."

Nico looked hesitant. "I don't want you cooking, but I do like the distraction. You already seem happier."

"What can I say?" Terza shrugged. "Cooking is my passion."

"Okay, but are you good here? I could always walk you over to your parent's house."

"No, that is a bad idea. They can *never* know this happened."

"O-kay," Nico extended the word, making him sound doubtful.

"I'm serious." Terza released her hand. "Please promise they will never know."

Nico raised his palm. "You have my word." He stood and walked to the back kitchen door. "Lock up behind me, okay?"

Terza stood and met him at the door. "Don't worry, I will."

Nico used his palm to brush the hair away from her forehead, and from the skin above her brows. "I'm going to wait outside until I hear the deadbolt."

"Thank you."

"After I get back, I'll text you when I am right outside the front door."

Terza exhaled with relief. "That sounds perfect. See you soon."

"Ciao."

"Ciao."

After Nico left, Terza promptly secured the deadbolt. She then checked the lock on the door leading to the Tiepolo Mercato. Terza knew she had locked the front door but checked it anyway. It, too, was locked.

Feeling safer, Terza set out to prepare their meals. She thought about calling Moheenie but decided against it. With her nerves still tender, Terza needed to focus on something other than her recent trauma.

CHAPTER TWENTY-THREE

Preparing their dinner made Terza feel surprisingly normal, although her thoughts still drifted to the shiny blade of Ruby's butcher knife. She hoped that time would take away its memory. Terza decided to serve the Chicken Parmesan on top of capellini, with a small dinner salad on the side. She placed a large pot of water on the stove to boil and began chopping the fresh vegetables for their salad. Terza made plans to bake the Chicken Parmesan right at 7:30 p.m.

She placed a red-and-white checkered tablecloth on one end of her large concrete kitchen island and then added an Italian-style straw Chianti bottle with a candle in the bottleneck. Terza looked at the candle and promptly removed it. *This isn't a date*. She then placed two plates side by side, added matching cloth napkins, utensils, and water glasses. *Hopefully we can enjoy wine together another time.*

Shortly before 7:30 p.m. Nico sent her a text:

I should be leaving here in 15 minutes.

Terza replied:

Great. Is it safe to put the Chicken Parm in the oven? It takes about 30.

Nico responded:

Sounds good.

Terza stared at her screen until her eyes grew blurry. She realized that Nico was actually joining her for dinner, even though the situation had resulted from a traumatic event. She would be alone with him, just like their first, and only, date. Terza reminisced about the time Nico brought her champagne. *And chocolates and flowers. What happened?* Terza sensed that Nico felt the same attraction she did, especially after he took her out on their first date. *Why didn't he call? Why didn't we have a second date? He seemed to forget all about me.*

Knowing she may never have the answers, Terza felt it best to start fresh. She would enjoy his company with zero expectations. If Nico is interested, he can let her know. If not, perhaps she should reevaluate her feelings for Conner.

Terza turned down the flame under the boiling pot of pasta water. The capellini would cook in three minutes or less. She then placed the Chicken Parmesan in the oven to bake and stirred the marinara sauce. It felt good to stay busy.

Nico sent a text announcing his arrival, prompting Terza to look out the window next to her front door. She was glad to see he had not changed from his jeans and Army green T-shirt. They could look casual together.

He waved at her through the window before she unlocked the door.

"I am happy to see that you are taking precautions." His full mouth hinted at a smile.

Terza winked. "This just might be my new M.O., or shall I say *Modus Operandi*?"

"I'm also glad to see a smile on your beautiful face once again. I was worried that we may have lost it for good."

"Thank you for the compliment, but don't worry. I'm not going to let Ruby Slippers get to me. Besides, I'm busy making us what I hope to be a delicious dinner."

"Since you like to cook, and I like to eat, we should make a great team. Lead the way. It smells amazing in here."

Nico followed Terza into her catering kitchen, where he washed his hands before sitting at the cloth-covered island.

"Dinner should be ready in about fifteen minutes." Terza stood next to her plate. "We have a few minutes before I need to make the pasta. Would you like your salad first or last?"

"I am very happy you asked. I actually prefer to eat my salad last." Nico grinned. "It's Italian style."

"I hear you." Terza rested an elbow on the counter. "So how did everything go?"

"Good. We finished the booking paperwork, and Ellington stayed on to interrogate Ruby. I'm going to meet up with him again in the morning."

"Don't you typically have two or more present during interrogations?"

"Yes, we do. Ellington asked another detective to sit in. He thought it best for me to make sure you get home safe and sound."

Terza felt a tinge of surprise. "That seems extra nice of Detective Ellington."

Nico nodded. "He's really not a bad guy."

Terza angled her head. "Tell me, how did you know I was in danger?"

"We have been tracking Ruby for the past few days. When I saw that she was in Little Italy this afternoon, I paid close attention to her whereabouts. Before you came out to the trash dumpster, she had been hiding in the alley for over an hour."

Terza felt a surge of shock. "You *knew* she was there?"

"Yes, but at that point she wasn't committing any crimes. We were close by and knew you were safe."

"It didn't feel that way." Terza's voice fractured. "I thought she was going to slice me up big time."

"I would have never let that happen." Nico placed his palm tenderly on the top of her hand.

Terza looked into his dark eyes. "Thank you for that." She paused. "Did she kill Sloan?"

"We think so but are hoping for a confession. That is another reason we were tracking her movements."

"Hold that thought." Terza moved to the stove. "Let me get the pasta going and check on our meal. You can catch me up while we are eating."

"May I help?"

"No, thank you." Terza tossed him a smile. "Stay seated. There really isn't much to do."

Nico relaxed onto his stool while Terza dropped the capellini into the boiling, salted water. She then removed the Chicken Parmesan from the oven and allowed their main course to rest. A few minutes later she tested the pasta. Satisfied of the perfect al dente doneness, Terza used a spider sieve to remove it from the water. She placed a portion on each plate, added a generous serving of marinara sauce, and then artfully positioned the chicken breast. Using a ladle of marinara sauce, Terza drew thick lines of red on the white plates. She then grated from a block of parmesan, allowing the freshly shredded cheese to rain down. After a final touch of finely chopped flat leaf Italian parsley, Terza placed her masterpiece in front of Nico.

He stared at his plate. "I could get used to this." Nico inhaled dramatically. "Terza, it smells incredible!"

"Thank you. I hope it tastes as good as it smells!"

"How can it not? Plus, the entire plate looks outstanding. I like this swish of sauce."

"Sometimes people prefer extra sauce with each bite. There is already marinara sauce directly on top of the pasta, but you can add more from the side if you want."

Nico continued to stare at his dinner. "The side of sauce looks much better than just serving it in a cup."

"I hope so!" Terza grunted.

Nico glanced up at her. "Is this how you prepare every dish?"

"I try to make each serving look like a work of art." Terza lowered her plate before sitting. "If possible, that is."

"This looks so good I almost don't want to eat it." Nico cut a slice of chicken.

"That's my goal, until you taste it. Then I hope you will come back for more."

They sat in silence while taking the initial first bites. Terza enjoyed being next to him. She felt safe and secure. She could also smell the woodsy scent of his cologne and wondered if Nico had freshened up just for her.

"Wow, Terza, this tastes even better than it looks. Thank you very much for inviting me to dinner."

Terza finished chewing. "It's my pleasure. Thank you for saving my life!"

"My pleasure, as well."

Terza watched Nico practically devour his food, while she picked at her plate. "Would you like some more?"

Nico hesitated. "I feel bad about eating when you're obviously not hungry."

Terza took his plate to the stove and prepared another serving. "Please, don't worry about me. I tend to graze all day while we are cooking."

Nico accepted the second Chicken Parmesan with a mischievous grin. "This is such a treat. I was expecting to eat fast food tonight."

"It's nice to see you enjoy my cooking."

"It's nice to spend time with you."

Not knowing how to respond, Terza just smiled, electing to remain quiet.

Nico placed a forkful into his mouth, winked at Terza, and then chewed with satisfaction. He enjoyed several more bites before asking, "Shall we address the elephant in the room?"

Terza examined the four corners of her kitchen before answering. "I don't see any elephants, just my vintage cat clock."

Nico rocked his head in time with the moving tail. "I think my grandmother had one of those."

Terza chuckled. "So did mine. When I saw this one, I just had to buy it. Plus, the wagging tail reminds me to get home and feed Olive."

"I take it Olive is your cat?"

"My cat and the ruler of our house." Terza laughed. "She is going to be one unhappy kitty when I finally show up tonight."

"I hope you're not unhappy with me." Nico's eyes grew serious. "After our first date I really wanted to take you out again."

Perspiration formed on Terza's palms. She lowered them to her lap and grabbed hold of the cloth napkin. Hidden from view by the concrete counter, Terza wiped the moisture from her hands. She drew in a breath. "I thought we had a nice time."

"We did. I did, at least."

"I did, too," she whispered. She met his gaze, returned it. "And?"

"I had to leave town," Nico said bluntly. "Right after we went out."

"You did? I had no idea."

"Well, I should have called you to explain, but I wasn't sure how long I'd be gone. You see, my mom fell off a ladder and broke her leg in two places."

"Oh, Nico, I'm very sorry!" Terza placed her palm on his forearm. "Is she okay?"

"She is now, but they needed my help with the winery. I took a leave of absence from work and seriously thought about reaching out to you many times."

"I completely understand."

"It's just that I wasn't sure how long my parents would need me. For a short while, I thought about relocating to Napa."

"Wow! Would you join the force up there?"

Nico shrugged. "I wasn't sure about anything. I returned home less than three weeks ago."

Terza removed her palm. "How is your mother doing, now?"

"She is feeling much better. Fortunately, she has progressed to a soft cast and is becoming an expert on crutches. I offered to stay, but my parents decided they needed to hire another employee anyway." Nico started laughing. "My mom practically pushed me out the door!"

"I'm sure she loved having you there."

"She did, but I think they were a bit concerned about my job. They know how much I enjoy my work and were worried about the amount of time I was losing."

"That's sweet. Did you enjoy working at the winery?"

Nico smiled. "Yes, it was kind of fun. I brought several cases home. Would you like to sample our Reserve?"

"Of course I would!"

Nico reached for her hand. "When you called to tell me about Sloan, I was really mad at myself."

"I don't understand."

"Every single day since coming home from Napa, I planned to call you. I was busy at work, and then when I got home at night it always seemed too late."

Terza squeezed his hand. "I understand. Thank you for telling me."

"I guess I lost my chance." Nico withdrew his hand and looked down.

"What do you mean?"

He lifted his eyes to meet hers. "You looked breathtaking the other night. I know I missed out, but I truly hope you are happy."

Terza tilted her head. "Are you talking about my so-called date?"

"Yes, you were wearing that amazing red dress. In fact, it matched the red Mustang perfectly."

"Nico, I was a plus-one for a wedding. Conner and I are just friends."

"Are you sure?" Nico's forehead creased.

"No, I'm *positive*." A pang of guilt swept through her. Conner was just a friend, but she knew he wanted more. Terza needed to be honest with him. Without realizing, she suddenly yawned.

Nico checked his phone. "It's late. I should take you home."

Terza placed a hand over her mouth. "I'm sorry. Suddenly I feel like I could sleep right here on the kitchen island."

"It is bigger than most beds!"

Terza knocked on the polished concrete top. "Yes, it is, but hard as a rock."

Nico nodded his agreement while skimming his palm over the smooth surface. He looked up at Terza. "Let me help with the dishes, and then I'll drive you home."

"I usually walk, but tonight I will gratefully accept the ride." She moved to the sink. "We can leave the dishes though. I can take care of them in the morning."

"Are you sure?"

"Yes. Let me fill the sink with hot water. I'll leave everything soaking."

They worked together like a long-term couple, with Terza at the sink and Nico clearing the table. Terza could tell he felt comfortable in the kitchen and guessed it came from helping his parents at the vineyard.

"Do you cook?"

"Do I, or can I?" Nico grinned.

"Both."

Nico carefully folded the red checkered tablecloth while explaining. "I can cook, but nothing like the kind of meals you prepare. I usually don't bother though, because it seems like too much work to feed one person."

"I understand. I hear that often from my friends." She dried her hands on a terrycloth kitchen towel. "I'm all set here if you are. I feel bad though. You didn't even get dessert."

"Next time." Nico touched his stomach. "Right now, I couldn't eat another bite." He joined Terza as she checked all the door locks, and turned off the lights. After they exited through her front office door, Nico used her keys to secure the deadbolt. He then escorted Terza to his gold-colored Lexus and pressed his key fob. A soft chime sounded before Nico opened the passenger's door.

Terza slid onto the luxurious leather seat and watched him walk around the front to the driver's side. "What a beautiful car."

"Thank you." Nico buckled his seat belt. "I looked long and hard before buying it. I wanted something solid that would last, and I also thought about a vehicle comfortable enough to drive me to Napa several times a year." He started the engine.

"I think you did well." Terza listened to the melodic hum of the motor.

The drive to her condominium took under five minutes. Nico parked in a commercial spot on the curb, tossed a police parking permit in his front window, and then walked around the front to open Terza's door. He held out his hand, making her feel like a princess.

Terza reached for his palm. "I could get used to this."

"I hope so."

Terza's heart raced when their skin connected. She wondered if he could feel her shaking. If so, Nico never commented. He followed her into the elevator, insisting that he walk her all the way home. When they reached Terza's front door, she opened it. "Would you like to come in for a cup of coffee?"

Nico hesitated, making Terza wonder if she was pushing too hard. "Will you promise to give me a rain check?"

"Of course I will."

Nico leaned through her door opening to look inside. "So where is the famous Olive? I thought she would be waiting for you right here."

"Ha!" Terza grunted. "Olive only shows herself when Olive feels like it. She is very particular."

"What about Mustang man?"

Terza's eyes narrowed. "Is that your way of asking me if Conner has been over?"

Nico shrugged. "At least now I know his name is Conner."

Terza rolled her eyes. "I suppose you are going to do a background check?"

"I hadn't thought of that." Nico rubbed his chin.

"Let me save you some time." Terza placed both hands on her hips. "Yes, Conner has been in my home. We are friends. No, he has never met Olive. Conner works for the DEA, so you probably have crossed paths."

"Wow, he works for the DEA?" Nico raised a brow. "He must be a good guy if he's in law enforcement."

"Conner is very sweet."

"Tell me then, who has Olive met?"

Terza counted on her fingers. "Let me see, Moheenie, my little niece Charley, and my mom."

"It sounds like she is partial to females."

"That's true."

"So how are you going to make it up to her?"

"If you are referring to the late dinner, I have a delicious can of salmon with Olive's name on it."

Nico chuckled. "I do believe your cat is spoiled."

"You have no idea. That is an understatement."

Nico leaned in to kiss Terza on the right cheek. "Lock up tight, okay?"

"I will. Thank you again. I thought I was a goner."

Nico pretended to tip his imaginary hat. "Glad to be of service." He turned to walk away, then glanced back. "Sleep tight."

"You, too." She quickly closed her front door, then locked both the door handle and the deadbolt. "The coast is clear," Terza called to Olive. "You can come out now!"

CHAPTER TWENTY-FOUR

BACK TO WORK

Thursday

After enjoying a morning off, Terza returned to Macaroni on Wheels shortly before 11:00 a.m. She wanted to clean the kitchen and finish some paperwork by the time Moheenie arrived at noon. It felt good to sleep in, and she hoped Moheenie had done the same. Fortunately, dreams of Nicholas Garza quickly replaced thoughts of her encounter with Ruby Slippers. But Terza could not wait to tell Moheenie. A lot had happened in a single day.

A knock sounded on the back kitchen door, and Terza heard Moheenie's voice. "Terza, it's me!" As Terza moved to unlock the door, she saw the handle turn. Moheenie had used her key.

"Good morning. Why is the door still locked?"

Terza quickly relocked the door and pulled a puzzled-looking Moheenie farther into the kitchen. "Do I have news for you!"

Moheenie narrowed her eyes. "What's up?" She hung her purse on the apron stand and slid onto a counter stool.

"You are not going to believe this!"

Moheenie's eyes went from slits to round circles as Terza recounted her confrontation with Ruby.

"She had a knife!" Moheenie screeched.

"I can still see it in my mind." Terza repeated everything Nico had told her about Joshua, his suspicions about Ruby, and Nico tracking Ruby's phone.

"Is she finally under arrest then?"

Terza's head bobbed. "Yes, as of now, but I think only for her attack on me. Nico said they're hoping she will confess to the murders."

Moheenie placed a hand over her heart. "This is so amazing, Tee. I'm glad you're alright. We knew Ruby Slippers was psycho." She exhaled loudly. "I am certainly happy Nico was tracking her."

"You can say that again." Terza bit her lower lip.

"Was it kind of nice seeing him?"

"It was." Terza smiled. "He came back after arresting Ruby, and we had dinner together."

"And..." Moheenie pressed.

"And, it was pretty darn good. He drove me home, walked me to the door, and said goodbye."

Moheenie raised her eyebrows. "Did he kiss you goodnight?"

"Of course not. It wasn't a date, Mo. He gave me a peck on the cheek."

"Ooh la la. That's something."

Terza allowed a slight grin. "It's a *little* something." She lifted her computer tablet off the counter and swiped the screen. "Let's see what we have left to prepare." Terza read through the menu. "We are down to the appetizers. Would you like to make the Polenta Bites, or the deviled eggs?"

Moheenie thought for a moment. "I'll take the deviled eggs. You are much better at polenta. What about the Spicy Frico?"

"I can handle that while working on the polenta." Terza lowered her tablet. "We are way ahead of schedule. I would like to leave here around two, arrive by three, and set up by four."

"You are so organized, Tee." Moheenie hopped off the stool. "I am constantly impressed."

"That's sweet, Mo. Thank you." Terza looked down at her ringing phone. "It's Nico!"

"Hurry and answer. Maybe he has news."

Terza pressed her green answer button. "Hi, Nico."

"How's my favorite chef? Are you still alright?"

Terza felt her face flush. "Yes, I'm fine, thank you. Moheenie and I are wrapping things up for the Escape Room party I told you about."

"I won't keep you then."

"No, it's okay," Terza rushed to explain. "We're almost finished." She looked to Moheenie who was mouthing the words *ask him*. Terza nodded. "Is there anything new?"

"Not entirely."

What does that mean? Terza thought.

"I may have an update soon," Nico continued.

"Thank you. As you can imagine, I'm really anxious to know more about Ruby."

"Are you available Saturday night?" Nico suddenly asked.

"Uh, yes. What's going on?" She sensed him vacillating.

"I thought it would be nice to have dinner together."

As in a date? Terza asked silently. "That would be lovely," she responded out loud.

"Great," Nico said. "Shall I pick you up at seven?"

"Seven is perfect. May I ask where we are going so I know what to wear?" Terza and Moheenie shared a smile.

"I was thinking about the seafood restaurant on Harbor Island."

"That sounds wonderful."

"Okay, see you Saturday. Ciao."

"Ciao, ciao." Terza's eyebrows shot up, along with the curve of her smile. "We have a date!"

"I could hear that. Where is he taking you?"

"He mentioned the seafood restaurant on Harbor Island, but now I'm not sure which one."

"They are all good, but I bet he is taking you to the one with the romantic view." Moheenie grinned. "What are you going to wear?"

Terza suddenly felt rattled. "Yikes! I have no idea. The nights are finally starting to chill, so I want to be warm." She rubbed her palms together while thinking. "But I can't wear a parka!"

"I vote for your red boots." Moheenie removed two cartons of eggs from the refrigerator.

Terza nodded. "Hmm, great idea, Mo. I just might know of the perfect outfit." Terza returned her focus to stirring the polenta, while Moheenie prepared the herbs and spice mixture for the deviled eggs.

"What are you going to do about Conner?"

Terza exhaled loudly. "I was thinking about inviting him to family dinner on Sunday."

Moheenie looked sideways. "Two different dates in the same weekend?"

"No, silly!" Terza grunted. "I want to get together with Conner so we can talk."

"How are you going to talk at family dinner?"

Terza rested both hands on her hips. "You are one funny girl, Moheenie Lakalaka Brickman! I plan to talk with him on the way home."

"*After* he has been wined and dined?"

"Exactly!"

Several hours later they were busy setting up for the Escape Room party at the home of Randolph and Jennifer Giralt. As each guest arrived, the excitement escalated with anticipation of the upcoming mystery. When the game finally commenced, Terza and Moheenie paid careful attention to the clues, and without spoiling the fun, they solved the mystery and secretly escaped long before the others.

Friday

Exhilaration from finishing their final job for the week made Terza and Moheenie a bit punchy. Moheenie cranked up the music, and Terza danced her way to the refrigerator. The sandwich bar was a great success, and the leftovers conveniently provided them with a late lunch.

Moheenie added several deli meats to the stack of cheeses already resting in her palm. "Are we still going SUP boarding tomorrow morning?"

Terza watched as her friend layered meats and cheeses on a large Italian-style roll. "Seriously, Mo." Terza giggled. "How are you going to fit your mouth around that sandwich?"

Moheenie glanced up with a sheepish grin. "I couldn't decide which ones to use." She extended the sandwich. "Would you like half?"

"Sure. Now I don't have to make my own."

"So what about tomorrow?" Moheenie sliced the sandwich roll in two.

"Yes, I'm game if you are." Terza accepted her half. "The only problem is my hair. We need to go early so I can be home by noon."

"What's happening at noon?

Terza rolled her eyes. Moheenie should know better. "What's happening? I need to wash my hair and begin working with the mess of curls I'm going to have."

"Got it! By the way, maybe you should call Nico now."

"And say what?"

"Ask him if they've interrogated Ruby yet. Aren't you dying to know?"

"Of course, I am. I just don't want to seem pushy."

"If he tells you something on Saturday night, please remember it word for word."

"Shall I tape him?" Terza joked.

"Yes, that's a great idea!" Moheenie took a large bite of sandwich.

"Oh, I forgot to tell you. I called Conner this morning." Moheenie nodded while swallowing. "And?"

"It was good. I told him about Ruby Slippers—"

"You told him about the attack?"

"Not really." Terza nibbled on a small piece of meat. "I just told him that she was stalking me. Of course, I didn't mention anything about the knife."

"That's a good thing." Moheenie wiped the corner of her mouth. "I didn't tell Ranger either. We would be banned from trying to solve any kind of mystery in the future."

"I know! Even the book club mysteries, let alone real-life ones. Conner would have gone ballistic."

"What about family dinner on Sunday? Is he coming?"

Terza held up a palm while she finished chewing. "I never got the chance to ask him. Conner told me he is going away for a work assignment beginning tomorrow."

"Oh, where is he going?"

Terza shrugged. "It's the same as always. He can never tell me. But I think maybe it's a good thing."

"You just don't want to have *the talk*." Moheenie used air quotes.

Terza rolled her eyes. "You're right about that. But also, this may give me a chance to see if Nico and I are even a possibility."

"I'm sure you are, but what does your heart tell you?"

Terza considered Moheenie's question before answering. "I really think I may be falling in love. Even when I am with Conner, I think of Nico. In fact, I think about him all the time. It's like his image is locked into the back of my mind. I enjoy Conner because he is a dear friend, and it's easy. I know he likes me, and committing to a relationship with him would be simple. But the spark is missing when it comes to Conner."

"I understand, Tee, and I'm glad you're eventually going to talk with him. Conner is such a great guy, and he needs to find someone."

"He does. I only want the very best for Mr. Conner Reeves."

Moheenie flashed Terza a bright smile. "I do, too!"

Terza brushed the crumbs from her hands. "Are you ready to call it a day?"

"I am ready to call it a week. What time do you want to meet for the beach?"

"Is eight-thirty too early? We can grab a coffee on the way."

"Eight-thirty works for me. Are we taking the company van?"

"Yes, I'll go to my parent's first thing in the morning, load my board, and meet you back here."

"That sounds perfect." Moheenie stretched her arms to the ceiling. "We need some fun in the sun."

"I couldn't agree more."

CHAPTER TWENTY-FIVE

Saturday

Dressed in her swimsuit, light blue board shorts, and an orange rash guard, Terza fed Olive and left her condo a few minutes before 7:00 a.m. She walked to the Macaroni on Wheels parking lot, then climbed aboard their company van. Before long, she pulled into her parent's driveway, knocked softly on the kitchen door, and walked in. "It's me."

Her mother looked up from the dining room table. "Good morning, my love. Pour yourself a cup of coffee and join me."

Terza walked up to her mother. "*Buon giorno*, Mom." She kissed Benedette's cheek. "Where's Papa?"

"He's in the shower." Benedette lifted her cobalt blue mug. "Aren't you going to join me?" She lowered her face to the steaming liquid. "It's delicious."

"It smells wonderful, but I promised to have coffee with Mo. We're going SUP boarding this morning."

"I figured as much when I heard your van." Benedette smiled. "Good for you. I'm glad you have a day off."

Terza grinned. "I also have a date."

Benedette raised her eyebrows. "From the glint in your eyes, it must be with your detective friend."

Terza's grin grew into a smile. "It is! He's taking me to a restaurant in Harbor Island."

Benedette nodded her approval. "Very nice." She turned the page of her Bible. "Would you care to read with me this morning?"

"That would be special." Terza slid onto the chair next to her mother's. "Just like old times."

Benedette reached over and placed her palm on top of Terza's hand. "I'm glad you're here." She looked down at her opened Bible. "I'm in the book of Philippians."

Terza listened as her mother began reading from the first chapter of Philippians. Benedette ended the short book before Terza's father joined them.

"You're finished?" Ezio sounded disappointed. He walked toward Terza and kissed her forehead. "Good morning, my little gnocchi."

"Good morning, Papa."

"I can read your favorite verses again," Benedette told him. "Be anxious for nothing, but in everything by prayer and supplication, with thanksgiving, let your requests be made known to God, and the peace of God which surpasses all understanding will guard your hearts and minds through Christ Jesus."

Ezio's smile beamed. "Amen!" He winked at Terza. "You are talking with your mother right now."

"I am." Terza knew what was coming next.

"I see you are reading the Bible."

"We are," Benedette answered for her daughter.

"Then you, my little gnocchi, are my favorite child."

"Why thank you, Papa!"

Benedette shook her head and just laughed.

"I love you both." Terza stood. "I've got to get my board and meet Moheenie." She hugged her father, then leaned to kiss her mother. "Have a wonderful day."

"You, too, my love," Benedette responded. "Arrivederci."

"Don't fall!" Ezio told her.

"I'll try not to." Terza laughed. "Ciao!"

Terza left through the kitchen door and went to retrieve her SUP board. As she pushed it into the back of her van, Terza could still hear the words her mother read from the Bible. *Be anxious for nothing.* Was the book of Philippians really the next book in her mother's reading plan, or did she purposefully select the special scripture for Terza's sake? *How does she always know?*

When Terza returned to Macaroni on Wheels, she saw Moheenie's jeep already in the parking lot. Terza waved to her friend. The duo met behind the Rubicon and systematically transferred the second SUP board to the van. "I am desperate for coffee," Terza moaned. "What about you?"

"Count me in. Shall we just walk over?"

"I'm already walking!" Terza took off in speed-walk style.

Moheenie laughed. "Ha! You *are* desperate. Let's run."

Terza glanced down. "No way, not in flip-flops."

"I can run in flip-flops."

"That is only because you are Hawaiian from head to toe. You were probably born wearing flip-flops!"

"Oh, that would hurt! My poor mother!"

Later, with large, lidded coffees in hand, Terza and Moheenie returned to the catering van. They climbed aboard, looking at each other with ear-to-ear smiles.

"This is going to be such fun."

"Yes, Mo, it is!"

CHAPTER TWENTY-SIX

Looking back on her day, Terza reflected on the special morning with her mother, followed by the fun she had SUP boarding with her best friend, Moheenie. She now sat in front of her bathroom vanity mirror, with her damp hair wrapped in a white terrycloth towel. Terza felt fantastic, and her naturally bronzed skin seemed to glow with a kiss from their morning adventure in the sun. She sipped from a mug filled with hot English breakfast tea, inhaled the pleasant aroma, and then purposefully kicked off her slippers. "Here you go, my beauty. Enjoy!"

Olive immediately walked over to the faux fur slides, circled to find the precise position, and then snuggled on top. Amused, Terza watched her cat before finally removing the towel from her hair.

"Okay, let's get this show on the road." Terza took another sip of tea and then began to section her hair with pink plastic clips. "What do you think?" She regarded her reflection in the mirror. "Do I look like a Christmas tree?" Terza looked down at Olive, who could obviously care less. Her cat was content to sit on Terza's slippers and sleep the day away, even with the sound of Terza's loud blow-dryer.

After finishing her hair, Terza prepared an avocado toast snack before starting her makeup. When she finally applied the finishing touches, she lightly sprayed her favorite perfume and stepped in front of her full-length mirror. "Okay, Olive, time to wake up." Once again, Olive completely ignored Terza.

She analyzed her outfit selection, wondering if Nico would appreciate or be shocked by the colors. Red with purple was a bold move, but Terza liked how they looked together. She had chosen a purple knit dress with elbow-length sleeves. She cinched the waist with a bold, and bright red leather belt, an exact match to her red leather boots. Terza slipped into a red knee-length coat, wearing it open to reveal the purple of her dress. Finally, she selected a matching purple clutch. Terza was excited, nervous, giddy, and slightly panicked as she walked to her nightstand and answered the ringing landline.

"I'm in your lobby," Nico told her.

"I'll be right down."

"No, please buzz me up. I have something for you."

Terza punched in the numbers to activate her door code before lowering the receiver. She then walked to her front door and stood waiting in the opened doorway. Terza caught her breath when Nico exited the elevator and stepped onto her marble corridor. He looked exceptionally handsome in his black slacks and beige silk dress shirt. Nico glanced her way and flashed Terza a luminous smile.

"Hello, gorgeous."

"What are you holding behind your back?"

Nico grunted. "You'll see soon enough."

When Nico reached Terza, he greeted her with three gentle kisses, beginning with Terza's right cheek. He then brought his left hand forward and presented her with a bottle of Pol Roger Champagne.

Terza accepted the bottle. "My, my, Pol Roger. Thank you, Detective Garza. I am very impressed." Terza opened her door wider. "Please, step inside." She placed the champagne bottle on her dining room table and turned as Nico extended another bottle.

"This is from our Grand Reserve."

Terza took the second bottle and studied the label. The burgundy rectangular brand featured the name Garza in elegant script made from gold-embossed letters. "This bottle is gorgeous. Thank you very much, Nico."

"I hope you enjoy it. My family takes great pride in their wines, especially the reserves."

Terza carefully placed the wine bottle next to the champagne. "I'm sure I will, but this is all too much."

"Are you kidding? You deserve even more for helping us solve another case."

Terza's eyes grew wide. "Then it's really solved?" She reached for his hand. "Tell me, please."

"Not now! Let's talk over dinner."

Terza sighed. "Okay, but only if you promise to tell me everything."

"I promise." Nico wrapped his arm around her waist, leading Terza toward the door. "By the way, you look incredible."

"Thank you. Do you think the colors are too bold?"

Nico stepped back to examine Terza's entire outfit. "I'm Italian, so I like bold. You look stunning from head to toe." His eyes moved higher. "I really like your hair."

Terza's fingers touched her tortoise-shell comb. "I couldn't decide whether to wear my hair up or down, so I went halfway." She giggled softly. "All of these compliments are making me blush." Terza motioned toward Nico's attire. "You also clean up well."

"Do I now?" He grasped her hand. "Shall we go?"

Terza smiled. "We shall."

As they drove to Harbor Island, Terza attempted to question Nico about the case. He laughed and refused to answer any questions until they were sipping on a glass of wine.

"You will not answer *any* question at all?" Terza joked. "What about the color of this magnificent automobile? I can't tell if it's silver or gold."

"I can answer that one. This is a Lexus GS, and the color is called Atomic Silver."

Terza flashed Nico a smile and then sat quietly to simply enjoy the nearness of him. When they arrived at the restaurant, she learned that Nico had made reservations for a window seat. He held out her chair, sat opposite, and peered directly into her eyes. "I'm glad you're here."

"So am I."

After Nico ordered the wine, a fruit-forward Pinot Noir, he toasted to the solved murder and finally revealed the killer. "You will be pleased to hear that Miss Ruby Kamoze will be going away for a very long time."

"Did she confess?"

Nico's head bobbed slowly. "That she did, and thanks, in part, to you, once again."

"What happened?"

"At first, we thought she would never break. But when we finally got her to confess to the murder of Sloan Kamoze, Ruby ended up acknowledging both." He took a sip of his wine. "Your video of the upside-down sofa cushion clinched it for us."

Terza's eyes widened. "How so?"

"We enlarged a photo of the cushion and told Ruby that her palm prints were clearly visible under our special lighting?"

"Is that true?" Terza asked, not believing a word.

Nico laughed. "Of course not, but don't tell that to Ruby Slippers, as you call her."

"Did she buy it?"

"Not in the beginning, but then we showed her enlarged photographs of clothing fibers. Since they were the same color as the shirt she was wearing, Ruby finally looked trapped. I kept pressing by insisting that her clothing fibers were found around Sloan's chest area, where Ruby had obviously suffocated Joshua's wife. She finally snapped and screamed her confession about both murders."

"What was her excuse?"

Nico grunted. "She claimed that both Yvette and Sloan had stolen her brother. I've got to tell you, that chick is insane."

"Psycho is the correct word. Tell me, how did you know what shirt Ruby was wearing on the morning of the murder?"

"Good one." Nico nodded his approval. "I was wondering if you would pick up on that." He looked at her with a sideways grin. "We have access to cameras, too, you know."

"We looked! I don't remember a video of Ruby Slippers on the morning of the murder."

"You saw her car," Nico reminded Terza.

"Yes, but we could not tell if Ruby was the driver, let alone see her clothes."

"What about the street camera?" Nico continued to grin.

Terza arched a brow. "Are there cameras on the frontage road?"

"Yes, indeed. We have a recording of Ruby on the morning of the murder. She was trying to sneak to and from her vehicle parked at the Palm Tree Inn."

Terza's jaw dropped. "You do? Thanks for not sharing!"

Nico shrugged. "I can't tell you everything. But I do have you to thank."

"I'll take it, but why?"

"Finding the right street camera took some research. We didn't pull the video until you told me about seeing Ruby's vehicle at the Palm Tree Inn." He tipped a pretend cap. "So, I thank you, Miss Tiepolo."

"All in a day's work." Sadness suddenly enveloped Terza.

"Is everything okay?" Nico asked. "I thought you'd be pleased."

Terza lifted her eyes to him. "Really, I am. I was just thinking about Joshua."

"I feel bad for the guy. He turned out to be a big help to us, though."

"Please tell me." Terza bit her lip. "How did he help?"

"It seems that he was already feeling uneasy when Sloan died in the exact same way as his first wife, Yvette."

"We all were."

Nico nodded. "Yes, and when they reopened the investigation of Yvette's death, you know Joshua was called to Los Angeles. He spoke with the detective and shared his growing apprehension. Then, when Joshua returned to San Diego, he met with Ellington."

"By this time did you suspect Ruby Slippers?"

"Yes, we did, but the case was not solid."

Terza felt her heart race. "That means Joshua also suspected Ruby, didn't he?"

Nico nodded aggressively. "At the time we met with Joshua, Jacob Radovan had already spoken with the medical examiner in Los Angeles. Now there were two reasons to reopen the case and resume the investigation. Originally, Ruby had an alibi that seemed legitimate. From what I can tell, the detectives checked it out, but obviously not well enough. She was supposed to be at a conference in Denver when Yvette Kamoze died."

"Where was she really?"

Nico rolled his eyes. "According to her mobile logs, Ruby Kamoze was with Yvette at the time of her death."

"Are you kidding?" Terza shrieked. "Why didn't this come out during the initial investigation?"

"That I don't know. I can only assume that Ruby was never a suspect. From what I can tell, they thoroughly checked Joshua and then pretty much ruled it an accident."

Terza placed a palm over her heart. "This is incredible. If Ruby was locked up after Yvette's death, Sloan would still be alive."

"My thoughts exactly."

"Ruby certainly grew smarter."

"What do you mean?"

"Last time she never bothered to hide her whereabouts, with the exception of the fake conference. But this time, it seems she went out of her way to stay off camera. Plus, didn't you say that she turned off her phone?"

"You're right," Nico confirmed. "I am thinking that when Ruby murdered Yvette, it was a crime of convenience, not planning."

"Do you mean she was at the right place at the right time to push Yvette down the stairs?"

"Yes, that is exactly what I mean. And then when Ruby realized she got away with it, I think she deliberately planned to murder Sloan."

"Why would she also push Sloan down the stairs? Two wives suffering the same type of death causes suspicion."

"Suspicion on the husband."

Terza looked up in thought. "But Ruby adores her brother. I don't understand why she would want to point the finger at him."

Nico narrowed his eyes. "I'm not positive about that one. I think perhaps it's her way of punishing him."

"For marrying a second time?"

"Exactly."

Terza mentally locked each portion of their conversation into her brain so she could effectively share the news with Moheenie. Then Terza and Nico enjoyed a succulent fresh fish dinner, with Terza ordering halibut and Nico selecting the salmon.

Later, while standing at her doorway, Terza yearned for their special night to last forever. Nico treated her as a true gentleman by kissing her on the cheek, and politely explaining he had to be up early. But Terza had her doubts. She suspected him of purposefully using restraint.

When they finally said their goodbyes, she closed her front door and leaned against the inside smooth surface.

Terza pressed her eyelids together and imagined kissing Nico goodnight. *If only*.

CHAPTER TWENTY-SEVEN

Wait on the Lord

After changing into her pajamas, Terza snuggled under the covers and reached for her remote. She pointed it at the television, turning it on to consider her options. When nothing captured her interest, Terza pressed the *off* button and dropped the remote onto her soft comforter. She then reached for the New King James Bible on her nightstand and turned to the Book of Philippians. Terza read, and reread verses 6 and 7 from Chapter 4:

> Be anxious for nothing,
> but in everything by prayer and supplication,
> with thanksgiving,
> let your requests be made
> known to God;
> and the peace of God,
> which surpasses all understanding,
> will guard your hearts
> and minds
> through Christ Jesus.

EPILOGUE

Case Closed

Sunday

Shocked that she got up in time to attend first service, Terza went straight from church to her favorite coffee shop. With a Grande Americano in hand, she selected an outdoor table and immediately sent Moheenie a text:

I have news.

Moheenie responded quickly:

Do you know?

Terza typed her response:

Yes, do you want me to tell you?

Moheenie replied:

No! Where are you?

Terza responded:

Hanging out with a guy named Romano.

Terza ended with happy face Emojis. Moheenie knew exactly where to find Terza, and Terza knew Moheenie was on her way. Terza's Americano was only half-empty when Moheenie's Jeep pulled up to the curb.

"I'm going to park at *MOW*," Moheenie called out her window. "See you in a minute."

"Do you want coffee?"

"Yes, please!"

Terza ordered a second Grande Americano for Moheenie and added two blueberry scones. She returned to the outside table as Moheenie walked up wearing navy blue yoga pants and a pink T-shirt.

"Good morning." Moheenie sat across from Terza. "How was church?"

"It was great. I'm kind of surprised that I made it to first service."

Moheenie bobbed her eyebrows. "Late night, huh?"

Terza laughed. "Not in the least! I was home and in bed by ten. I just didn't sleep much."

"Did Nico kiss you goodnight?"

Terza shook her head. "Just the right, left, right cheek peck. We had such a nice time though. I was kind of hoping to finally know."

"What do you mean, Tee?" Moheenie rested an elbow on the small round table. "Finally know what exactly?"

"Don't get me wrong. I'm not complaining. Nico was a true gentleman, and I feel very blessed." Terza sipped her coffee while collecting her thoughts. "I really feel like I'm falling in love with him, Mo." She paused. "I was hoping he would kiss me passionately, just like Conner has kissed me before. I am so confused. I truly do not think I'm in love with Conner, and yet my knees go weak when we kiss. I need to know what it will feel like with Nico."

"You silly girl. I know how you'll feel."

"You seem so confident."

"You're right. I am very confident." Moheenie grinned. "Close your eyes, and think back to the time you were kissing Conner."

Terza closed her eyes and cautiously tried to remember each and every detail. Suddenly her lids popped open. "I was thinking about Nico!" She screeched, before placing a hand over her mouth. Terza glanced around, grateful that the other customers were busy having their own conversations. "The entire time Conner was kissing me I was pretending he was Nico. How did you know?"

"Because I can tell how you feel about Nico, and I know how you feel about Conner."

"You are one smart lady, Mo."

"Why thank you."

Terza lowered her eyes. "But now I feel even worse about deceiving Conner."

"Don't worry. You'll have the talk, and then he'll move on."

"Well, I hope he doesn't move on too far." She looked up. "I love him as a friend."

"It will all work out. Now, tell me every single detail, beginning with who did it."

Terza sat up straight for her big announcement. "Ruby Slippers." She then proceeded to outline the entire case, including how Ruby had been fooled by the upside-down pillow and the mention of her clothing fibers.

"That was smart of the detectives. I'm sure it was Nico's idea and not the other guy."

"Do you mean Avery Ellington, the *third*?" Terza laughed. She told Moheenie about the street-front cameras and how Ruby Slippers was filmed trying to sneak to and from the Kamoze's house.

"I knew it!" Moheenie's palm hit the table. "Too bad Ian couldn't get us any images from that angle."

"Maybe he could," Terza explained, "but he didn't want to hack into the city. Porch and parking-lot cameras are one thing, but hacking into the city public works department could get him into trouble."

Moheenie nodded. "You're probably right."

Terza then explained how Joshua Kamoze had suspicions about the similarity in both deaths and how he reported them to the detectives in Los Angeles and San Diego. She ended by sharing the information about Ruby's fake work conference and the tracking done on Ruby's mobile phone. Terza held up her palm for a high five. "We did it. We helped solve another murder."

"We did, didn't we?" Moheenie slapped Terza's palm. "Thank goodness for Ian."

"You're right, Mo. He really came through. Plus, I need to thank Conner when he returns. He also helped."

Moheenie smiled. "That may be a great opportunity. Ask Conner over for family dinner as a way of thanking him. Then, after dinner you can talk about your future together as friends."

"*Just* friends," Terza added. "Yes, that's a fantastic idea, Mo. Thanks!"

Moheenie extended her paper coffee cup for a toast. "To us." She touched Terza's cup. "We are the dynamic duo of crime solving."

"To us." Terza stood. "Shall we walk over to *MOW* and erase our murder board?"

"Great idea." Moheenie joined her side.

When they entered the Macaroni on Wheels kitchen, Terza retrieved the murder board from between their two refrigerators. After resting it on their kitchen counter, Terza pulled an eraser from one of the drawers. She held it high into the air. "Are you ready to say goodbye to our latest case?"

Moheenie leaned over the board. "Only two names left. I forgot that we already erased Belinda Benson."

"I wonder if she will finally warm up to Joshua. I feel very sorry for him."

"So do I. Do you think we should go and see him? You know, maybe to pay our respects."

Terza thought for a moment. "Maybe. I was also thinking about calling Sloan's friend, Carnegie. She could probably give us some good advice."

"That's a great idea, Tee. Call her now."

"Don't you think it's too soon?"

"Not really. You could call to tell her about Ruby," Moheenie suggested.

Terza slowly reached for her phone. "Why not?" She scrolled through the list of contact numbers and pressed Carnegie's name.

Carnegie answered after two rings. "Terza, I was just going to call you! I heard about Ruby. Are you okay?"

Terza felt a twinge of surprise. "Yes, I'm fine. Thank you. How did you know?"

"From Joshua," Carnegie explained. "He was kind enough to keep me informed. Joshua knows how close I was to Sloan, and he feels awful that Ruby came after you, too."

"He feels awful?" Terza repeated. "Moheenie and I feel like creeps for suspecting him in the first place."

"Join the club," Carnegie told her. "I had my suspicions about Joshua, too. How could you not?"

"I agree, but we still feel badly for him. Now he has lost two wives and basically his sister as well."

Carnegie made a gagging sound. "Good riddance to her. What a wacko!"

Terza nodded in agreement. "Moheenie and I were wondering if we should go and pay our respects to Joshua. We could bring him some dinner."

"That would be nice, but he is already gone."

"Joshua's gone?" Terza echoed, mostly for Moheenie's benefit. "Where did he go?"

Moheenie moved closer to Terza in an effort to hear. Terza pressed the speaker button and gently placed her phone on the smooth concrete surface.

"Joshua decided to move back to Jamaica. He packed up the few items he wanted to take with him and left yesterday."

Terza and Moheenie stared at each other in shock. "I have so many questions. I don't know where to begin. What about his house and his job?"

"Joshua quit his job. His parents are driving down to pack up his house and place it on the market."

"Hi, Carnegie, it's Moheenie. You're on speaker."

"Hi, Moheenie. It's nice to hear your voice."

"What about Sloan?" Moheenie asked. "Aren't they going to have a service, or something, when her body is released?"

"Yes they are, Mo, but in Jamaica," Carnegie announced. "As you can imagine, this has been extremely difficult on the entire family. Joshua's parents just found out that the daughter they brought into their home, and raised with love, is responsible for murdering their son's two wives. It must be devastating."

"I can't even begin to understand their pain," Terza said.

"What are their plans?" Moheenie asked.

"After Mr. and Mrs. Kamoze sell Joshua's house, they are going to rent out their home in Los Angeles and join Joshua in Jamaica."

"Are they moving to Jamaica for good?" Terza asked.

"Joshua didn't say," Carnegie explained. "I know the plan is to bring Sloan's ashes and join their son as soon as possible. What happens after that most likely depends on how quickly Joshua emotionally recovers."

"Wow!" Moheenie sighed loudly. "What a tragedy."

"Yes, it is," Carnegie agreed. "On a lighter note, I may have a catering job for you both."

"That's nice to hear," Terza said. "Thank you, Carnegie."

"It's my pleasure. I'll give you a call next week."

"Sounds good," Terza said. "Thank you for letting us know about Joshua. Bye, Carnegie."

"Have a great day," Moheenie added.

"Same to you both. Goodbye."

Terza ended the call and stood shaking her head. "Two weeks ago, we were catering a surprise birthday party for Sloan and getting to know their wonderful friends. This is all very heartbreaking."

"I wonder if Joshua will stay in Jamaica," Moheenie pondered.

"I guess time will tell." Terza lifted the large chalkboard eraser and slowly wiped through the letters of Joshua's name. "Joshua must have felt something in his bones."

"What do you mean?"

"Do you remember how Joshua was away from his phone for so long on the morning of the murder?"

"I do. At that time he had no idea about Sloan, so what was he doing?"

"I bet he was thinking about Ruby. He probably noticed how odd she acted during the party and needed time to think it through."

"Too bad he didn't find out *before* she murdered Sloan."

"That's an understatement." Terza finished erasing the entire column under Joshua's name. The only column remaining had the heading for Ruby Slippers. "Are we ready to be done with her, too?"

"Definitely ready."

Terza aggressively erased the entire white board and then used a wet paper towel to wipe away any black residue. "Ruby Slippers, consider yourself erased."

"Amen to that."

Terza contorted her face. "You know her attorney is probably going to plead insanity on her behalf."

"I'm sure you're right."

"Fortunately, she's not our problem." Terza returned the whiteboard to its place between the two refrigerators.

The best friends said their goodbyes, and Moheenie left for the day. Terza remained at Macaroni on Wheels just to organize some paperwork. When her office phone rang, she slipped onto her desk chair to answer. "Macaroni on Wheels. How may I help you?"

"Oh good, you're open," a female's soft voice responded. "I wasn't sure if you'd be open on Sunday."

Terza briefly thought about explaining her method of forwarding her office phone calls to her mobile phone. Instead, she said, "We are usually open Tuesday through Saturday, but I'm always happy to help."

"That's nice to hear. My name is Everly Lane, and I kept meaning to call you all week. The days just seemed to get away from me."

Terza chuckled. "I know exactly how that feels. My name is Terza Tiepolo, and I'm the owner of Macaroni on Wheels. Are you interested in our catering services?"

"Yes, please. But first let me ask, do you only cater Italian food?"

"No, we are full service. Did you have a special menu in mind?"

"I did," Everly said. "I was hoping to serve Paella."

"I adore Paella," Terza told her. "And I can provide you with several options. What date did you have in mind? Our holiday bookings are beginning to stack up."

"That's why I wanted to call you right away. I'm actually planning a Valentine's party, but didn't know how early I should book it."

"Oh, I am very sorry," Terza told Everly. "You were right in wanting to book in advance, but we already have an event on February fourteenth."

"Forgive me," Everly said. "I meant to tell you that my party is on the thirteenth of February, the day before Valentine's Day."

"That's a new one," Terza commented. "Fortunately I don't even need to check our catering calendar. I know that specific day is open."

"That's great! You see, this past Valentine's Day, a group of us were lamenting over having no special plans. We came up with an idea of celebrating together, but all of the restaurants were booked solid. So I had an impromptu party on the thirteenth of February, and we decided to make it a tradition."

"I love it!" Terza clicked open their catering calendar. When the month of February filled the computer screen, Terza asked, "How many guests are you expecting?"

"I'm not sure yet," Everly answered. "Fifteen to twenty, if that's okay. I will know more after Christmas."

"That's perfect. Will you be hosting the party at your home?"

"Yes, at my condo. I live in Pacific Beach."

"Okay, I have you down for February thirteenth and just need your contact information to get started. Look for an email from me this upcoming Tuesday or Wednesday. I will send all the information you will need to plan the perfect party."

"Thank you, Terza. I will watch for your email."

"You're welcome, and thank you for calling Macaroni on Wheels. It was nice speaking with you, Everly."

After ending their conversation, Terza logged out of her catering calendar and opened her search engine. Paella was a dish with many variations. She hoped to discover some fresh ideas before presenting them to their new client.

The End

Look for the third book in S.K. Derban's Macaroni on Wheels series.

Case of the Paella Party – A Macaroni on Wheels Mystery, Book 3.

TERZA'S COOKING TIPS

Straight from the Macaroni on Wheels kitchen

How to Use Parmesan Cheese Rinds to Enhance Sauces
Save those Rinds!

There are many benefits to grating your own parmesan cheese, with the main benefit being the ever-precious rind. Freshly grated parmesan cheese is better for you, as it is just cheese with no additives. Oftentimes it is also less expensive, and your arm gets to exercise while grating! This is how we use the parmesan cheese rinds in the Macaroni on Wheels kitchen:

When grating parmesan cheese, grate only to the hard rind portion.

Save the entire rind in a zipper bag and store in the freezer. The more rinds you have, the better. So eat more cheese!

Prepare your tomato-based sauces as desired and bring to a boil.

Add the frozen parmesan cheese rinds to the boiling sauce, turn down the heat, and let it simmer. I typically add two frozen rinds for each quart of sauce.

Remove the melted rinds before serving. You will notice an extra richness to your already delicious sauce.

Buon appetito,
Terza Tiepolo

Thank you again for reading *Case of the Curved Staircase.* In Case of the Paella Party, the final book of the Macaroni on Wheels series, readers will be introduced to the Slim Man band. Their music is featured as one of the playlists enjoyed by Terza and Moheenie while they create amazing meals. Slim Man, an award winning musician, cook, and author has graciously agreed to share his mouthwatering recipe for Pesto Sauce. You can listen to his extraordinary music, purchase CDs, make reservations for an upcoming concert, order cookbooks, and join in the fun at https://www.slimman.com ...Thanks Slim!

PESTO SAUCE

Reprinted from *Slim Man Cooks Volume 2*
https://slimmancooks2.com/
This is the Slim recipe for pesto. It's a little different than my dad's. Sorry, Paps! I had to give it a Slim Twist...

NOTES:

The Italian name for pine nuts is *pignoli*. Just thought I'd toss that out there.

I toast the pine nuts in a dry pan over medium heat until golden. Shake it baby, shake it. Don't burn your nuts!

I use the extra ¼ cup of toasted pine nuts for sprinkling.

I sauté the smashed garlic on both sides in a small pan with a tablespoon of olive oil for a minute or so. It takes the edge off the garlic, softens the taste.

I use fresh Parmigiano-Reggiano cheese if possible. It ain't cheap, but it's worth it!

Grate it fresh. She's a-so nice that way!

INGREDIENTS:

- ½ cup pine nuts (1/4 cup for the pesto, ¼ cup for sprinkling)
- 1 tablespoon olive oil
- 2 cloves garlic, smashed with the broad side of a knife and peeled
- 2 cups fresh clean basil leaves
- ½ cup olive oil
- ½ teaspoon salt (I use kosher, mazel tov)
- 1 cup freshly grated Parmigiano-Reggiano cheese (plus a little extra for topping)

HERE WE GO!

Put the pine nuts in a small sauté pan over medium heat.

Toast and shake until golden.

Remove to a small bowl.

Put 1 tablespoon of olive oil in the same pan.

Add the garlic and sauté for 30 seconds or so.

Flip the garlic over and sauté on the other side for another 30 seconds or so.

Pour the garlic and oil into a small bowl.

Put the basil, ½ cup olive oil, ¼ cup of the toasted pine nuts, the garlic, and the salt in a blender and blend, baby, blend.

When everything is smooth, transfer to a bowl and slowly stir in the grated cheese by hand.

Or use a spoon!

DISH IT UP!

Put some over baked salmon, broiled shrimp, roasted chicken, or over pasta.

Sprinkle some of the extra pine nuts on top, or stir into the pasta, and...

MANGIAMO!

ABOUT THE AUTHOR

S.K. Derban resides with her husband in Southern California. Although born in the United States she moved to London within the first three months, and remained in England until the age of five. Her father, an American citizen, was a decorated veteran of the Second World War. Her British mother was involved with the London Royal Ballet Company, and a great fan of the arts.

After returning to the United States, Derban's life remained filled with a love of the theatre, and a passion for British murder mysteries.

S.K. Derban's personal travel and missionary escapades are readily apparent as they shine through into her characters. Readers are often transported virtually across the globe. She has traveled to Hong Kong on five separate occasions to smuggle Bibles into China, and has been to Israel on seven missionary trips. Derban's other adventures include visits to Bangkok, Greece, Egypt, Italy, and the Caribbean.

Beginning with her faith in the Lord, S.K. Derban relies on all aspects of her life when writing.

She hopes her books will allow readers to go on holiday without having to pack!

Visit S.K. Derban at https://childofthecarpenter.com/

OTHER BOOKS BY S.K. DERBAN

UNEVEN EXCHANGE

A brave woman confronts mortal danger with faith that reminds:
"For the battle is not yours, but God's..."

CASE OF THE BAYFRONT MURDER

With mystery solving skills sharper than her chef's knife,
a young caterer strives to remember:
"All things are possible for one who believes..."

CIRCUMVENT

When perfection turns to panic, an isolated couple must learn:
"For we walk by faith, not by sight…"

FOR NO APPARENT REASON

A calloused murder, a chance discovery—
two unplanned events become the catalyst that proves:
"In all things, God works for good…"